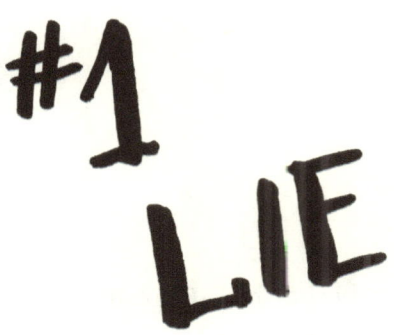

#1 LIE

USA Today Bestselling Author

T. GEPHART

#1 Lie
Published by T Gephart
Copyright 2018 T Gephart

ISBN-13: 978-0-6480231-7-3
ISBN-10: 0-6480231-7-6

Cover by:
Hang Le

Editing by:
Nichole Strauss, Insight Editing Services

Interior Design & Formatting by:
Christine Borgford, Type A Formatting

#1 LIE

DEDICATION

To the women who checked in, emailed, texted, messaged me. I don't know what I would have done without you, this book is for you.

CHAPTER #1

I HAD A dream.

Not like a Martin Luther King kind of dream—Lord, don't get too excited. But a dream nonetheless, and a girl had to start somewhere.

Born in Shreveport, Louisiana, the less sexy cousin of New Orleans, excitement didn't come easy. And while our city didn't have the allure or craziness that Bourbon Street offered, Shreveport had the third largest film industry right behind California and New York.

Yep, you heard that right.

We were number three.

And I wasn't sure how, but I wanted in on that.

All through high school, those film trucks rolled into town. And while I had no idea what I wanted to do with the rest of my life, the sight of a new production crew setting up would make my excitement spike. Other girls dreamt of hooking up with the leading man but I had another fantasy that kept me up at night.

And no, I didn't want to be an actress.

Please, the good Lord had a hard enough time directing me, so there was no hope a mortal man could.

Plus, while I wasn't ugly by anyone's standards, my auburn

hair, porcelain complexion and small frame didn't exactly scream Hollywood material. I swear I must have been the only person in L.A. who wouldn't have a tan.

I wanted something different, to be part of the noise in another way. And I knew that if I wanted to be involved at a grassroots level, then I'd have to go to where number one was.

California.

Try telling your Southern Baptist parents you want to skip town and move out west. Yeah, that conversation was fun. You'd have thought I was confessing to joining a cult, to become one of the many wives to a serial killer with bad teeth and even worse personal hygiene. Ewww, just because you're a sociopath doesn't mean you can't visit a dentist every six months and have a shower once a day.

But all of that aside, my relocation of course had them horrified. So we compromised, I agreed to stick around through college—LSU as previously attended by most of my family—and then if I didn't change my mind they would give me their blessing.

Spoiler alert. I didn't change my mind.

So with my communications degree in hand—and the thirty million prayers uttered by my parents—I moved to Hollywood, landing an assistant job with Jeremy Levin, one of the biggest agents in town.

Crazy.

I know what you're thinking, that I'd slept my way to the amazing job opportunity. How else could a girl with zero experience end up working for such a prestigious company? Well, save your judgment. I was a lot of things, but whore wasn't one of them. I was brilliant and able to handle chaotic while still maintaining a smile; they had no choice but to hire me. And I *may* have embellished my resume. But a few little white lies never hurt anyone, right?

And over the last four years, those tiny lies had faded into insignificance because, despite what I *hadn't* done, I was an amazing assistant.

Life was awesome.

Or at least it was, until it wasn't.

"Shit."

Like a Martha Stewart version of anthrax, a million tiny foil hearts exploded onto my desk as I opened the envelope. I didn't need to read the ivory linen cardstock to know what it was, the panic setting in before the tiny hearts had a chance to settle.

It was my cousin Lana's wedding invitation, and I was in a shitload of trouble.

It wasn't that I hated my cousin or her future husband; in fact I loved every member of my family. And I was genuinely happy for Lana and Clay. My issue wasn't even with the institution of marriage, hoping some day—when the time was right and I found the perfect guy—I too would take the walk down the aisle.

No, the chill that travelled down my spine was from additional script that would undoubtedly be written next to mine.

I took a deep breath, hoping a serious and freaky unexplained case of amnesia had rocked the entire state of Louisiana as my fingers slid out the invitation. Or maybe Lana and Clay decided they were going to be cheap and keep the numbers down.

But no, there it was, my worst fears confirmed in embossed gold lettering.

Jessica plus one.

Double shit.

My head shook as I evaluated my stupidity, wondering how someone who was at the top of her game in her professional life could have made such an epic misstep.

Okay, so maybe it wasn't *such* a mystery.

The reason I was staring at plus one instead of just my name was because I hadn't wanted to disappoint my gran.

Shelly McClain—my gran—wasn't an inch over five-feet tall and weighed less than a hundred pounds. I was a carbon copy of her when she was younger—although I'd gained four more inches on her height and at least twenty more pounds—inheriting her fiery personality. She was never without her signature bright pink lipstick, balanced perfectly on high heels even though she needed a walking frame and swore like a sailor whenever the Saints took the field.

And those weren't even half of all the reasons why she was my most favorite person in the world.

For the last four years I had called her every other week religiously, possibly even more than my own parents. I'd tell her about the people I'd met and the places I'd been, and she would tell me about the new Catholics who had moved in down the street. They were from New Jersey, and she didn't trust northerners.

So naturally, when I was summoned home with news of Gran on her deathbed, I was inconsolable. I would have done or said whatever I had to in order to guarantee the woman I had loved and admired my whole life would be able to rest in peace.

And her dying wish was to know I had found my soul mate.

Out of eleven grandkids, I was the only one who hadn't been tied to a significant other. Dated a plenty sure, but settle down? Um, no.

Looking for a man to be my "forever" wasn't a priority, at twenty-six, I had plenty of time for that. But as I looked into her pale blue eyes, the grey lashes that framed them straining to stay open, I did something I never thought I was ever capable of.

I lied to my gran.

It wasn't that I hadn't lied before, generally speaking I had no problem with a few little white lies, and at work it was an almost daily occurrence. Hell, in Hollywood it was harder to come by honesty than it was to find real freaking boobs.

And while most of the lies I'd told could be fixed by a few Hail Mary's, this one was on a whole other level. Lying to my family was something I'd *never* done. I was positive I was going to burn in Hell for it, but I did what I had to do. And I'd take eternal damnation if it meant Gran would go happy.

And as my fingers caressed her frail pale hand, I whispered tales of a man who made my heart stop. Filled her head with fiction on how wonderful he was, kind, considerate, funny. I spun untruths of his incredible talent, love for his family and how amazingly handsome he was—all the things I knew she would want to hear. And as the wrinkles around her eyes crinkled and a faint smile spread across her lips, I didn't have it in me to stop.

By the end, I had almost convinced myself of my mystery man's existence and was almost disappointed he wasn't real. Spared from giving his name because she was too tired to keep her eyes open any longer.

Although it seemed her meeting with Jesus would have to wait, with the Heavenly Father insisting Gran needed to be on earth a little longer. It was either a miracle, or Gran was just too stubborn to die. And knowing her, my money was on the latter.

But with this seriously awesome reprieve came the realization of what I had done. The tiny lie I assumed would have no consequences ended up biting me in the butt. And now, with my cousin's wedding next month, I was either going to have to fess to what I had done, or find a solution.

And confessing wasn't an option.

My family was loud and boisterous; they loved hard and were loyal to a fault. Things were more straight forward for them. It was either black or white, good or bad—there were never any shades of grey. You worked your ass off, you lived well and you went to church on Sundays. But making up stories of fictional boyfriends to tell your dying grandma? Well, I might as well have killed her myself and rode through town wearing her head as a hat. Slightly dramatic but no less accurate.

No.

I couldn't tell them the truth.

There *had* to be another solution. One that allowed me to somehow emerge from this relatively unscathed and not be disowned by my family.

I refused to admit defeat.

Besides, I was a girl who could get things.

And when I said *things*, I meant *anything*.

While my job title was Assistant to Jeremy Levin, my real role was in procurement.

Whether it was finding a director who was shooting in the Siberian Tundra, a rare bottle of wine in the cellar of a forgotten French vineyard, or an elephant—I was your girl. There was no challenge too great, with the thrill of it giving me a reason to get up in the morning.

Sure, I did boring stuff like set meetings and answer phone calls, but underneath my cute pencil skirt and business jacket, I wore a superhero cape.

This was what I was born to do, and Jeremy—who took the lion's share of the praise—knew exactly how hard I worked, rewarding me handsomely for my efforts.

So instead of hyperventilating at my desk like a loser, I needed to treat it the way I would if this were someone else's problem dropped into my lap with the directive to "fix it."

"Jessica, you get those tickets for the Laker's game?" Jeremy's head popped out of his office. "I want courtside and a late dinner reservation at—"

I waved the envelope in my hand, stopping him from finishing his sentence.

The envelope wasn't the one housing the offending wedding

invitation—its vision in my periphery making me nauseous—it was the other one that had been sitting on my desk since ten a.m., exactly an hour after he'd mentioned he might like to take a client out this Friday.

"Courtside." I watched as he strode over to me, taking the envelope from my hand and checking the tickets inside. "And you have a reservation at ten for *Madres*. Back corner table as always," I added, not missing a beat.

His smile was slight but apparent as he tapped the envelope on his palm. "Good."

"Also, your anniversary is Saturday." I stood up from my desk and handed him a red gift bag. "You bought Hilary a pair of Cartier diamond earrings, and there's a suite booked for the two of you at the Beverly Wilshire."

Stress spread across his face as he looked to the bag dangling from his fingers in horror and then back to me. "Are you fucking with me, Jessica? My anniversary is next week."

"That would be a negative, Jeremy." I shook my head, remembering last year when his wife had tried to surprise him. She'd organized Pierre Moreau, a famed chef, to come to their house and cook them dinner. Jeremy not realizing the significance of the date had blown her off and had dinner with a client. They were still in couples counseling. "Your anniversary is Saturday and Hilary will have your balls if you forget another one."

Ordinarily the words "fuck" and "balls" were frowned upon in the workplace. Even a misplaced "ass" would get you a visit to HR. But working with Levin Murphy Talent Agency had taught me that there was nothing *ordinary* about my job. Not only did we bend the boundaries of acceptable workplace conversation, but half the things that came out of my mouth were either seasoned with well-chosen expletives or full of shit. The ability to be a proficient liar was necessary when you worked in the entertainment industry, and clearly I was pathological.

His hand tightened around the gift bag, nodding his head. "Fuuuuuuck. She would not only have my balls but she'd have our friends at Cartier make them into a necklace to match the earrings." He leaned across my desk, the look of gratitude easing across his features. "I owe you. Go out and get yourself something and charge it to my account. Just don't get too crazy and buy a car or yacht. And dinner is on me tonight. Pick anywhere you want and we'll go out, my treat."

"Thanks for the offer of dinner, but I have plans tonight." I looked down at my desk, the menacing invitation not forgotten. I figured it was going to take at least one evening to come up with a solution.

While augmenting the truth was fine in my professional dealings, it wasn't cool when it came to my family. Maybe I'd been in Hollywood too long, my dad had always worried I'd end up worshiping the Devil.

"And I am going to need some time off next month to attend my cousin's wedding in Shreveport. Just a few days, four at the most."

He screwed up his face, giving me the same look of distaste he always did when we talked about the *other* LA. "Awesome, you're heading back to the armpit of America, how exciting for you."

"My family is there, and it's not so bad." I smirked, unsurprised by his response.

"Yeah, not so bad if you don't like civilization," he scoffed. "Please tell me your cousin isn't marrying another cousin."

I laughed, well versed in most people's skewed view of the South. While some of us *were* a bunch of backward hicks who rode in pickup trucks with missing teeth, that wasn't always the case. Although, my cousin Trevor was once arrested drunk while in his underwear shopping for toilet paper in Big Lots. But that wasn't because he was from the South, that was because he was stupid. There was one in every family.

And while I could bat my blue eyes and bless-your-heart as much as anyone, I had toned it down since moving to L.A.

"No, you'll be happy to know they are unrelated. I'll be sure to give them your best. I can probably wrangle you and Hilary an invite so you can see for yourself. I'm sure y'all would looooooove it." I let my accent thicken on the last part.

He barked out a laugh before turning serious. "Yeah, I'd rather slam my dick in a car door. But you enjoy Shitport, just don't get any wild ideas about moving back. I know your parents hate that you live here and will put the hard word on you. And I don't want to have to go down there to drag you back, you know I hate gators unless they've been turned into luggage."

"My life is in this L.A., I'm not moving back." I rolled my eyes, tempted to give him a heart attack and tell him I was considering it. "And the last time I was there my grandma was about to die, it was natural my folks tried to talk me into staying."

He shook his head, taking a step back. "Yeah, sure whatever. Go, enjoy your hick wedding and schedule Katrina to cover for you while you're gone." He nailed me with a hard look as he paused in the hall. "But tell her that if she cries like she did last time, I'm going to hire a fucking temp."

"Roger that." I saluted, watching him again retreat to his office.

Katrina was not only one of our secretaries, but she was also one of my best friends. She was dying to be promoted, wanting more excitement than her admin job gave her. But as much as I loved her, I wasn't sure she was ready for the 24/7 that came with being an assistant.

Still, I'd let her fill in for me whenever I needed cover, hoping to help her aspirations along. Sadly, Jeremy wasn't too fond of her, finding her too chatty and emotional. God forbid anyone show human traits. He only forgave mine because I could think on my feet and pull his ass out of a fire.

So while she was more than competent to do the work, her downfall was her inability to deal with the stress involved in our day-to-day. The last time, one yelling client later and she was in tears in the bathroom. Which is why you needed to not only be qualified to work at Levin Murphy, but to have nerves of steel as well. Something that would hopefully serve me well if I ended up hiring an escort to be my date for the wedding.

Okay, that was a terrible idea.

I really needed to work on it some more.

"Hey, Jess."

While there was nothing sexual about the words, his voice curled around my name erotically all the same. Then again, it wasn't like he could help it; sex appeal was so deeply ingrained in his double helix, it was as much a part of him as those gorgeous chocolate-colored eyes.

My gaze lifted, giving him a warm smile as he settled into the sofa across from me. "Hello, Dave."

Dave Larsson was the younger brother of superstar Eric Larsson. Eric was part of Hollywood's elite, gracing the pages of magazines and touted as one of the hottest actors in town. He also had a body that made atheists find religion and a smile that disintegrated panties. And while his younger sibling hadn't reached the same level of professional success, he was no less impressive in the looks department.

With a slightly darker complexion, delicious brown eyes and fantastic brown hair, he had women creaming their pants before he'd even open his mouth. He was funny too, his wicked sense of humor making him even more desirable.

And sure, I'll admit when I first met him I'd fantasized about testing his washboard abs with my tongue just like everyone else.

But alas, he was *forbidden*. Because along with being hot, talented and funny, he was also a client, which put him strictly in the no-go territory.

Such a shame too because I really would have liked to tongue his abs like the fantasy.

"Jeremy will see you in a minute." I gave him another smile, buzzing Jeremy to let him know his next appointment had arrived.

"You know," he leaned back, his strong forearms folding across his chest as he shot me a devilish smile, "we could skip the whole meeting part and *you* could tell me what the part is. I know that you've probably read the script and have seen the director's notes." He wasn't even attempting to be subtle, trying to get the insider scoop and flirting shamelessly like he always did.

"Nice try, Larsson." I grinned, not even considering it despite his best efforts. "But I wouldn't deprive you of the joy when Jeremy tells you."

"Yeah, yeah." He chuckled as he shook his head. "One of these days you're going to cave."

I was positive if I ever did cave, it would only mean trouble. And not just for my job, but for my hormones as well.

"Dave!" Jeremy burst through the door, lifting his arms in the air like he was welcoming his best friend. "How's my favorite Larsson?" He curled his knuckles like a prizefighter in Vegas, punching air as he moved closer.

Dave rose to his feet, rolling his eyes as he grinned. "Stop bullshitting me, Jeremy. I know Eric's your favorite."

"Please, *that* prima donna." Jeremy waved his hand like the notion was ridiculous. "I just pretend to love him more because he has the bigger ego and needs constant reassurance." He mock punched Dave in the gut. "Now *you* you're my guy. Look at you." He took a step back, as if to admire him. "You've been working out. Hell, you must be at least two hundred pounds of solid muscle."

"Two-twenty," he answered, his lips curling in a grin. "You want to feel me up some more or you going to tell me about this audition?"

Jeremy shook his head laughing. "Yeah, fine. Let's go talk business. Jessica, hold my calls."

He slapped Dave across the back and welcomed him into his office. I was almost positive the meeting wasn't going to last long. That audition Jeremy had set up wasn't exactly one I'd think Dave would be excited to take.

It seemed both of us were destined for misery today.

Sadly, the company didn't make it any better.

CHAPTER #2

"HEY, WAS THAT Dave?" Katrina scampered over, her smile doing little to convince me she hadn't been staring at him the whole time he was at my desk.

"Yes, it was." I rolled my eyes, knowing she had a massive crush on all the Larsson boys. "Don't stare at his ass when he leaves though, it was creepy when you did it last time."

She had the decency to look shocked. "I wasn't staring at his ass. I was trying to read the label of his jeans."

"Sure, that sounds convincing too." I rolled my eyes again, clearly a prerequisite for both dealing with Katrina *and* Jeremy. I wished my only problem was whether or not to stare at Dave Larsson's ass.

"Actually, while I've got you here you're going to need to fill in for me when I go home for a wedding. It's next month."

Her face lit up, excitement dancing across her features. "Yay! Lana is getting married. Thank your lucky stars she didn't ask you to be a bridesmaid. That dress you had to wear at her sister's wedding—hideous." She screwed up her face in disgust, remembering the burnt orange dress I'd had to endure. It had been fall-themed wedding, sadly that didn't do wonders for my dark auburn hair and pale skin. And I had curves too where the other bridesmaids hadn't, the tight fabric making me look like a distended pumpkin. I still refused to look at the photos. "And of course, I'll cover for you. Whatever you need, I'm your girl."

"Thanks, and trust me, a hideous dress is the least of my problems." I took a deep breath. "They're expecting my boyfriend to come."

The only two people who knew of my stupidity were Katrina and our friend Liz. Both had been convinced I'd done the right thing, even commending me for my quick thinking. But apparently I had a responsibility to come clean at some point and that was where our opinions differed.

"Shit, you haven't told them yet?" Katrina's voice lowered, side eyeing suspiciously like my family might be lurking around the next corner.

"What was I supposed to say?" I threw my hands up in defeat. *"Hey, remember when I talked about that guy I was dating and told you all how wonderful he was? Yeah, I made the whole thing up."* Wow, saying it out loud made it sound even stupider than I thought. Who made up fictional boyfriends? What was I? Twelve?

"Surely they'll understand." Katrina tried to be sympathetic. "I mean, it was for a good reason, your heart was in the right place."

She was right about that. My heart *had* been in the right place, but I doubted that would matter to my black-and-white family.

I sighed, letting the breath slowly ease out of me as I closed my eyes. "Trust me, they're going to be disappointed."

I was just about to share my previously bad—and currently the only one I had—idea about hiring a prostitute when my cell rang. The letters M O M lighting up the screen as I cursed not so quietly under my breath.

Not sure how she did it, but that woman had a sixth-sense. And I was almost positive her call was not one of coincidence.

"Hi, Mom." I pulled a face at Katrina, her eyes widening as she looked on. "What a great surprise."

That, of course, was another lie. Not that I didn't like hearing from her, but there was nothing *great* about the surprise. I was beginning to wonder if the truth was ever going to make an appearance again, certainly not from my mouth.

"Baby!" She still called me baby even though I was twenty-six and had a younger brother. "I know you're at work but I've been trying you catch you for weeks and never seem to get you at home. I was fixing to send out a search party." She continued, barely taking a pause, "I wanted to make sure you got Lana's invitation. She thought you might be offended by the plus one, but you never did tell us your mystery man's name. I told her you wouldn't be, but you know your cousin. Anyway, with all the excitement of Gran Shelly pulling through, and you being so busy at work, I never did find out his name. Now, you know I don't like to pry, but I haven't heard from you in ages and I need to know what to tell your aunt to put on the place card. Besides, it's been so long since you called your momma, if I didn't know better I'd say you've been avoiding me."

I shook my head wondering in what world I thought any of it was going to work out okay. Dodging calls would only go so far, and clearly my mother wasn't going to tolerate radio silence forever. "Mom, don't be ridiculous, I just thought you would be busy. Your attention should been on Gran Shelly, I mean what a miracle. Praise the Lord."

Despite my affirmations, I wasn't overly religious. I believed enough to think there was a heaven and hell, but wasn't convinced that time on your knees could win you favors. All though if it did, I'd happily spend some time on them to get me out of my mess.

Katrina looked at me, biting back her smile at my Jesus praising and probably wondering—like I was—how long I could keep up the deceit.

"I'm so glad Lana didn't end up cancelling," I added, hoping to deflect a little longer. "I know how excited she was. And *yes*, I got the invitation last night. I just didn't get a chance to open it until now."

I'd sidestepped the whole name thing but I knew there was no getting out of it. All I'd really done was successfully stall her for a few seconds, hoping that in that time I'd come up with something good. I always did my best work under pressure, and now would not be the time for that theory to come undone. Plus, I had praised God. Hopefully that—the praise—had gotten his attention and he was willing to throw me a bone. Or at least, give me a small reprieve.

"Oh, I'm so glad." Her voice sweetened, but she didn't sound convinced. "Now, put your momma out of her misery. I want to hear all about the sweet boy you're bringing home with you. He *is* coming to the wedding, right?"

"Errr." I paused. *Now would be a good time for that help, God.* "You know, I just got it. I mean, I haven't even had a chance to ask him." My mouth spat out words that didn't sound confident.

I hated being in this position, but it didn't seem like I had a lot of options either. I was far too deep in the hole to just casually toss out the truth now.

A smart person would have realized the jig was up, flown down there on the weekend and set the story straight. Cry a little, act remorseful, and then promise to never do it again while sipping on sweet tea and complimenting my momma's cooking.

The combination of crying and begging would probably be the only thing that would save my ass, but I'd probably still have to wear the shame like a metal chain around my neck for the next one hundred years, or until I died. And I wasn't a fan of big gaudy jewelry so you could see how the option wasn't overly appealing.

So instead, I left the *shame necklace* for another time and tried to brainstorm ways to try to stop the mother of all snowballs from spiraling out of control.

And like the miracle I'd been praying for, a loud bang filled the air, Jeremy's door flying open with a very unhappy Larsson storming out.

"Dave," I said absently, my eyes tracking his delicious body as he stalked through the doorway like a lion.

I assumed he wasn't going to be pleased at Jeremy's pitch, but I'd never seen him so angry.

"Dave?" His name echoed, the second mention coming from the phone I was still holding at my ear. "Oh, that's a lovely name. Strong, classic, manly. I thought he was going to be called something like Tad or Razor, thank God he has a sensible name. Tell me, baby. Is he a Christian?"

Shit.

Shit.

Shit.

"Momma, I need to go. I will call you back." I hung up the phone before she had a chance to say goodbye, stepping from behind my desk. "Dave, wait."

I ran out in front of him, stopping him from leaving the office. He didn't look happy, his body looming as he looked down on me. He seemed taller than the six-three listed on the back of his headshot, but maybe it was because I wasn't usually standing right next to him. And wow, Jeremy was right. Dave *had* been working out.

"Dave, come on, calm down and come back into the office." Jeremy followed him out, engaging in damage control. "I'll get Jessica to get us a drink. I had some water flown in from the Himalayas."

Dave looked at me and then at Jeremy, his jaw tensed like it had been clamped shut and his teeth were grinding. Fierce looked good on him—and while I was positive he wasn't attempting to look sexy—angry and pissed off made him look even hotter. *I bet it would be even better naked.*

Dear. Lord.

His hotness didn't make me forget my family drama. All that shit—the chains of shame, the disappointment on the face of my parents—was still very much a concern. Not to mention that not only was I expected to bring home a man, but also I had now unwittingly given my fake boyfriend a name. *Well played, mouth. You are an asshole.*

But those problems were going to have to wait a minute as I attempted to help Jeremy calm down Dave so the rest of the building wasn't treated to a sexy version of Godzilla. Not to say they wouldn't enjoy it, especially if he ripped his shirt off and treated us to those astounding abs. But some asshole would probably take pictures with their phone. There was a PR nightmare waiting to happen, besides, I didn't want to share the fantasy with anyone.

"Katrina, can you go grab the water?" I turned to find her still standing silently beside my desk. She was looking at Dave with a lust that most women would have the decency to hide. Probably fantasizing about climbing him like King Kong scaled the Empire State, or maybe it was just me who was thinking that?

But finding some professionalism, she nodded briefly before scampering off, and probably glad it wasn't her this time in the crossfire.

"And Dave," my voice softened as I turned my attention to him. *Climbing him is not an option.* "Maybe we go back in Jeremy's office and—"

"Another dog food commercial?" He didn't give me a chance to finish, looking at me before turning to Jeremy. "Come on, dude, I've already done that. You promised me this was a lead."

Yep, I knew it wasn't going to fly and had even warned Jeremy about it before the pitch. But of course, he hadn't listened, telling me how much cash they were throwing at it, convinced there was *no way* Dave would say no.

"And you were so great at it." Jeremy's smile widened, his arms spreading out to the side. "That's why they want you back, to roll out a series of ads. Not only that, but there are going to be billboards, magazine spreads." He smacked Dave on the shoulder in encouragement. "You could be like that English soccer player who sounds like an idiot. The ladies *love* him."

Dave shook his head, not buying Jeremy's hard sell. "*David Beckham* sells his own shit. He's not pushing someone else's dog food. Pretty sure he also played sports every once in a while too. And why the hell do I need to be naked? I don't mind nudity when the script calls for it, but this is a pet food commercial. *This* is the big break you promised me?"

WOW.

Naked.

There was no way that had been on the original brief, because that was not the kind of detail I would have forgotten. Just the thought of all that *man* being stripped down made me need to fan myself. Lordy, I could barely take him clothed, but . . . naked? Yeah, sure as shit would have gotten my attention.

"No one is going to see your junk, if that's what you're worried about," Jeremy laughed. "It will be covered by the food. That's the beauty of it. It adds to the character."

"Here's the water!" Katrina power walked, balancing a tray of crystal glasses and a smile. "I sliced some lemon and lime too."

Silence.

The tension cut through the air like a hot knife through butter while I thanked Jesus, Katrina hadn't been around to hear about Dave's exposed *junk*. I was having a hard enough time keeping myself in check; I couldn't be responsible for controlling everyone else's hormones as well.

"Why don't we take this back to Jeremy's office," I suggested, thinking we should probably be offering him something a lot stronger than water. Lord knows I could use a drink. "I heard the director is *really* good."

The director is really good?

What the hell did I say?

Clearly, I'd missed a cloud of locusts or something, because the day of the apocalypse had obviously come to pass and there I was grasping at straws. *JJ Abrams* could be the man behind the lens and it wouldn't change the fact that Dave would be naked, covered in dog food like a poor man's version of *American Beauty.*

"No." He looked at me and then turned to Jeremy. "Find me something else. *Anything* else. And preferably a *real* role this time." He walked over to Katrina and picked up a glass, gulped the entire thing in what looked like one long sexy swallow then waved goodbye.

Damn. He was hot.

"He's right, you know," Jeremy said under his breath as we watched Dave leave.

"Yeah, he is." I sighed, nodding to Katrina that she was free to take her Himalayan water and leave. She didn't need to be asked, giving me a we're-going-to-talk-later look and heading back to her desk. "You do need to find him a better part."

"No, not about that," Jeremy scoffed. "I meant when he said I liked Eric better." He laughed.

"You're a jerk." I leveled my stare at him. "You think Eric will be pleased with the way you treated his brother? I wouldn't be surprised if Dave doesn't have him on speed dial right now."

While I'm sure many women would have applauded his effort to get Dave naked and visible for the general population, it still was a shitty thing to do. I liked Dave, unlike some of the assholes who walked through our door, he was never sleazy. Plus, he spoke to me like a real person, not like I was just the hired help.

"Shit, you're right. Call him and smooth it over." Jeremy

pointed at the phone with urgency. "If he wants to toss away good money, fine, but I don't need the family to close ranks and pull their talent. Eric is one of my best earners."

I shook my head as I huffed out a breath. Jeremy could be the biggest prick sometimes, but I guess in the industry, nice people finished last. And as much as I hate the way he sometimes conducted his business, cleaning up the mess was one of the things I did best. Coming from a big family meant I was used to the chaos, or maybe I was just secretly hedging my bets in case there really was judgment at the pearly gates. You never know. And if the California sun was murder on my skin, the fiery pit of Hell wouldn't be a good thing. "You can go now. I have work to do."

Jeremy shot me a grin, knowing I would handle it like I always did. He didn't even look back as he headed back to his office to focus on another client. I hoped for both our sakes he didn't piss that one off too. Lord knows if he did, I was going to ask for a raise.

I cursed softly as I dialed Dave's number and waited until he picked up.

"Wow, found a part so soon? Must be my lucky day," he laughed, the sarcasm dripping from his voice. "I'm not doing the dog food commercial."

"Hey, it's Jess," I said, gripping the phone hoping my smile was beaming down the line.

"Did he think by you calling me I'd agree? C'mon, Jess, you know I'm still out."

To his credit, he didn't hang up which was what most actors would have done. Hell, it's what I would have done, but not before telling them to kiss my ass a few times. Especially if I felt like I was being handled, which ironically, was exactly what was happening. I'll admit that wasn't my favorite part of my job, but when it came to talking people off ledges, I was pretty damn good at it.

"No, I know," I started, in no way intending to talk him into it. "I do still think Jeremy is trying to do the best for you, but I'm not asking you to reconsider. I just want to make sure you knew that we took your concerns on board, and that we are committed to finding you the right role."

He laughed, his earlier sarcasm missing in action, with his chuckle sounding genuine. "You seriously didn't regurgitate the company line did you? You're better than that, we both are. So just tell Jeremy to pull his head out of his ass and find me something decent. There *are* other agents, you know. Maybe it's time I shopped around."

He could be bluffing, but there was no way to tell. And I wasn't about to gamble. He might not have been a huge fish, but losing a client wasn't an option.

My eyes fell to the invitation on my desk, and I had possibly the most brilliant—or stupidest, jury was still out—idea I'd ever had.

"Dave, I think I might have something for you." I reached down and picked up the invite, the tiny foil hearts sticking to my fingers. "It's an independent project. Very small budget."

Was I actually going to do this?

I wasn't sure I hadn't blacked out, the suggestion almost so preposterous it made trolling for hookers sound sane. I was also fairly sure I was breaking about a hundred employment rules, not to mention possibly risking my job.

But clearly, desperate times called for desperate measures, my sanity the least of my concerns as I sunk even lower into deceit. I mean, it was okay as long as we both got something out of it, right?

Lord, I better pack my sunblock—I was going to Hell.

"Really?" Dave hummed into the phone. "I don't have a problem with independent or small budget as long as it's a decent role."

"It's a lead."

Shit.

Too late now, my mouth had volunteered us for the biggest sham of the century before my brain properly evaluated the situation. I guess I'd told so many lies, what was another one. I was almost positive there was going to be no amount of Hail Marys getting me out of this one.

"Don't tease me, Jess," he purred into the phone, his voice more seductive than he'd probably intended.

"I'm not. I promise." I looked at the date on the cardstock and cringed. "But you don't have a lot of time to prepare. Shooting starts next month."

I wasn't sure if it made me the worst person in the world—lying to my family and Dave—or if I was brilliant. I mean, who best to play the role of a fake boyfriend than an actual actor? In its purest form, the idea was genius. Or at least that's what I told myself as I picked up the shovel and dug even further into the hole.

"I'll come in and pick up the script." His response coming so fast there was no time for further internal debate. Ready or not, we were doing this.

Assuming he agreed.

And that was a big IF.

My eyes shot to Jeremy's closed office door, and I almost threw up in my mouth. Images of Dave sauntering in, asking for the script that didn't exist, for the part that didn't exist, made me dry heave. To say I hadn't worked out all the particulars was an understatement. And as good as I professed to be, there was only so much I could spin on the fly, especially with my boss only a few feet away. It would be like jerking a guy off in a confessional; while the element of taboo was hot as hell, even I had standards.

"Meet me tonight and we can discuss it. It will make it less formal." *Sure, that didn't sound suspect.* The suggestion was thrown out like we were meeting up for a drug deal. I wasn't convinced I didn't sound like a lunatic.

"I have plans tonight, won't be free until later, like around eleven?"

"Eleven is perfect," I answered a little too eagerly, my concern over it sounding shady less than my need for him to agree. "There's a twenty-four hour coffee shop downtown, The Americano. I can send you the address."

A bar probably would have made more sense. I had contemplated it, hoping that after a drink or two, my idea wouldn't sound so crazy. The drinks were for me of course. But as tempting as it was to blame alcohol for the insanity, I needed both of us to be sober when he heard my pitch, and hopefully accepted. Last thing I needed was dubious consent added to my growing rap sheet of sins.

No, at the very least we should *start* sober, after that it was anyone's guess how it was going to go. There was always the chance he would run, cowering from my hideous idea like it—and in turn me—were infested with cockroaches. And if that happened, there was a huge possibility I'd have to drink myself into oblivion. *Couldn't attend a family wedding because I was passed out drunk in a pool of my own vomit, sorry Lana.* That would have to be Plan C, the prostitute was still standing strong as a solid Plan B.

"I know the place. I'll meet you there around eleven." He took a breath. "Thanks, Jess, you were probably the one who pulled the strings and I appreciate it."

I shook my head, his sincerity making me feel like a total ass. "Well don't thank me just yet." *Literally.* "See you tonight."

After a quick goodbye and ending the call, the realization of what I'd done and what I was about to do became extremely apparent.

If I had half a brain, losing my job would have been my number one fear. But instead of being concerned about possibly joining the percentage of the population who were unemployed, I felt energized—excited almost—with rational thought leaving the building as the fever of delirium took over.

Dave Larsson wanted a lead role with more substance than the stupid commercial Jeremy had offered him. I needed a guy to play the part of boyfriend for a couple of days.

If both of us were to each get something out of it, then what was the problem?

And sure, he wouldn't be getting any recognition or exposure like a *regular* job. He'd also be paid less than the commercial had promised. But think of the good karma it would attract; it would be like his fast-pass into Heaven. Not to mention I'd beg, cheat or steal to get him something worthwhile to star in next. There was a script currently on my desk that was perfect for him. And Jeremy owed me, and he owed Dave too. Plus, I would still pay him; I wasn't expecting him to do it for free. And he'd get to sample some of the best southern cooking known to man. That had to be worth something?

It would be a job like any other, only the script would be more fluid and he wouldn't have any pesky cameras pointed in his face. And while the five grand I was intending to pay him wasn't huge, I'd cover all the expenses too.

It would be like an adventure. How could he possibly resist?

I refused to eye the invitation on my desk any longer, shoving it back into the envelope and tossing it into a drawer.

In a few hours, I'd find out either way and refused to accept any outcome other than the one I had in my head.

Dave would say yes, we would go home, play the part of the loving couple, and then "break up" after the wedding. I would be saved from being excommunicated by my family and move on with my life with no one none the wiser.

What could possibly go wrong?

CHAPTER #3

I WAS INVINCIBLE.

At least that was what I had convinced myself of, my positive affirmations ringing in my ears as I went about my day. And I wasn't just trying to inflate my ego; I really was brilliant at fixing problems.

In the last few years I had learned a lot. Not only about the industry, but about myself too. My biggest take away? Don't take things personally.

Whatever happened tonight wasn't about me; it was business. So while it was easy to be worried about the rejection, or even be embarrassed I was in the predicament from the start, he was either going to say yes *or* walk away. Neither was going to make me any less of a person, which was why as I sat in The Americano waiting for Dave I felt an odd sense of calm.

And yes, with my level of expertise and impressive contact list, I probably could have found a legitimate date. Possibly even—gasp—a boyfriend in the next few weeks, but I didn't want the baggage that came with it. Plus, dating in L.A. was a minefield.

The last guy I'd been out with was a self-confessed vampire. He'd worn prosthetic fangs and had a coffin in his living room. And while I had sort of been caught up in the whole *Twilight* phenomena like a lot of teenage girls years ago, *Edward* isn't so sexy when he's a pasty white guy from Pasadena who was unemployed and broke.

Hiring a professional made sense, and it really was the best solution. And while man-for-hire sounded slightly skeevy, it wasn't like I was paying him to sleep with me. Please, I wasn't *that* ridiculous. He was an artist, and I was merely giving him an opportunity to perform. Realistically, I was providing a public service.

In fact, the more I thought about it, the better the idea sounded. It really was a win for everyone involved. I didn't even worry about what his rationalization was for meeting me so late. He could be moonlighting as a freaking murderer and I hadn't given it a second thought. Clearly, my predicament far outweighed stupid stuff like personal safety.

"Been here long?" Dave's voice broke me from my thoughts of all the *awesome* as he shuffled into the booth. "Sorry, I'm a little late." His lips pulled into a frown as he checked his watch. "Shit, Jess, I didn't mean to keep you waiting."

I'd been so absorbed with "The Best Plan Ever" to even notice his lateness, but found his annoyance with himself endearing. Think we could rule out murderer for the time being. There was a positive. "It's fine, I haven't been waiting that long."

Of course that had been a lie, I'd been there for over half an hour. Which was something I had been doing a lot lately.

Lying I mean, not waiting.

But if Dave could play fairy godmother to my Cinderella and help me get to the ball, I'd wait a hell of a lot longer than thirty minutes. Bibbidi-bobbidi-boo.

"Good." His lips spread into a grin, the light hitting his warm brown eyes. "I've been thinking about you all day."

Before I melted into the cheap vinyl of the booth, I reminded myself he meant *me* in the vaguest sense of the word. Or maybe he *had* been thinking about me—and my stellar personality—but that was incidental. Because as much as I would have loved to be taking up room in his cerebral space, I was a cursory visitor. An interloper, and what he was really giving time to, was the potential proposal I had to offer.

The *indecent* proposal.

Of which he knew nothing about.

So considering what I was about to ask him, I had no reason to be neither hurt nor offended. It wasn't personal, remember?

I had *no* problem with a sexy man—who made angels cry when he looked at them—sitting across from me to not feel attraction. For when he looked at me, for his interest to be only business. In fact, it was easier that way. Lord knows I'd thought about him in ways that weren't professional, so one of us needed to keep our head screwed on straight. And as my eyes flicked over his lickable hot body—his muscular chest housed in a fitted T-shirt, his strong arms resting on the table in front of him as he met my eyes—that person was probably not going to be me.

"I'm so glad, Dave. I really hope we can work on this together."

Please, baby Jesus, if there ever was an opportunity I needed proof of your existence, now was the time.

Taking a deep breath—and saying a quick prayer to the Virgin Mary, just in case—I stopped prolonging the inevitable. Besides, it was already skating dangerously close to midnight, and I didn't know if he needed to continue his murderous activities, so dragging it out wasn't smart.

I cleared my throat, sitting up straighter as I spoke, because the voice of my mother whispered in my ear telling me posture was always important. "It's a romantic comedy. A smart, successful woman takes her boyfriend—who is madly in love with her—to meet crazy, but loveable family in Shreveport, Louisiana. Hilarity ensues." I spread my fingers out either side of my face as I jazz-handed my enthusiasm. "Obviously, you would play the role of the talented, successful and extremely good looking boyfriend."

His brow rose slowly. "It doesn't sound very funny. What's the angle? And who is directing it? They cast the female lead yet?"

All those questions were perfectly valid, if we were discussing a film.

Which we weren't.

And I as much as I wanted to lay down some more foundation work before coming clean, I decided the Band-Aid approach would work best—rip it off without hesitation. Besides, what was the worst that could happen? He flipped me the bird, told me to go fuck myself and then grumbled about me wasting his time? Pfft, that was nothing compared to the damnation I was going to get from my mother.

"Sooooooo." I chewed on my bottom lip, forcing a grin. "Well see, the funny part is that it isn't actually a movie."

"So, it's T.V. series?"

"No."

"A play?"

"Not that either." I waved my hand, trying to make it sound better than it did. "It's more a real-life drama."

He leaned in closer, his eyes widening in either interest or utter disgust, I wasn't sure which. "Like a reality show?"

"As in, I'm the fucking dumbass who told my dying grandma I found a soul mate and now I need to produce a man for my cousin's wedding. But it just can't be any guy, he needs to be convincing and pretend to be in love with me. Then I need to think of something suitably devastating where he breaks my heart so I have a reasonable explanation for our split. And then I can go on with my life. Hilarity ensues." I jazz-handed again.

He laughed, relaxing back into his chair. "Oh, I see the comedy. You're kidding. Great. Good one. Now, what's the real job?"

"Dave, I'm not kidding." But how I wished I were. "The job is *you* helping *me* fool my family into thinking we're a couple. Attend the wedding. Break my heart. End scene. You'll get paid for it, and of course all of your expenses will be taken care of."

I mean, it was the least I could do. While I was positive Dave Larsson wasn't hurting for money, I wasn't about to take advantage of him either. It only seemed fair that I compensate him as best I could for the time and the effort. After all, he was a professional.

And this was business.

Professional business.

He stopped laughing; his voice dropped as the warmth left from his tone. "Is this some kind of fucking test you and Jeremy cooked up to see if I'll just take anything? I mean, I assume he thinks I was being overly dramatic today when I turned him down, but I'm not an idiot either." He looked around, scanning the tables around us. "Where is he? He sitting around laughing his ass off or did he just send you to do his dirty work, expecting a full report later?"

"He doesn't know," I added quickly, trying to salvage the situation. I hadn't even considered he'd think it was a joke or that my boss was in on it. "This isn't a test, and Jeremy knows nothing about it. In fact, I'm probably risking my job and my reputation by even suggesting it. But I'm sort of desperate and it seemed like a good idea."

Maybe it was one of those things that sounded better in my head than it actually was. Like deciding at four a.m. it was easier just to stay awake rather than get only a couple of hours sleep. In no world is no sleep a good option. And possibly, hiring a man date isn't one either. Who knew?

"It was stupid, but I'm sort of stuck now."

Stuck was an understatement, and if he didn't say yes I was faced with the very real possibility of putting a Want Ad in the paper. Or cruising Sunset and promising some poor asshole he was going to be staring in a new version of the Truman Show. I wasn't above Craig's List as a last resort either, or trolling a Wal-Mart. I'd come this far, there wasn't much further I could drop into the pit of dumbassary.

He stopped, looking at me in what I assumed was a moment of compassion. "You're serious?"

No, I would make up something like that because I liked the idea someone would mistake me for an escapee from an asylum.

"Yes, yes, I'm serious." I nodded, a little too excited that he hadn't left yet. "I need a man, but without the complications. And preferably someone who can be convincing so I can somehow come through this unscathed."

"Why don't you just tell your family that you made the whole thing up? They're your family, surely they'll understand."

It was my turn to laugh. "Are you kidding me? You have not met or know my family. In their eyes, there is never a reason to lie to them. Ever. It doesn't matter if it was for good intentions, or you had a good reason—to them, it's one of the biggest sins there is. They will not understand, trust me."

If I thought there was a chance, I would have already come clean. But there wasn't, so the road, however treacherous, needed to be continued.

"What about if you break up with him before the wedding? People break up all the time."

He was adorable.

Trying to be helpful even though it was a possibility I'd already thought of myself.

"No. If I break up with him before the wedding, I will have to spend the entire trip needing to explain why." My family weren't the type of people who'd let that one slide. They'd need dates, times—a Machiavellian storyline complete with plans for revenge. It had been by the grace of God, I'd managed to go three months avoiding the subject—my grandma's recovery saving my ass. *Thanks*

Gran, I owe you one.

But my reprieve was about to run out. "It will mean I need to pretend to be miserable because the love of my life broke my heart. And I don't have the energy to pretend to be sad. Not to mention dealing with one of my meddling aunts trying to set me up with someone because they'll feel sorry for me. The last time one of them did that, I had to sit through a family dinner with a guy called Ford. He wore a purity ring and insisted there were demons testing his resolve against fornicating. I caught him staring at my breasts at least five times, so you can see how none of those scenarios work for me."

He fought a grin, possibly trying to not laugh. Either at the absurdity of a twenty-six-year-old woman conjuring up an imaginary man, or Ford's battle with the temptation of my demon breasts. "So instead, you would rather orchestrate this huge production, hire a random guy to play the part of your boyfriend and hope they don't find out?"

"Firstly, you aren't a random guy. I know you, you know me. Totally not random." It wasn't like I'd pulled over on a street corner and picked him up while cruising in my car. We'd already established that had been plan B, and I was still hoping plan A was going to pan out. "Besides, if you are as good of an actor as you claim to be then they won't find out, will they?"

"Are you trying to dare me into doing this?" His eyes gleamed, his mouth twitching at the edges.

He was definitely interested, and from the look on his face, money wasn't going to be a motivator. At least I hoped it wasn't, considering I hadn't disclosed the amount I was paying him yet and it wasn't going to be a lot.

No. He was either bored, or intrigued, and I didn't care which one got me over the line as long as he agreed. Hell, he could think I was a tragic basket case and do it purely to fulfill his measure of charitable service.

"I could try appealing to your ego, but I figured you'd be more receptive to a challenge." I grinned, answering honestly. "You know, I could always ask Nick. He has a break in his filming schedule next week. I'm sure he'd love to help me out."

His younger brother had also won the genetic lottery that seemed to come with their famous last name. And while he wasn't as successful as older bro, Eric, he'd landed a role on a Netflix drama and was enjoying steady work and rising stardom. And while I'm sure Dave was happy for his younger sibling, I assumed there was some rivalry there. Or at least, that was what I was counting on.

A manly rumble vibrated up his throat and his eyes smoldered. The combination making him even sexier than his already good looks seemed to achieve. I totally got Katrina's fascination with him. "Low blow, Jess. But I'm sort of impressed."

Oh thank God, because I was positive Nick would have turned me down flat. While it was true that he had break in his film schedule coming up, it would have taken some fancy talking and a sacrificial virgin to get him to agree to more work after filming six months in a row. I'd be surprised if he didn't already have some vacation lined up in Cancun or Hawaii, maybe even both because why the hell not.

"So, does that mean you are considering it?" I tested the water, not wanting to seem too confident in that he'd agree.

He leaned back, getting comfortable in his seat, the hesitation seeming to be gone as he smirked. "Sure, I'm considering it. But it will cost you."

Reaching across the table and kissing him in thanks seemed over the top, but I was so relieved I had to stop myself from leaping into his lap. Plus, that wouldn't help sell this as a business proposition.

No, we were keeping this professional, remember?

Instead, I laid out what I felt was fair and hoped he didn't think I was a cheap bastard. "Five grand, plus your flight, your own hotel room, per diem and any additional expenses. I'll even buy you a new suit if you want."

Hell, if I thought it would help, I'd offer to buy him a plane ticket to join Nick on his Cancun/Hawaii extravaganza right after. Hookers and blow? Sure, whatever.

"Wow, I wasn't talking money. And thanks, but I think I can cover my own suit." He winked, intriguing me even more.

"Then what? I don't expect you to do this for free, this is a job like any other." And while I was happy for him to say yes out of the goodness of his heart, this was a strict business transaction and I didn't like owing favors.

He rolled his eyes, his grin remaining. "Fine, we'll agree to five grand. But we can share a room. It will not only keep up the charade, but save the unnecessary cost in expenses."

I laughed, thinking it was sweet that he was concerned about my budget. And while I wasn't a big dog getting around town in a Bentley, I wasn't doing too badly either. "I can afford two rooms, Dave."

"Are you listening to my terms or you going to argue?" His brow rose, daring me to object.

"Fine, go on."

He nodded, appeased as he continued. "You're not paying me per diem or fucking expenses. That's ridiculous."

I shook my head, ready with my rebuttal. "If you were on a shoot—"

He cut me off. "If I was on an indie film I'd be lucky to make five hundred dollars a day and get a room at a Motel 6. And wasn't it you who sold this as a small budget, independent production? So save the money and the argument."

"Okay, whatever, we can haggle later." I waved him off knowing the battle I needed to win wasn't a salary negotiation but him agreeing to do it in the first place. "So, what's it going to cost, if money isn't what we are talking about?"

"Tit for tat."

"I'm sorry?"

"I'm going to be your boyfriend, wow your family with how amazing I am and how wonderful our relationship is. Then I'm going to go along with whatever fate you decide that ends us. But when this is over, you are going to be my date to the opening of Jimmy Ferrara's exhibition."

Hold the freaking phone.

Jimmy Ferrara was a modern day Picasso who had been wowing both critics and regular folk since being discovered in New York two years ago. Plucked from obscurity by gallery owner Eve Thorton, his pieces were hitting the market in the hundreds of thousands. And while his *messes on canvases* weren't my particular brand of vodka, I had to hand it to the guy—he knew how to market himself. Which was why the first two months of his exhibition at the Hans Weckman gallery sold out within minutes of going on sale. And to be clear, even I—the master of acquisitions—had only managed to secure two tickets to the opening.

Jeremy's lovely wife had been desperate to go and he was only too happy to take her. After all, it was more a status thing to be at the excusive party hardly anyone could get into to. To laugh, drink, laugh, and compare penises—whatever men tended to do in business settings masquerading as social gatherings. I hadn't even been able to get a ticket for myself.

"You have tickets to the opening of Jimmy Ferrara's exhibition?" I didn't even try to hide my surprise. "I didn't take you as an art fan."

Or to have those kinds of connections.

"I'm not a fan of his art. He's a hack who fried his brain with too much heroine in the 80's and somehow survived. His shit is overpriced and ugly. But I also know the Big Three are going to be there and face time in a relaxed setting with three of the biggest directors in Hollywood is not something easy to pass up. But if I go by myself, it looks like I'm there to do business. I need a woman to help keep up with the charade while I'm there pretending to look at the shit on the wall. And I'm not the kind of guy to take a date and ignore her the whole night while I try to make conversation with other people. Which is why I'm going to take you."

"You still haven't told me how you got a ticket."

A devilish grin twisted on his lips. "And, I'm not going to. So, we have a deal or not?"

"Fine, I'll come with you to the exhibition." Not a hardship since I'd been curious to go anyway. "I'll do enough staring at the art for both of us. And I'll be perfectly fine entertaining myself while you network."

"Good. I knew you would." He seemed satisfied even though I was clearly getting more out of our arrangement than he was. Still, I wasn't about to argue the point.

I met his eyes, wanting verbal and binding confirmation that he was agreeing. "So, do we have a deal? Are you actually going to do this?"

"Looks like you got yourself a boyfriend." He smirked. "When you said filming starts in a month, I assume you meant that's when the wedding is."

My fingers fumbled into my handbag and pulled out the invite. "Ummm, yes. It's three weeks from Saturday."

"Right, so that gives us some time to work on our backstory, how we met, what we like to do together, favorite sexual position—stuff like that."

"My family isn't going to ask what our favorite sexual position is. And if they did lose their damn minds and ask, they'd have to torture me before I'd answer."

He shook his head, waving his finger at me as his grin widened. "Uh-uh, Jess, if we do this, then we do this. You don't get to pick and choose what you think is important. You aren't embarrassed are you?" The last part seemed to please him.

"No, of course I'm not embarrassed." I lowered my voice, looking around at the mostly empty coffee shop.

I liked sex. No, *like* wasn't strong enough a word. I *loved* sex. But talking about it with someone you barely knew was weird, wasn't it? And there'd be a cold day in Hell before I'd talk about it with my parents. "I just don't see *why* we would discuss my sex life with anyone."

He watched me silently for a minute before reaching across the table, his fingers slowly caressing mine. My eyes widened as I watched the erotic glide of his thumb across my knuckles, making me swallow hard.

I couldn't remember the last time we'd touched. Probably a handshake? Definitely not more than that, and it had never been like this.

His hand barely grazed mine but was surprisingly sexual. "Trust me, I know what I'm doing." His voice rumbled. "And if we're going to sell us as a couple, you can't get weird on me when I ask a question like that or when I touch you."

Yeah, no shit.

I didn't doubt for a minute he didn't know what he was doing and it had nothing to do with his acting experience.

"Of course. I won't get weird." I made promises I had no idea if I was going to be able to keep. "I will be totally cool with touching and questions."

Especially the touching.

You are not going to have sex with him, I reminded myself.

Not that I was tempted. Please. I didn't sleep with clients.

And even though he was gorgeous and pretending to be my love interest, I knew I was paying him to be with me. There was a line, and I was positive I wouldn't cross it.

At least I was mostly positive I wouldn't.

No, I was sure. Positive, positive.

Do not cross the line, Jessica.

"There's one other thing," I added, wanting to get the important stuff out while I could still think straight. I pulled my hand back from his, saving it from any further finger seduction he had planned. "And this is sort of awkward to bring up, but I need you not to mention anything to Jeremy."

It sort of went without saying that what I was doing wouldn't exactly be kosher with my boss. I'm not sure he'd go so far as to fire me, but he would definitely not be pleased. Not to mention how bad it would look to other clients.

"Actually, our little agreement needs to stay confidential. You can't tell your brothers either." Because let's face it, who knew if one of them would spill and foil my plan.

He shook his head, shooting me a grin. "No one will know. I'll be your dirty little secret."

Those words thrilled me more than they should have.

Not sure why I did, but I trusted him, which was ridiculous because I didn't really *know* him. Sure, I'd seen him in the office plenty, had many conversations with him and could probably recite his height, weight and most of his resume off the top of my head. But all the stuff I knew about the man he was underneath it all had been garnered incidentally. So I wasn't sure if it was accurate.

"Do you have a girlfriend?" I heard myself asking. Probably something I should have asked before agreeing to share a hotel room with him. Still, if we were going to have to deal with a jealous significant other, it was best I knew now.

His eyebrow rose like he was surprised I asked. "Are you

concerned or you just making conversation?"

To be honest, I wasn't sure.

Not that it mattered, either way it wasn't *my* problem.

I shrugged, relaxing a little. "A little of both. Besides, if you expect me to answer which sexual position is my favorite, I think me asking if you are in a relationship would be an easy one for you."

"I was on a date tonight actually," he said with no hesitation. "Not a girlfriend. Just a date. It's not serious or exclusive," he answered with little emotion.

Well, I guess I should have been thankful it was a date and not a killing spree that had kept him detained. And whoever she was, she obviously hadn't been important, or very compelling, because he'd left her to come meet me. I'd hope that after a date with me, a man wouldn't run off to meet another woman. Except, I wasn't another woman, I was a job opportunity. Which made this ok, and me not a harlot trying to steal her man.

Blink. My brain was hurting.

I was really over thinking it.

I waited.

Waited for him to ask me the same question, but he didn't.

Instead I stared at him with expectation, trying to will the words from my mind to his.

"Something else you want to ask?" He looked at me with curiosity, missing the telepathic messages I'd been sending him, but unable to ignore the crazy eyes.

Not sure why it made me feel awkward, but it did. I was good with someone yelling at me or being able to achieve the impossible at work, but put me into a personal situation and I'd suddenly became an idiot. "I just thought you might want ask me the same thing."

He chuckled softly, his body leaning forward across the table as he whispered. "I sort of assumed you needing me meant that you weren't in a relationship."

Shit.

Of course.

I knew that.

"Yes, yes," I fumbled, stupidity seeming to be a theme I was keeping. "I'm single. No man. Which is why I need you." I took a breath, looking at him with apology. "I'm sorry, I don't know why I'm acting this way."

I wasn't sure where to lay the blame. If it was my mouth, my mind, or if the two of them were conspiring against me. But my lack of confidence was of serious concern, especially if we were going to convince my family we were more than passing acquaintances.

"I'm not a psychologist nor do I pretend to know how women think." He chuckled again as his eyes caught mine. "But if I had to guess it is because this is out of your comfort zone. Which is cool, we can work on it together."

I didn't care what Jeremy said. Dave Larsson was most definitely my favorite.

"You are so sweet." I took his hand—the same one that had given me goosebumps when it rubbed my fingers unintentionally erotically—and gave it a squeeze. "Thank you so much for understanding."

"Stop thanking me." He squeezed back as a gentle laugh traveled up his throat. "You still owe me my date. And I'm probably going to ignore you and be a general asshole."

It was my turn to chuckle, the idea that Dave thought his intention to mingle with important people and network would be seen as being an asshole was hilarious. "You can be as asshole-ish as you like," I grinned, "I'll be using you just to get in anyway."

Dave's beautiful chocolate eyes filled with wonder as the smile spread across his face. "Oh, we're perfect for each other."

Lord help me, I had to agree.

Professionally, I meant.
As co-stars.
Right?
Right.

CHAPTER #4

WHAT SHOULD HAVE happened last night was a quick meeting.

Like a bandit, get in, get out, and hope no one got hurt.

Because there were only two possible outcomes. Either he would agree, or tell me I was insane—neither required more than an hour. Less time if you didn't wait for the men in white coats to come and take me away.

I hadn't anticipated conversation.

I dropped the hey-can-you-pretend-to-be-my-boyfriend bomb in his lap, and he didn't bat an eye. Instead, he ordered an espresso and *chatted* like it wasn't the craziest thing he'd ever heard.

For. Two. Whole. Hours.

Even if I was subpoenaed and testifying under oath, I'd still be unable to recall the conversation. Maybe excessive caffeine made you stupid—not likely—or his voice had the ability to lull me into a relaxed trance. Either way it only meant bad news, my mouth spilling shit I hadn't wanted to say.

Thank God I'd never been trusted with matters of national security, who knew what me and my mouth were capable of.

It had been a while since I'd been out with a guy and it wasn't a work meeting or a date. They'd kind of become one in the same really, the initial *dates* feeling more like job interviews. Trying to work out whether or not he was suitable for a fulltime position. And half the time, they were more candidates for a casual basis.

Like hiring staff for the holidays, my dating life was more seasonal than long term.

And I was totally fine with that.

But with Dave there was no need for the interview. It was like having a new friend and we were in on the same private joke. Which was why I hadn't wanted to leave even though I had to get up early.

I felt weirdly hung over, intoxicated only by the conversation.

Oh, and I hadn't called back my mother.

Her missed calls and not so subtle *Call Me* text taunted me from behind the screen. She could only be avoided for so long.

I groaned, hauling my ass out of bed and into the shower. I was going to need to be as alert as possible to deal with my mom.

LeeAnn Dawson was a former Miss Louisiana who was anything but a southern belle. Born into money, she got a business degree so she could help run her daddy's construction company. And after my parents got married, she took over the business and expanded it into a national operation. She kept her blonde hair perfectly coiffured and a loaded nine-millimeter in her Chanel purse—she was not a woman you wanted to mess with. Which was why I needed to return her call as soon as I got to work.

"Hey, Mom." I pressed the phone to my ear as I sat down at my desk. "Sorry about yesterday, I was swamped at work."

"Jessica Lynn Dawson, have you been avoiding me?" She didn't bother with the greeting. "I tried calling four times and even left you a text message. Please tell me that heathen you work for did not keep you there all night."

To say my mother wasn't fond of Jeremy was an understatement. She'd said he had the demeanor of a traveling salesman peddling snake oil and didn't appreciate his hedonistic—her word, not mine—lifestyle. I preferred to ignore it rather than defend a man who cared very little about what my parents thought of him.

"No, I wasn't here the whole night. I was out with Dave."

Oh, I knew what I was doing, and while not technically a lie, it was building the foundation for my further deceit. It was a necessary evil I told myself, planting the seeds now, so later our relationship flower would be able to grow.

"Is that so?" Her voice softened. "You finally going to tell me about the man you've been dating? Or am I going to have to hire an investigator and get the scoop myself." She took a breath; the pause in the conversation not usually meaning good things. "I've been trying to be patient and give you your space, especially because I'd been so busy with Grandma Shelly. But I'd be lying if I wasn't beginning to wonder if you weren't keeping him from us on purpose."

Great, now I had to try and convince her that the lack of details hadn't been premeditated. Still, it was easier than telling her the truth. "Mom, of course not. It's just been crazy here and I didn't want to bother you when I knew you had your hands full. You'll get to meet him when I come back for the wedding. We're going to fly in Friday before the wedding and stay until Sunday. Lots of opportunity to get to know him."

"I thought you said you were coming in on Thursday? I was hoping we could have a family dinner so you could introduce us to Dave properly. And Melanie was looking forward to going shopping." I could hear the warning in her voice, knowing how displeased she would be if I changed plans.

Shit.

When I'd agreed to fly home on Thursday it had been before the whole fake boyfriend fiasco. My sisters-in-law, Mom, and I had offered to use the opportunity to go shopping with my older sister who was expecting her second baby. Of course if we proceeded as planned it would mean leaving Dave at the mercy of my brothers, brother-in-law and father while I was gone. And while I didn't doubt his acting ability, even Denzel Washington would struggle. Especially having less than a month to prepare. Not even a year would be long enough.

"Errrr, I don't know if I can get the time off work," I offered, thinking it was the most believable excuse.

Jeremy—who wasn't supposed to be in till later—picked that exact moment to emerge from the elevator and catch the tail end of the conversation, eyeing me with suspicion.

"Time off work for what?" He didn't bother waiting until I was off the phone, asking the question as he came to stand in front of my desk.

I forced a tight grin, waving him off as I continued to talk to my mother. "Oh, hi, Jeremy. Yes, I know how busy this time of year is."

I'd hoped my telepathy was working better this morning than it had been last night. With all the brainpower I could muster, I begged him to go into his office, promising him I'd fill him in later.

Not that I'd tell him the whole truth, because I wasn't insane, and valued employment. But the mortified version, which I hadn't concocted yet, but would sound amazing as soon as I had.

"Is this about your hillbilly wedding?" He cocked an eyebrow totally missing my mental clues and misreading my exaggerated hand gestures. "Why are you acting weird? I already told you to take off whatever days you needed as long as we had cover."

No, I mouthed silently, shaking my head as my mother's voice filled my ear. "See, the heathen is fine with it. Fly in Thursday like we had planned."

Damn it.

I narrowed my eyes, shooting Jeremy mind bullets I knew wouldn't register as I responded. "Sure, sounds great. I'll let you know what time we're flying in and when we're checking into our hotel."

"Hotel?" I heard the sharp intake of air, not even attempting to hide her shock. "No child of mine is coming home and staying in a hotel when we have perfectly good bedrooms here."

We'd been through it before, and usually I relented, happy to stay in my old bedroom. But there wasn't a snowball's chance in Hell I was staying with my parents this time around. It would mean Dave and I would have to be in character the entire time, and have my parents eye him suspiciously if he ventured anywhere near my room. Not that we were going to do anything sexual, but we need evening meetings for debriefing and possibly regrouping, something we couldn't do if we were constantly under surveillance. I was exhausted just thinking about it. Besides, one slip up and we'd be exposed, and my mother was a shark when it came to noticing stuff, she could smell the blood in the water.

"Mom, my accommodation is non-negotiable." I made it clear my mind had been made up and I wouldn't be bending. "I'll be staying at the Hilton, downtown. We can argue about it later."

She huffed out a breath, knowing that when I dug my heels in there was little more she could do to convince me. "I swear, I have to wonder where you get this stubborn streak from, but fine, if that's what you want, then that's what you want. Throw good money at that god awful place." The distaste rolled off her tongue.

"Thanks, Mom, we'll speak later."

"Do not avoid my calls Jessica Lynn," she gave me one last warning, "I still don't know anything about the man who is dating my youngest daughter. While the lack of details might fly in Hollywood, it's not going to suffice for us."

Jeremy waited until we said our goodbyes, his hands in his pockets as he eyed me. "You want to tell me what that was about? I'm not fluent in hand waves and evil eye stares."

"I lied to my mother," I explained, wondering if I got credit for telling half the truth. "I was trying to get out of going home the Thursday before the wedding."

"I thought you *wanted* to go back. Is there something I'm missing?" He looked at me with confusion.

I groaned, trying to explain further was too hard and would only dig myself into an even deeper hole. "Trust me, you don't want to know."

"All you needed to say. The less I know, the better." He held his hands up. "Now, onto important things. You smooth things over with Dave Larsson? I have a meeting with Eric at ten and I need to work out how much ass I need to kiss." The smile on his face told me he wasn't as worried as he pretended to be.

I rolled my eyes, unable to hide my grin. "You need to find him a better role. I'm giving you a script and you need to read it. It is perfect for him."

"Yes, yes. I will." He crossed his heart as he moved toward his office. "I promise."

I shouted after him. "Don't burn me, Jeremy. I went to bat for you."

I'd promised Dave we'd find him something better and I was committed to making that happen. Not just because of what he was doing for me, but because he'd earned it. He was a great guy and talented too, and he sure as hell was hot enough to carry a lead. Amazing how I'd suddenly felt more invested in his future when yesterday morning I hadn't. Must have been the lingering remnants of the trance I'd been in. That was the only explanation.

THE DAY WAS like any other. Phone calls, meetings and about a million Post-It notes on my desk with messages and reminders for Jeremy.

Katrina and I met for lunch like we did most days, eating in the break room while we chatted.

"So, you never told me what happened with your mom?" she asked between bites of her quinoa salad.

I swallowed, conveniently not having mentioned my arrangement with Dave. "Nothing really." Which was pretty much the truth. "You know me, I'll work something out."

She nodded, agreeing that I'd find a way to somehow come out of this in one piece. "Did you call Dave?"

"Dave?" I almost choked on my sandwich. "Why would I call Dave?" I tried to scoff in disbelief.

"Ummm, because he left angry yesterday after Jeremy was a douchebag." She narrowed her eyes, looking at me like I'd grown an extra head. "Weren't you tasked with smoothing it all over?"

"Yes, of course I was. Sorry, my mind is on other things. He's all good." My smile hopefully reassured her that I wasn't acting crazy.

She leaned in closer, her smile widening. "Great, I was thinking of asking him out."

I coughed again, my poor esophagus taking a beating as I tried to clear my throat and breathe at the same time, the words wheezing out. "On a date?"

"Of course on a date, did you not see how hot he looked? I figured the worst that can happen is he turns me down, and I'll never know unless I ask." Her lips spread into a grin of self-satisfaction. "And, if he says yes . . . well." She fanned herself dramatically.

"He's a client, Katrina." I hoped pointing out the obvious would curtail her ideas of hooking up.

"So?" Her shoulder lifted, giving me a shrug. "Technically there is no reason why we can't date. We're not responsible for any of his bookings, there's no conflict of interest."

Katrina was right. There were no official rules against us dating clients. Most people didn't because it would be awkward when a breakup inevitably happened, but Jeremy was the only one who was ethically bound not to pee in the pool. I just didn't think it was smart, and given how stupid I'd been lately, I wanted to hold on to as much intelligence as I could.

"I don't think Jeremy will see it that way."

Katrina scoffed, amused by my suggestion. "Unless Jeremy is going to lose money on it, he won't give a shit. Besides, he hasn't even said yes yet."

Well, she had a point.

There was the very real possibility he'd turn her down. I mean, he hadn't seemed to notice her whenever she was staring at his ass. And while she might not have a problem dating clients, maybe he did.

"I thought you'd be more excited for me?" She pouted, her eyes clouding with disappointment that I hadn't been more supportive of her dating my fake boyfriend.

Not that I'd told her he was my fake boyfriend, no she was just supposed to innately know that he was off limits.

"Of course I'm excited. It's great. You should totally ask him out and I bet he says yes." *No need to oversell it, dumbass.* "And if he turns you down it's probably just because he doesn't want to mix business with pleasure."

I was being ridiculous. There was no reason Dave could not date Katrina. We had a business arrangement. I was paying him money for services to be rendered and I certainly didn't expect for him to be celibate for the next few weeks. He'd been on a date last night, could have been screwing her brains out before he'd met up with me. Hell, he might be screwing someone's brains out right now and I have no say in the matter.

"Awesome." She grinned. "I'm going to call him after lunch."

I forced a smile, continuing to fake my enthusiasm. "Great. Let me know what he says."

It was so not great.

CHAPTER #5

THE DAY HAD seemed to drag on forever and when I finally got home to my apartment, I felt dead on my feet.

I was already on my second glass of wine when I called my mother. I'd kept details of Dave fairly generic, just mentioning we'd met at work and that he was an actor. She wasn't pleased that he didn't have a *real job*, but was glad he was at least employed. And lucky for me the minor debrief had been enough information to satisfy her.

Well, at least until she got a chance to meet him.

Which would be happening soon.

* *Insert sarcasm* * I could barely contain my excitement.

Instead of cooking dinner, I grabbed a bag of *Goldfish*, collapsed onto my sofa, and polished off the bottle of wine. It seemed like a solid idea and one I was pretty happy with when I was sipping the last of the Shiraz from my glass.

It was also doing wonders for my mood, the tension easing out of my body as I watched mindless television. I'd barely even noticed when my phone buzzed beside me.

"Jessica Dawson," I answered, not bothering to check the caller ID.

"Hey, Jess, it's Dave."

The bottle of Shiraz made its presence felt as my skin flushed at the sound of his sexy voice. My body scrambled, trying to sit up straighter even though he couldn't see me. "Hey, Dave." I unsuccessfully tried not to slur. "What can I do for you?" The words came out slow and unsteady.

"I was looking forward to reading over my casting notes." He chuckled. "However, my inbox is missing the all-important file."

My hand lacked coordination as I attempted to slap my forehead. "Shit, I totally forgot."

Last night before we said goodnight, we'd agreed it would be useful to get to know each other a little better. A crash course on all things important. Things that might be significant—like favorite food, tastes in music, where we went to college—stuff that most people would know about their significant other. I had started compiling my Jessica Dawson dossier earlier today, but stalled out after hearing about Katrina's *fantastic* idea at lunch. I had intended to finish it when I got home but then wine happened.

Shit.

"I can have it to you in the next hour." I harnessed all my effort to be able to continue talking and turn on my laptop. "I was almost done."

"It can wait till tomorrow if you're busy."

I tried to focus on the saved document, thanking God it was mostly completed. "No, no. I'm not busy. I can totally do this."

Not sure why I didn't just agree to give it to him tomorrow, because I wasn't at all convinced I could even type my name let alone write a sentence. But in my head, it made sense. I didn't want to be the weakest link that let down the team, and his email was already sitting in my inbox, mocking me as it flashed as an unread message.

He paused, a few seconds passing before he spoke. "Are you

drunk?"

"No. No. Not all," I assured him, shaking my head with vigor for confirmation. "I've just had some wine, but it's fine. I'll finish and send the email."

I hung up before he could argue or confirm my inebriation, and set about adding more information. Not sure why I had struggled earlier in the day, my fingers flew along the keyboard as I added bits and pieces of information. I should have done the whole thing after a bottle of wine, the process seeming easier than I first thought. And without bothering to proofread, I sent the email and congratulated myself on a job well done.

No wonder Hemmingway was an alcoholic; writing while drunk was super easy. It was literally the

Best.

Thing.

Ever.

But my celebration didn't last long as fatigue took over. Between the late night from yesterday, the eventful day, and the wine, I barely had enough energy to walk to my bedroom. I didn't even bother with pajamas, stripped out of my clothes quickly before commando crawling into bed with my phone in my hand.

And against my better judgment—I mean, why start being sensible now—my fingers swiped the screen, opening Dave's email. Unlike my detailed attachment, he'd including all his notes in the body of the email. In point form, he listed snippets of information, like a cheat sheet on all things Dave Larsson.

It felt so naughty, reading about him as I lay naked underneath my sheets, my eyes widening when I got to the part where he said he slept naked. I wondered if at that moment he was doing the exact same thing. Like phone sex by email without the dirty talk, his voice took up residence inside my head as he whispered to me his secrets.

And while my position at Levin Murphy had meant I already knew a lot, I relished the private delicious morsels he'd included. It was a rare man who could be just as sexy on paper as he was in person, but Dave Larsson was a freaking unicorn.

I WOKE UP with my phone on my face and a headache. Slowly, I lifted each eyelid, testing how offending the light was in the room before I made a full commitment to opening them. It wasn't so bad, the heavy drapes that hung on my bedroom window saving me the full assault from the morning sun.

"Ugh," I groaned, peeling the screen from my face and taking a layer of epidermis with it as the glass lifted from my skin. I rolled over onto my stomach, squinting as I tried to focus on the time. It was nine a.m. and I was going to be late.

Shit.

Normally, I would have leapt from my bed running around like a madwoman trying to break the space-time continuum while getting ready and refusing to accept the inevitable. I was always shocked when I was still late, but gave myself credit for trying. But as I slowly ambled out of bed, I felt a strange sense of calm.

Maybe I was still drunk, I reasoned, making my way to the shower with no sense of urgency. It was weird, and other than the headache, I felt sort of . . . great.

Relieved. Relaxed.

That must have been one hell of a bottle of Shiraz. I made a mental note to check out the label and buy a case of it. Not that I had plans of becoming an alcoholic, but to keep for the times where I needed a mental vacation. Not everyone could afford a trip to the Bahamas whenever life got too intense, so I'd happily make do.

The spray from the shower felt good on my skin when I finally got in, the suds washing down my body, my long hair pressing against my back as I took my time before stepping out and patting myself dry.

I was still reveling in my good mood when a fragment of a memory snapped into focus as I pulled on my underwear. The lower half of my body feeling a tingle I usually associated with a night *well* spent.

No.

No, please tell me I didn't.

I ran to my bedroom and grabbed my cell, my finger scrolling to access the call register before I confirmed what I already knew.

There at the top of the list was the name Dave Larsson, the call made a whole hour after I'd sent the email.

Okay, no need to panic. I didn't necessarily know *what* we'd spoken about, I could have simply asked if he'd received the email, and to clarify if it was Belgium waffles or buttermilk waffles that were his favorite breakfast food. Or I could have potentially babbled for thirty-five minutes and fifty-six seconds to his voicemail, I mean anything was possible.

Although, you'd have thought it would have cut off before then.

Shit, this wasn't looking good.

Maybe the sexy thoughts that flashed through my memory were part of a dream I'd had later. Like after we'd hung up. That made sense. I'd once dreamt I'd had sex with Jason Momoa and that hadn't happened. It was totally plausible that I *hadn't* asked Dave Larsson to say naughty things to me while I touched myself and orgasmed in his ear.

Dear. God.

Damn that fucking Shiraz.

The phone that was still in my hand lit up with an incoming call, and thankfully it was just from the office. It was easier to deal with my boss rather than the man that I might have—or might not have, we couldn't be sure—had phone sex with last night.

"Hey, Jeremy, sorry, I woke up with a headache and am running a little late." I didn't bother saying hello, knowing exactly why he was calling. "I'll make up the time."

He laughed, his voice missing the anger or impatience I was expecting. "Relax, it's Dave. I'm sitting at your desk. I figured if you saw this number, you'd definitely pick up."

Oh God, my feelings of relief vanished as I tried not to hyperventilate.

"Hey, Dave." I tried to sound normal, grabbing clothes out of my closet as I attempted to dress with one hand. Clearly I couldn't be trusted around him naked, and I didn't want to risk asking for a repeat of whatever happened last night that I couldn't remember. "What are you doing at the agency? I didn't think we had a meeting scheduled."

The question was rhetorical because I knew for a fact there was no meeting. And Jeremy didn't know how to set things up in his calendar which meant he didn't set it either.

"There wasn't a meeting scheduled. But apparently you left a script on Jeremy's desk yesterday for a role I'd be perfect for. It's not a lead, but a major supporting role for a big budget feature. It's good, Jess. It is *really* good."

The feelings of *really good* were felt on both sides of the call. Happy for him that Jeremy listened to me and called him, and happy for me we were avoiding last night's shenanigans. Maybe it *had* just been a dream; just me, my hand and no one else whispering dirty things in my ear.

I offered up silent thank yous to the heavens as I buttoned up my blouse and zipped up my skirt. Getting dressed one-handed was tough, but I'd managed it. And just like that, no longer being naked was something else to be thankful for.

"That's great." My excitement genuine as I continued giving unspoken gratitude. "I didn't think he'd had time to read it, let alone call you. And the role really is perfect for you, the script has been on my desk for a week."

"Yeah, it is great. Except he didn't call me. You did."

Say what?

"I'm sorry, what?" I checked the date, making sure I had only slept in and not skipped a whole day.

I had zero recollection of making a call about the script. I had barely spoken to Jeremy about it, with a bright pink Post-It sitting on my computer monitor reminding myself to harass him about it today.

"Last night, you called me."

And there it was. All my feelings of gratitude were shelved as the call that I'd hoped we'd avoided suddenly was thrust into the spotlight. So not only had I touched myself while breathing heavily over the phone—well done, Jess—but I'd also discussed a script that my boss hadn't properly vetted.

Brilliant.

"Funny thing about that call." I sat on the edge of my bed, feeling the blood drain from my face. "I was drinking and Jeremy should have called you about that role. It was unprofessional of me, and I'm really sorry." Not to mention inappropriate.

I wasn't sure if I was glad I couldn't remember the details—saving myself the embarrassment—or annoyed I didn't have the conversation tucked away for private enjoyment later. Clearly it had been pretty outstanding for me, my body still buzzing from last night's sextivities, not sure how it rated for him.

"Fuck professionalism, you were awesome and I was incredibly glad you called."

Well, that confused me.

It wasn't the first time I'd had phone sex. Sure, it wasn't my favorite thing to do, preferring to be with a man in the flesh than heavy breathing through a phone. But I wasn't adverse to assisted self-love with the right person. But usually the person on the other end of the line had at least seen me naked, and wasn't someone I had to see at work because that would be kind of awkward. And as wonderful as I liked to imagine myself to be, I'd never been told I was *incredible*. Was it possible for a man as sexy as Dave Larsson to have been having subpar sex?

I closed my eyes, hoping the darkness would help me focus better, but sadly it didn't.

"You still with me?" he asked when I didn't respond. I had been too busy wondering if I was a goddess in the sack or he had been subjected to really unfortunate lovers.

"Yes, I'm here." I rubbed my temples, the headache that had started to fade making a reappearance. "The phone call is a little fuzzy, want to refresh my memory a little?"

He laughed, not sounding surprised. "After you emailed, you called and begged me not to read it."

"Okay." I held my breath, waiting for him to continue.

"Then you mumbled stuff which I really didn't understand, and told me that if I didn't read it you would return my kindness by tipping me off about the part."

Oh thank you, God.

While I had probably still sounded like a raving lunatic, at least I hadn't asked him to talk dirty to me while I touched myself. Sad that I needed to make the distinction, but there I was, making it nonetheless.

"Yeah, I probably had a little too much to drink." There was an understatement. "Thanks for not reading the email, it probably made zero sense. I'll send you a replacement later today."

I totally ignored that part about mumbling because clearly it wasn't important. And as for the phone sex, it had obviously been one-sided using my active imagination. And I was completely okay with that. In fact, I was better than okay, I was fucking elated.

My eyes rose to the heavens, my thanks to Virgin Mary offered up in gratitude.

All in all, I was pretty pleased with myself. I assumed any pleasure I'd given myself last night had either been before or after the call. Yes, I probably shouldn't have drunk dialed Dave and made a fool of myself, but there were worse things in the world. And if I wasn't so thankful that the only thing I was guilty of was sounding like a lush, I might have been embarrassed.

"Errr . . . Jess." It sounded like he was trying to suppress a laugh. "You called an hour after you sent the email. I had already read it."

No.

No.

No.

"I thought you said . . ." I replayed the conversation, and realized that he'd only mentioned what my side of the exchange had been, and not his.

"Trying to tell you I'd already read it was like trying to nail Jell-O to the wall. I've spoken to telemarketers that were less insistent. If you ever decide to give up your job with Jeremy, Verizon will hire you in a heartbeat." He chuckled, finding humor in my stupidity. "It was only after you'd told me about the part that I was able to get a word in edgeways. And when I came in this morning and I didn't see you, I assumed you were pissed off that you'd told me even though I'd read it. I had a whole elaborate apology planned. It was epic, I'm kind of bummed you missed it."

I didn't answer, heavy breathing on the phone like I assumed I had last night. Well, at least I was consistent.

My lack of response prompted him to continue. "But when Jeremy asked me what I was doing at the office, I figured I had nothing to lose so asked him about the script. We went over it together, and he got me an audition."

I opened my mouth and then closed it again, my brain unable

to formulate exactly what I needed to say.

"Jess?"

"Hmmm?" It was the best I could do, offering him only syllables while I died of mortification. And I still hadn't read the email, unsure how bad it was with my imagination not doing me any favors.

"I know it was information you hadn't meant to share, but I swear on my life I tried to stop you."

I wasn't sure what was worse, him feeling bad or me not remembering. And for God's sake, what the hell had I said? "Um . . . so the email." My throat tightened as I tried to swallow.

His voice lowered, vibrating against my ear. "It was actually kind of hot. Made for fascinating reading. I have a few questions though so I'll call you later. So much we need to explore. See you, Jess."

And before I'd had a chance to say goodbye, the line went dead.

"Fuck," I cursed, tossing the phone on my bed as I straightened my skirt and blouse.

It had been fascinating reading? What the hell had I'd written? I grabbed my phone trying to not hyperventilate. *Ha, good luck with that.*

Last time I checked, I didn't possess super powers to spew out literary brilliance. It would have been easier if I'd just had phone sex with him, my finger hovered as I opened the sent message addressed to Dave.

Shit.

My heart slammed against my chest as I scrolled through the contents, speed-reading through the paragraphs.

It started innocent enough—birth date, education history, detailed reports of members of my family. That had been before I'd partaken in the Devil's drink, typed out earlier in the day when I still had some sense—or sobriety—either would do. But then it turned into something else, like I had been possessed by a demon, the powers of the Shiraz compelling me.

I'd taken his suggestion of *favorite sexual position* and run with it. It got dirtier and more personal as I went on. My sexual chronicles of the past were only less mortifying than my aspirations for the future. Because admitting you lost your virginity on prom night was fine as long as you didn't follow that up with your fantasy of smothering yourself in chocolate sauce and having a threesome with *Ragnar* and *Rollo* from *Vikings*. Who knew The History Channel would be so goddamn sexy? Still, not something I needed to broadcast to a MAN I BARELY KNEW.

It was okay, I tried to rationalize. It would all be fine. I would just merely admit that I was bored and had a little fun with it. And possibly I'd taken it too far but that none of it was true. I mean, some of it was true, but not all the crazy stuff. That stuff was most definitely not true.

I contemplated picking up the phone and telling Dave the whole thing was off. He'd already got his audition for a more suitable part like he wanted, so he probably didn't even have the time for my nonsense anyway. And if I thought it would save me the embarrassment of seeing him, I'd have probably done just that. Worked out some other solution to my date problem. Screw it, I hadn't even tried Tinder yet. Even a trained monkey could swipe right.

But unfortunately, I would be seeing him regardless, probably more so if he got the part.

Fine.

It would all be fine.

I was onto my second pep talk and still wasn't convinced. But I was out of ideas, running late and needed to get to work.

Fine.

It would be fine.

Nope, the third time didn't help either.

CHAPTER #6

JEREMY WAS ANNOYED I'd been late until I dropped a latte and croissant from his favorite bakery on his desk and told him I'd been busy picking up scripts. It wasn't unusual for me to swing past a studio on the way to work, and I had done it on numerous occasions.

This time it had been a lie of course, with the scripts having been delivered yesterday afternoon and I just hadn't gotten around to reading them yet. But it was either tell him the lie, or setting a fire and having the place evacuated.

Sadly, that's what it had come to.

Katrina, on the other hand, didn't seem to be buying it. She waved off my offer of coffee, coming at me like a heat-seeking missile the minute I'd sat down.

"He was back. And oh my God did he look good today." She fanned herself for effect. "He even asked me where you were, the two of us having a twenty-minute conversation while he waited for Jeremy. Can you believe it? He is so fucking fine I thought I was going to pass out."

My lips edged into a bogus smile as I faked ignorance. "Who are we talking about?"

"Dave Larsson." Her hand softly slapped me across the arm.

"That is twice in one week, I think I might be in love with him."
She sighed, her attention switching to whatever fantasy she had in
her head rather than to me.

I pretended to be busy, looking uninterested as I turned on my
computer. "That's great, Katrina. I'm so glad you guys got to chat."

Apparently my response wasn't as excited as she'd hoped,
prompting her to yank on the back of my chair and spin me around.
"I asked him out, Jess."

Well, now she had my attention. "Ohhhh." I meant to tack on
a suitable adjective but didn't get the chance; the surprise stunning
me into silence.

"He said yes." She danced excitedly in place, her face beaming.
"I'm still in shock."

She wasn't the only one.

I wondered if it was too late to go back to my other option
this morning and set fire to the office? It seemed I'd been jumping
from one metaphoric fire to the next in the last few days, so maybe
a real one might help. I'd throw in some white sage and smudge
the place while I was at it, hoping to exorcise the evil spirits that
had suddenly cursed my freaking awesome life.

"That's . . ." I paused, swallowing my first instinct which was
to just string a bunch of swear words together. "Great. Really
great. So Great."

It was so *not* great.

She spun around, feeling all the joy I wasn't. "I know." The
celebration paused for a second as she focused on me. "But I have
one tiny little favor I need to ask."

"What is it?"

"You have to come too."

Huh?

When I assumed things couldn't get any worse this morning,
I had been sadly mistaken. "I'm sorry, what?" I asked on the slim

chance I'd misheard.

"I know, I know. I'm sorry." She shook her head, her eyes trying to convey an apology I didn't believe for a second. "But he didn't say yes right away so I panicked and told him it was a group thing. And we have that party to go to tomorrow anyway, so I figured we'd just have dinner before. You know, give me a fighting chance to wow him before we are around a crowd. When I told him you were coming, he agreed."

My eyes rose to the ceiling, wondering if I was being punished. There was no other explanation why the situation was going from bad to worse. We hadn't even gotten to Louisiana yet and I was all ready neck deep in sinful deceit. At this rate, I was going to spontaneously ignite the minute I got anywhere near a preacher.

"Katrina, as much as I would love to be the third wheel on your," I waved my hand at her, "attempt to *wow* him. But don't you think it's going to look suspicious when it's just me and you?" Because I assumed the man wasn't blind and would smell a set up. Oh, and sitting across the table from him and trying to eat dinner after email-gate sounded like a good time as well.

She threw her head back and laughed, her eyes widening as she gripped my arm like she already had a plan. "Well yeah, of course if it was just the *two of us*. But I figured we could invite Liz, and surely we could ask some of the guys from the office. Matt from accounting will say yes in a heartbeat, and he has lots of friends."

"Katrina." Her name was huffed out in exasperation. "I swear, you drive a woman to drink." And considering my liver had yet to recover from last night's escapade, things were pretty dire if I was considering returning to the Devil's elixir.

"But you love me, right?" She batted her eyes, feigning innocence. "And because you love me, you'll come."

There were a lot of things I wouldn't do, and being coerced into accepting invitations sat rather high on that list. And yet, in the last few days I had bent twice, both times because I cared about the person making the request.

Damn being nice.

"Fine, I'll come," I agreed, shaking my head at my stupidity. "But you're making the dinner reservations and inviting everyone else. I am not asking people to be part of your charade, especially not Matt from accounting or any of his friends." I already had a bucket load of my own deceit; I didn't need to be borrowing anyone else's.

She threw her arms around me, her gratitude and excitement manifesting itself into a hug. "You are the best friend ever. And I will totally take care of everything; I will even organize a car."

Well, not driving meant I could drink, so at least this potential disaster had *that* going for it. Okay, so I wasn't giving up alcohol; that had been a stupid idea and one that was shelved for the foreseeable feature. Maybe I should steer clear of red wine though, that could be the compromise.

Now I just had to get through the day and most of tomorrow and prepare myself for a group "date" with Dave. Seriously, it was too late to hire a gigolo, right?

I am never going to lie again.

I MANAGED TO survive the day despite rocking a slight hangover and a truckload of last-night's regret. Thankfully it had been busy so I was able to make it through without thinking too much about my impending night out.

And when the day was over I went home, shut down all my electronic devices, shuffled under my covers and closed my eyes.

The next day was more of the same, minus the hangover of course. I didn't even get a chance to eat lunch, Katrina having to go it alone as I continued to work through. I hadn't minded so much, grateful for the distraction until it was time to go home.

Oh, I hadn't forgotten about my commitment to the group dinner. It wasn't like I slipped, fell and had given myself a concussion. Although as I got ready to face my fake boyfriend who was on a real date with someone else, I wondered if faking a brain injury wouldn't have been smarter.

Ugh, it was a little late in the game now to try to change the play so I guess I was going to have to stick with the original plan. Besides, I was putting too much stock into this.

Dave had probably already forgotten about the email, the phone call and everything else I had done which could have been classified as weird. Besides, they were isolated incidents on what was an otherwise unblemished record, so I was fixating on the negative for no good reason.

And with those words of wisdom tucked into my proverbial pocket, I finished getting ready and waited for the car.

I left my long mane of red curls loose, sweeping the front away from my face. And threw on a dress that maximized my thin waist and curved hips. It also did nice things for my boobs, the smoke-and-mirror silhouette making my B cups look more like a C.

Not that I was trying to impress anyone, no. I just wanted to make sure I looked *fancy* enough for the party we were going to go to after. The thirtieth birthday of a model I barely knew wasn't my idea of time well spent, but it was a friend of Liz's, and it beat sitting around my apartment spending the night alone. It was a good thing we were eating before we went too because I highly doubted there was going to be any food there.

My phone buzzed with a message the driver was waiting for me downstairs, so I grabbed my purse and phone, locking up behind me as I left my apartment.

I was glad to not have to worry about parking, the driver holding the door open for me as I climbed inside the black Lincoln.

Shit.

"Jess." The amusement in his voice evident as he cocked his head to the side. "Ready for our first date? Or was the coffee shop our first? I'm just trying to keep a mental tally so I can keep track of our special anniversaries. I read an article on BuzzFeed that said it was important."

I shuffled into my seat, shutting the door behind me as I tried to get a handle on my shock. "Heyyyyy. You're here . . . in the car. I thought you were meeting us at the restaurant. And I believe you're on a date with Katrina, not me."

Wearing dark blue dress pants with a crisp white shirt, it wasn't just his presence that was throwing me off my game. He even had a hint of stubble on his jaw, making his vibe sexier than it needed to be.

"Really?" He sounded genuinely surprised. "She didn't mention that, only asked if I wanted to come have dinner with all of you guys. I thought this was a *group* thing?"

I hadn't meant to expose Katrina's plan, that I—along with everyone else—were the decoys in what was a poor attempt at asking him out. But I hadn't expected him to be in the car, or look that good, or be in the car.

Shit. I'd thought that twice.

"It's a group thing. Totally a group thing." My attempt even worse than Katrina's as my words fooled no one.

He shook his head, his smile tightening as the car started moving. "If I'd known she was asking me on a date, I'd have said no."

"Really?"

I wasn't sure if I was surprised or relieved by his revelation, but the new development had renewed my faith in God. And no, not because I was jealous and glad he didn't want to date her. It was for far more selfish reasons than that. Us talking about Katrina and her misguided intentions meant we didn't have to discuss me, my drunken email, or the phone call that followed.

I was a terrible person.

"I like her, and she is great. But I'm not interested in Katrina in *that* way." He added, his eyes flicking to mine, "She's not my type. Plus my girlfriend would be pissed."

"Dave, you know you don't have to stop dating just because of me," I said even though I'd happily have him be celibate during our fictional relationship.

Because that was fair and made perfect sense.

Not.

He shook his head, leaning in closer as he smirked. "Are you trying to sabotage my first time as a lead? I *literally* just got out of the *doghouse* and you're trying to put me back in? Frankly, Jess, I'm a little shocked you'd be so unsupportive."

I laughed, the reference to his famous commercial quickly changing the tone.

"Just don't hurt her, and let her down easy, okay?" My conscience finally decided to show up and be concerned for my friend who was probably going to be crushed.

"I'll be a perfect gentleman, I promise." He rested his hand on his heart. "Stringing women along on isn't my MO."

He was right about that. Despite looking the way he did, and having a famous last name, he could have his pick of beautiful women and leave a trail of broken hearts in his wake. But he didn't. Or at least, none that we knew of.

I relaxed in my seat, my tension slowly easing. "I know, you're one of the good guys."

"I wouldn't go that far." He laughed as his eyes darkened. "So, let's talk about your file. It was very . . . detailed."

All my earlier feelings of relief evaporated as I was thrown head-on into a conversation I was hoping to avoid. I assumed the time would come and we would address my lapse of judgment, but I was hoping that wouldn't be this evening.

There was a choice to make. Either I stutter around like an idiot—something I'd done far too often recently—or just own the fact I had overshared information of a personal nature.

"Well, you said you wanted to know everything, so there it is. You know everything." I met his gaze, not allowing it to drop for a minute despite the temptation to look at the floor.

"Mmmm," he hummed as he stroked his chin. "And it made for fascinating reading. Reverse cowgirl, huh?"

Heat flushed across my skin but I still didn't look away. "It's underappreciated in my opinion."

He blew out a breath. "Yeah, I'd have to agree. Maybe we should start an appreciation society, I'll happily volunteer to be its president."

"Big of you."

"So is the rumor," he said with a smirk. "You read mine?"

I coughed, fighting oxygen as I nodded slowly. His had been nowhere near as scandalous as mine. "I think it's only fair you give me a little more to work with now you've read mine."

The car slowed, coming to a stop in front of Katrina's apartment, our time alone approaching its end very quickly.

"I'll send you more before our big debut." He winked. "And I know we have to keep this on the lowdown, but I'm really looking forward to meeting your family."

"Huh?" My eyes widened. Like a bucket of ice water had been tossed in my face, the future dirty email getting sidelined with the mention of family. "Dave—"

I didn't have a chance to finish—probably for the best because I had no idea what I was going to say—the door opening as Katrina stepped in.

She looked like a million dollars, dressed in a figure-hugging piece of couture that could reverse erectile dysfunction. Clearly she wasn't leaving this up to her warm and bubbly personality.

"Oh hey!" She looked surprised to see me in the car. "I thought we were going to get you guys after me?" She looked to the driver who had yet to shut the door.

"Sorry, Ms. Wagner, I must have read the brief in the incorrect order. My apologies."

Her smile faltered for a second before she looked at Dave and beamed. "No apologies necessary, we're all here now. Let's get to the restaurant, Liz is meeting us there."

Dutifully I allowed Katrina to dominate the conversation as we drove, with Dave graciously answering all her questions. He remained polite, but as promised nothing he said or did could in no way be construed as overly interested.

But God love her, Katrina kept trying, leaning suggestively so he could get a better eyeful of her cleavage and pursing her lips in a perfect pout.

She didn't seem deterred he had yet to fall under her spell, remaining upbeat as we arrived at the restaurant. Dave continued to be incredibly sweet, holding the door for her as she strolled into the crowded eatery.

In a city where almost everyone had some level of fame, Dave was relatively small fry. Of course he was recognizable, drawing looks from diners as we walked in. But when they saw he was the most famous person in our posse, they went back to their Wagu steaks and overpriced salads with little fanfare.

"Larsson." Liz stood offering her hand while she sipped an Old Fashioned. "Or should I say *wocf*." She finished with a smirk.

While Liz Langley completed our group of three amigos, she was firmly on the Dark Side. An actress, who had worked with both Dave and Nick in the past, she was no stranger to the company we were keeping, or the cursory looks we'd no doubt attract. She also was from Texas and had very little tolerance for bullshit, one of the reasons why we'd became friends four years ago when Jeremy signed her on.

Dave laughed, tipping his head as he shook her hand. "You'll be sad to know my days with pampered pedigrees are over, I'm moving on to bigger and better things."

"Oh, how sad." She laughed, taking a sip from her tumbler. "But it is good to see you in the company of the two-legged variety." She tipped her drink in our direction.

"Hey, gorgeous." I reached over and gave her a hug before taking my seat. "Hope you weren't waiting long."

"Not at all." She greeted Katrina before she retook her chair. "I was just enjoying a pre-dinner drink."

The additional members—ring ins—of our group hadn't arrived yet, leaving us to order our own pre-dinner drinks while we waited, a waiter walking over to me first. "I'll have soda and lime, and can we also get a Cosmopolitan and a Dos Equis, please." I ordered for the rest of the table, a habit when we all went out.

"Soda and lime?" Liz held her hand up, stopping the waiter from walking away. "Put a shot of vodka in it for her, she isn't driving."

I shrugged, agreeing that my abstinence from the feel-good juice was probably not going to last the night. How long had I held out? A few hours? I would totally suck in a hostage situation. "Fine, add the vodka."

He nodded, making his way to the bar to fill our order.

Dave smiled at me with appreciation before turning his attention to Liz. "So tell me, Liz, how's cable life treating you?"

"How did you know what Dave wanted to drink?" Katrina leaned into whisper while Dave was momentarily engaged in conversation with Liz. "I know *we're* predictable, but I *know* his drink preference isn't written in his employment file. I've read it like five times, I'd have remembered if it was."

She was right about that, it wasn't written there. Instead, I had read it on the specially prepared fake boyfriend dossier he'd given me. Which funnily enough I'd read five times too.

"Oh, you know." I played it down, pretending like it was no big deal. "It's my job to know stuff like that. Favorite drinks, places clients like to go, who they follow in sport. Lord knows, Jeremy wouldn't be able to remember."

Her look of concern eased, my explanation seeming to make sense. "Of course." She shook her head, a smile crossing her lips. "I should have known you'd have insider information. You can give me all the extra dirt later."

I hated not telling her the truth, that instead of being a walking talking Hollywood encyclopedia like I'd just implied, I'd been given a helping hand courtesy of the man himself.

But the fewer people who knew about our arrangement, the better. Too much was on the line—my job, my reputation, my family disowning me—so for now, it would have to stay my dirty little secret. Ironic since that's what Dave offered to be. And even my closest friends, with whom I shared almost everything, would have to remain in the dark.

"You found a date yet for Lana's wedding?" Liz asked, pulling me back into the conversation. "Or should we shop for funeral dresses for when you tell your mom the truth?"

"Nobody yet." I smiled, deliberately not looking at Dave. "I still have a few weeks though."

"I know a guy you can use," Liz offered. "I dated him for a week, good take-home-to-momma material, but has a weird doll collection." She shivered at the memory. "Creepiest thing ever, but as long as you stay out of his bedroom, you're good."

Dave laughed, covering his mouth as he pretended to cough into his hand.

"Thanks, I'll take my chances finding someone on my own."

I kicked him deliberately under the table.

My threat of violence did nothing to curb his grin, tilting his head to the side as he spoke. "Now, Jess, I don't think you should rule out Liz's suggestion so quickly. Doesn't one of your aunts collect dolls?"

"How did you know that?" Katrina asked, her brow knitted in confusion.

And it was a fair question, the information not something a lot of people knew. Unfortunately, Dave and I had info-loaded each other and were both having trouble remembering where the line was of what we should publically know.

"I must have mentioned it to Dave when Nick went for that audition for that horror movie last year." I stumbled around the explanation like a drunkard trying to find a light switch in the dark. "You know, freaky dolls are scary."

"Actually you told Nick and Nick told me, but yeah it was when he went for the audition," Dave continued seamlessly, his bullshit story rolling of his tongue like it was utter fact. "We toyed with idea of sending you a Chucky doll anonymously. You can thank me for convincing him that was a shitty thing to do."

My eyes widened, not needing to pretend I was horrified. "Umm . . . thank you?"

"Ladies." Matt arrived with a friend in tow, saving my ass. "Sorry we're late, the traffic was terrible."

Katrina introduced everyone. The additional company distracted her from our near miss as the waiter delivered our drinks before taking an order for our newcomers. Matt sat next to me while the guy he'd walked in with—Joe—almost fell into the seat beside Liz. He wasn't even trying to hide his excitement, his jaw hitting the table as he stared at the blond, blue-eyed starlet he was obviously not told about.

We ordered more drinks and dinner as the conversation flowed easily. Matt was a nice guy—good looking, great job and warm personality. Which would have made him prime dating material except, despite knowing him for a while, there had never been any chemistry between us. Joe, who was new to our group, was having trouble stringing words together. He was miraculously still managing to charm the pants off of Liz, her laughter getting more animated as the night wore on. All the while Katrina was doing her best to beguile Dave.

It was strange watching the interaction, her slow sexy dance of seduction while he politely and gently rebuffed her advances. He was kind and attentive, listening to everything she had to say while making sure he engaged everyone else in conversation as well.

"She's really into him, huh?" Matt leaned in, whispering in my ear.

I discreetly leaned back, trying to work out who we were talking about. "Liz?"

"No, Katrina. She hasn't taken her eyes off him for a second."

Oh?

Oh!

My head snapped to him, my eyes following his as he glanced over at her. She was laughing at something Dave had said, her eyes closed as she tossed back her head.

"I knew this was a group thing." He shrugged, his puppy dog eyes looking slightly defeated. "But I thought maybe I'd have the chance to . . . you know, get her alone for a minute or two."

My heart squeezed for him, not having realized that he had feelings for her other than a friendship I thought we all shared.

"There's still time, and I don't think anything is going to happen beyond this date." I offered words of encouragement. "Maybe I can distract Dave for a while, give you a chance to talk to her?" I pretended to not be as excited as I was at the prospect.

His eyes lit up with hope. "You'd do that?"

"Of course. Let's get the check and when we get to the party, I'll say I have some business to discuss or something. While we're gone, you can show her how awesome you are." Giving him an encouraging punch in the arm.

He nodded, giving my hand a squeeze. "Right. That's exactly what I'll do. Thanks, Jess, you're the best." I was fairly sure that I wasn't, but arguing the point wasn't going to be beneficial for anyone either.

That I would enjoy being Dave Larsson's distraction was another story entirely.

CHAPTER #7

KATRINA, DAVE AND I pulled up to a beach house in Malibu shortly after ten, finding the *party* in full swing.

Liz had arrived before us—her driver breaking the land speed record—while Joe and Matt got there soon after.

The supermodel's birthday had apparently attracted quiet a crowd, the house packed with beautiful people and a few token regular folk added for diversity.

"Hey." I grabbed Katrina before we got too far involved in the noise. "Mind if I steal Dave for minute, there's a director he should meet."

She smiled, looking at Dave before turning back to me. "I don't mind tagging along. Who we meeting?"

"I'll keep you company," Matt offered. "Let them take care of business and we'll grab drinks for everyone."

I had to hand it him, he wasn't the kind of man to let an opportunity slip through his fingers. Bravo, Matt. Bravo.

And either Dave had read the situation, or needed a break from the full body onslaught he'd been battling all night, tapping her arm as he moved closer to me. "It's probably best if I just go with Jess. It will no doubt just be boring conversation. Work, scripts, pretentious actors." He pulled his face into a fake grimace. "The less people that see behind the curtain, the better."

Katrina's smile dipped, her disappointment evident as she agreed. "Sure, take care of business. We'll get drinks."

"You trying to save me or her?" He laughed as he wandered through the crowd. "I don't think I can make it any more obvious that I'm not interested without being rude. I'm tempted to tell her I wear ladies underwear and my drag name is Luscious, but I'm positive she'd find a way to put a positive spin on it."

I looked back over my shoulder, Katrina and Matt disappearing as we turned a corner. "Well, hopefully by the time we get back she'll have recalibrated her target and *Luscious* can stay in the closet."

"Really?" A devilish smile twitched at his lips. "I saw the two of you whispering at dinner and assumed his interest was with you."

"Pfft, we weren't whispering; we were conspiring. Two different things."

"And here I thought I was the only man you were conspiring with, way to make a man feel special. After I confessed about my drag habit and everything."

"Oh, he's not even in the same league as you. Me and you—we're in deep."

He put his arm around me, pulling me in closer as he laughed. "Now you're just stroking my ego. I'd tell you to stop, but I not so secretly like it."

A rush passed through my body with the contact, goosebumps spreading across my skin. I was sure this was part of his rehearsal stage, but being touched felt nice even if it was under false pretenses.

His arm dropped just as fast, releasing me as we stopped suddenly. "So you thought any more on our breakup? Personally I think we should go with me deciding to join a secret underground fighting ring, I've always wanted to play Tyler Durden."

"Huh?" I responded, the conversation taking a sharp turn.

"Our *breakup*, the reason we are no longer together. I just figured if you knew what that was, then I could help build it into the character. Don't tell me we're just going to drift apart or something lame like that."

It made sense, but to be honest, I hadn't given it much thought. I hadn't given *any* of it much thought. I was just hoping to convince my family we were together in the first place, planning our spectacular demise was a problem I had yet to resolve.

My head tilted, the noise of the mingling surrounded us as I pondered. But as I looked him in the eyes, it was easy for it feel like it was just the two of us. Maybe it was because I wasn't trying to impress him, and he wasn't trying to get in my pants.

I liked it, feeling safe with him—with zero expectation.

"I guess you cheat on me, that would probably make sense."

It seemed the most logical and would definitely be a deal breaker. And at the risk of it being cliché, it was a very easy out.

He looked at me, his brow knitting in displeasure. "How does *that* make sense? Why would I cheat on you?"

"Because . . ." I stopped, searching for an answer. "I don't know, because people cheat. I don't know why. Maybe they think the grass is greener on the other side, or maybe they got bored, maybe they have trouble with commitment, or maybe they are—"

"Stupid." He finished my sentence, and not with the word I was going to use either. "That's the *only* reason to cheat. Because they are stupid, anything else doesn't fly."

I studied him, almost enthralled at his answer. Of course, I knew all men didn't cheat, but it was strange to hear one was vehemently against it. And I wasn't sure if I'd always been so jaded, or just learned to expect disappointment.

My head nodded slowly, agreeing with him even before I spoke. "You're right. There's no other reason to cheat."

"Fine, so I'm stupid and I cheat." He shrugged with a laugh. "In that case, you should definitely dump my ass, you deserve better."

God, he was so easy to talk to, effortless to be around, and I was just starting to see it now. I might never have seen this side of him, able to get a peek purely because of our arrangement.

"Heyyyyy, there you are." Katrina came around the corner, juggling a couple of drinks while a dejected Matt followed close behind. "Hope you got business taken care of, I want to let loose and dance." She looked at Dave with hope.

Clearly Matt's attempts had either not gone to plan or were shot down by Katrina, her interest in Dave still being at an all-time high.

He gave her a warm smile. "Yep, all done. But I'm not the dancing type, it brings back bad memories from junior prom."

I bit my lip trying not to laugh.

It was Katrina's turn to look dejected, handing him a beer while her mood visibly deflated. "Oh, well, that's too bad."

"I'll dance with you, Katrina." Matt smiled, and God bless the man because he wasn't out for the count just yet. "Come on, no point standing here when we could be out there making everyone jealous." He offloaded the beer he'd obviously gotten for me before yanking gently on her arm.

Her cheeks pinked, liking the attention even if it wasn't from the man she wanted. "Yeah, okay. Let's go." She took a sip from her drink and let him lead her away.

"May the odds be ever in his favor," I whispered to Dave as they disappeared. "He's really fighting the good fight."

"He sure is." Dave laughed. "You want to get out of here? I can tell you all about what happened at my junior prom and we can get a decent beer." He held up his Budweiser with disgust. "I think I'd rather drink the pool water than this shit."

I hesitated, tempted to say yes and it had nothing to do with the beer or hearing about his past. But I also knew that if I left with him, Katrina would be devastated, and I didn't want to do that to my friend either.

"As much as I'd love to, I can't." Every single ounce of disappointment I felt was real as I turned him down. "We should probably play it cool until we have to go away. I don't want there to be any unforeseen complications if we're seen together too much."

"Whatever you want, boss." He gave me a slow smile before he looked around. "But I'm serious about getting out of here. Send me an email with dates and anything else I need to know. I'll be ready to mobilize whenever you are."

My arms closed around him in a hug that surprised both of us. "Thanks, I will. No drinking this time, I promise."

"Jess," he laughed, the gentle vibrations felt against my cheek as I pressed it to his chest. "I think the email was more fun when you did, don't stop on my account. This time, I won't turn down the phone sex."

"What?" I pulled away from him in a rush.

He winked, his smile getting wider. "You heard me. You aren't the only one who's been telling lies."

It was like a bomb had gone off, my heart beating so fast I could hear it ringing in my ears even above the music.

"You can't just leave after telling me that." I grabbed his arm, holding it hostage so he wouldn't be able to leave. "You need to tell me everything."

He looked over the crowd who were oblivious to us and smirked. "Some other time, when we're alone. Email me the details, and say goodbye to Katrina and the rest of your friends."

And with the protest still lodged in my throat, he left just as he said he was going to. The crowd swallowed him up, his tall sexy figure disappearing into a sea of people I barely knew or liked.

Previously I had begged time to stand still so I wouldn't have to deal with going home, dreading attending the wedding. But now, I was dying to go.

And it had nothing to do with seeing my cousin get married.

IT TOOK KATRINA at least an hour to get over the disappointment of Dave leaving us at the party. She had really hoped to wow him, and was flummoxed as to why he hadn't fallen victim to her charms. But for all the interest Dave hadn't shown, Matt had, cushioning the blow and salvaging her night.

Liz had disappeared, taking her date with her. Not surprising, I'd become the third wheel as I'd predicted, which kind of sucked. That it was Matt instead of Dave with Katrina had made it at least tolerable.

And with his assurances that he would see Katrina safely home, I took the car service and left them to a budding office romance. Well at least tonight hadn't been a total loss.

Calling Dave the minute I was safely back in my apartment was almost impossible to resist. I had picked up the phone at least a million times before I locked it in the bottom drawer of my nightstand to ensure I didn't get up to any late-night shenanigans.

It was too much to expect I would resist in a sleepy haze, obviously that hadn't worked out for me the last time. And while I was sober, unlike the last occasion, I wondered if my curiosity wouldn't overpower my sense of responsibility. Let's face it, it wasn't just curiosity that was in the mix, he was gorgeous and funny, and there were parts of me that wouldn't mind getting very acquainted with the man who was to play the lead in my fake love saga.

He was not a prostitute, I reminded myself, trying to stop any further dirty thoughts and/or actions my brain was so willing to conjure up.

And by some miracle, and after some very serious tossing and turning, I was able to float into a sexually frustrated sleep that spawned dreams so bizarre I had to remind myself I hadn't been drunk.

You cannot sleep with him.

It became my daily mantra.

CHAPTER #8

LIZ MESSAGED THE next day with news that Joe had been fun but she wasn't looking for a repeat. It wasn't shocking by any means, with Liz going through love interests the way most of us went through underwear.

Katrina, on the other hand, couldn't stop talking about her newfound appreciation for Matt. That he worked with us was a bonus, asking me if I was cool with her spending a few lunchtimes with him. And of course I was fine with it, happy her attention was diverted from my fake boyfriend, and Matt was finally getting his girl. In a Hallmark movie, he'd send her love notes through the interoffice messenger, and I would be credited at their wedding for bringing them together.

Meanwhile, in my own Hallmark movie, I was a little perplexed about the feelings I was having for Dave. While it was perfectly normal to find the man irresistible, stirring up sexiness that made my whole body tingle—I was positive there were enough women affected to warrant a support hotline—but what I should be feeling was gratitude. Friendship. Shit like that. Getting all hot and bothered was not helpful or conducive, especially when on his side of the script, all he probably felt was platonic.

So, like most of the problems I'd been dealing with recently, I pushed it aside and lived in denial until one evening when my buzzer rang.

If those goddamn hippies from the next apartment had locked themselves out again, I was going to cuss their butter churning, crunchy granola asses into next week. *How hard is it to remember your keys?* Who said smoking weed didn't screw with your brain.

"Yeah," I spat into the intercom, ready to hear Nadia giggling into the speaker about needing to knit her vagina or something.

"Bad night?" His voice tingled up my spine like a haunting Georgian chant.

My heartbeat doubled its speed as I stared at the box on the wall. I hadn't been expecting company, sitting around in a pair of sleep shorts and tank top I'd thrown on hours ago.

"Dave?" I asked, wondering if I wasn't having one of those vivid dreams I'd had the last few nights. He'd come to my door, tell me how much he wanted to make my fantasies come true and we'd have dirty, passionate sex. What? I'd decided I was more an *HBO* kind of girl and not *Hallmark* after all.

"The one and only. Can I come up?"

I looked down at my lack of clothes, my boobs coming to full attention against the soft fabric of my tank top. I was definitely going to have to change before he made it to my front door. "Sure, let me buzz you in."

As soon as I hit the release lock on the outer gate, I sprinted to my bedroom and put on a bra, pulled on a dress and twisted my hair into a ponytail. There wasn't enough time to put on make-up—my earlier "face" now sitting on a bunch of wet wipes in the bottom of my wastepaper basket. But I splashed some water over my skin, sprayed on some deodorant and tossed in a breath mint for good measure. By the time I answered the door, I was trying to not gag on the mint I had accidentally sucked down my throat while gasping for air.

I'd probably have looked less of a hot mess if I'd just let him see my enthusiastic nipples.

"Are you ok?" He walked in, giving me a hard tap between my shoulder blades, prompting the breath mint to shoot out of my mouth and into the hall. Well at least it had been in there long enough to make it minty fresh, my breaths coming out more easily as I was no longer asphyxiating on candy.

"Yes," I coughed out. "All good."

His raised eyebrow hinted he wasn't convinced, closing the door behind us as he watched me clear my throat a couple of times.

"So . . . what brings you here?" I regained some composure and was able to talk without spluttering in his face.

I gestured for him to follow me into my living room, watching him sit on the sofa before I lowered myself into my armchair. I couldn't decide how I liked him better, casual in jeans like he was now, or in dress pants and a button down.

Naked, my subconscious whispered, because thinking it was bad enough but saying it out loud was off the table. I'd never seen him sans clothes but didn't need to test the theory to be one hundred percent sure that would have been my preference.

"Well, we can't be seen together, but we need to practice." He was completely oblivious to my indecent thoughts as he sat there smiling. "And I figured since I shared a house with Nick, it made more sense to come to you."

"Yes, of course. Practice. Makes sense." I rattled off half sentences as I wondered how he'd worked out which apartment I lived in. Sure, it wasn't hard to remember my address when the car service had picked me up, but there were fourteen apartments in our complex. Had he gotten lucky?

"How did you know what apartment I lived in?" I asked, not bothering to try and finesse out an answer.

He laughed, leaning forward in his chair as he looked me in the eyes. "Are you worried I'm stalking you? Relax, you wrote it in your detailed list. Along with every other place you've lived and a phone tree of your emergency contacts. I haven't committed them to memory just yet so I hope there's no pop quiz tonight."

Of course, I had given it to him. Were there any details I'd left for him to discover all by himself? There was probably no need for him to sleep with me; I'd given him the highlight reel in my notes.

"Okay, new rule. I don't want to speak of that horrible email again." I swished my hand through the air hoping he'd heed my new decree.

"Not ever?" He pulled his lips into a pout. "But I wanted to hear more about your chocolate ménage fantasy with characters from The History Channel."

I sighed, still cursing the Shiraz and my stupidity. "I'll never tell."

"Fine. I won't bring it up." He mimicked me with a flick of his wrist. "So tell me why you don't have a boyfriend?"

My eyes narrowed, wondering if he was testing me. "That information was contained in the body of work we are no longer discussing."

"Actually it wasn't." He shook his head, and for once he wasn't laughing or joking. "You said you moved to L.A. and getting into anything long term wasn't a priority, that doesn't answer the question about a boyfriend."

"Can't we talk about my favorite sexual position?" I offered, thinking it was easier to discuss that than something as personal as why I wasn't currently dating.

"Jess, be honest with me. I just want to understand, and I swear there is no judgment here." His eyes were so sincere that it was hard not to drop every defense I had and lay myself bare. I still didn't understand the whys, but trusting him just felt right.

Maybe it was because he was a genuinely nice guy, or maybe it had been his willingness to help me. *Or maybe*, it was because there were some people who were just naturally more trustworthy than others.

Inherently good, better than the rest of us.

I was still wondering which category he fell into, and feeling blessed I'd stumbled on such a decent and kind man to play house with when he took my silence as hesitation.

"Look, I'll even start. My last girlfriend was six months ago. We just didn't click and I was dating her out of habit. So rather than spend time committed to women I know I have no future with and then go through some bullshit breakup, I don't bother. I see women casually and date when the mood takes me."

I wished I'd been startled by his candor, but his honesty was something that rang true for me as well.

"I haven't found anyone I want to spend the night with." I found myself telling him stuff I hadn't even admitted to Katrina or Liz. "Not sex obviously, but spend *a night* with, so he's there the next morning. I've tried, but I inevitably find some stupid fault. Like I'm looking for an excuse. I've worried that I'm too picky, or jaded or even just destined to be alone. And being alone doesn't scare me half as much as being married to the wrong guy."

He nodded like he was agreeing. "I'm glad you don't settle. And you shouldn't, none of us should. So what is it about me that made you change your mind?"

My eyes widened so much I thought for sure they were going to drop out of my head.

"My character." He laughed, "I assume your family knows you well enough that you're not just going to pick up any dude and drag him home. So, we need some kind of hook for me."

His commitment to the role was both commendable and terrifying.

He *was* different. Not just in his ability to play the part, but he was one of the few guys I could see myself having a friendship with *and* wanting to sleep with. It was usually one or the other. And if there happened to be a man who straddled the line, then without a doubt, I'd get bored.

"Because I could see you as my friend, and not just a boyfriend. And I'd want to spend time with you, even if you weren't in love with me," I answered honestly, my words almost making me cringe.

Sure, I wanted him to believe me, and when we spoke it was so easy just to forget the bullshit. There was no need to pretend. But I didn't want to scare him into thinking I was buying into the story. I knew he wasn't going to fall in love with me, and the best I could hope for was an ongoing friendship and a cool guy friend I could count on keeping it real. And trust me, that was worth more than sex. Which was why I needed to make sure I didn't accidently sleep with him and screw it all up.

"I like it." He weighed my words without laughing or ridiculing me. "And reasonable, definitely something your family will buy."

My head nodded, agreeing with him. Because that was what it was all about, my family buying it. "Can I get you something to drink?" My feet dropped to the floor, feeling the need to stand and change the serious mood the conversation had taken. "You're probably going to need to learn to drink sweet tea, so that should be the other thing we work on."

I felt him follow me into the kitchen, leaning up against my counter as I went into my refrigerator and pulled out a pitcher.

"I've had sweet tea." He watched me with interest as I grabbed two glasses and set them down beside him. "They have it at Mc-Donald's."

I gasped, pausing before I poured to fully express my horror at his statement. Thank God we'd had this conversation now so we could clear up the misunderstanding.

"Please, that's like comparing Nike to Jimmy Choo. Sure, both are worn on your feet, but one is functional while the other is a work of art. Once you've tasted the real deal, you'll never want to waste your time with that cheap imposter again."

Not only was I was glad that I was pouring him tea I had made myself—wowing him with my diversity—but the intensity of the previous conversation had gone.

"Taste." I tipped the glass of liquid amber toward him. "The secret is not having the water too hot, it burns the leaves."

He took the glass, the edges of lips lifting as he brought it to his mouth. I watched him drink slowly, closing his eyes as he savored it. He might have said he'd had sweet tea before, but as far as I was concerned he was a virgin and I was his first.

"Wow, that is really good." His tongue seductively slid across his lips, collecting the remnants. "And yeah, it's different."

"Mmm." I took a sip from my own glass, not sure if my moan of approval was because he enjoyed it, or because my tea was that good. Probably a little of both which was why I took another sip.

"See, this is good for us. It will give me the edge." He chased down what was left in his glass before setting it down on the counter.

I finished my own drink, putting my glass down to join his. "Well, whatever I can do to help, just let me know. I'm no actress, but I've watched enough of them to feel like I can wing it. I've helped running lines and even blocked scenes and—"

Oh. My. God.

The rest of sentence was swallowed as his lips hit mine, his tongue teasing against my mouth as I stood there unable to move.

It was a runaway train I had no chance of stopping, my fingers curling and clocking him right in the gut before I realized he was kissing me.

OH MY GOD.

He. Was. Kissing. Me.

My lips still tingled from his, my hand flying up to my mouth as my eyes widened to out-of-skull-popping portions.

"Fuck." He laughed as he pulled away. "That didn't go how I'd planned it."

"I didn't expect you to kiss me," I huffed out, my lungs feeling like they needed to get better acquainted with air.

I was horrified.

Completely disgusted.

Not that he'd kissed me. Please, if I'd given myself half a chance I'd have threaded my hands through his hair and fused my lips to his mouth. But he'd taken me by surprise and I'd reacted before I'd had a chance to enjoy it, completely screwing myself out of the opportunity. Not to mention I'd just punched him.

Shit.

My heartbeat tried to regulate itself while my lips begged for another chance.

"Yeah, I guess the element of surprise didn't go so well." He chuckled, rubbing his gut lightly. "I just didn't want you to over-think it."

I shook my head, still shaking my metaphorical fist at myself. "I'm sorry, I was just surprised. Maybe we can try it again?"

My voice was hopeful but the rest of me could see it was a lost cause. He was probably not going to get any closer until he was fully padded up in a hockey mask and a chest protector. And who would blame him? It's not every day you kiss a girl and get a right hook as your reward. Thank you, Jesus he hadn't attempted it out in the living room where I had access to my purse. I'd have probably maced him and left the poor guy partially blind.

L.A. was a dangerous place, and I needed protection.

He hesitated, standing where he was as he looked at me. "Maybe we leave it for now and pick it up later, give my ego a chance to recover. Give me a call and we'll schedule a time. Hopefully, you'll be less surprised then."

"Sure. Of course. I'll call you." I nodded, thinking there was no way he was ever going to give me the chance again.

And rather than living in the mortification a second longer, I yawned pretending to be tired which prompted him to say good-night.

I'd wanted him to stay.

I'd wanted to kiss him.

I'd wanted to do more than that too.

Which was why when he walked out my door, I sagged against the wall and breathed a sigh of relief.

What the hell had I been thinking? He was not a *real* date, or even a prospect for a *real* date. He was doing me a favor and would probably run a thousand miles in the other direction if he knew what was going on inside my head.

No, I needed to keep it professional and keep it friendly.

And just to be sure, I'd decided I needed to keep my distance for a while. Because only the Lord knew what would happen if I got him close and alone again.

LIKE BRUSHING MY teeth and showering, not calling Dave Larsson became a ritual I was trying to form into a habit. Because I had no reason to call him, none that was important anyway. And if I wanted the plan to work—the one where I passed him off as my significant other—then I needed to not do anything stupid in the next few weeks. Sleeping with him would qualify as stupid.

There was a whole sea of other men to do that with. I could go and have as much meaningless sex as I wanted to. I wasn't in a relationship, and I very much doubted a man who looked as amazing as Dave wasn't partaking in some indiscriminate fishing himself. Even if he had joked he wouldn't. Of course for me, the desire for frivolous sexual relationships had diminished. I blamed it on being overworked, with my "sea" being polluted by conceited men who were boring and one-dimensional. Funny how I'd never noticed how slim the pickings had been earlier, not that it was important now.

And so passed my days.

Work.

Home.

Not calling Dave.

Not having sex.

It was a good plan which saw the days eat their way into weeks, the date of Lana's impending wedding getting closer. And I was more excited than I probably should be. Because maybe I couldn't sleep with him, but after this was over, we could hopefully settle into some kind of friendship.

As long as I didn't screw anything up.

Just one more day.

All I had to do was get through today, pack and then tomorrow we'd be on a plane. I was either going to convince everyone of my amazing love for him or have him bear witness to a failure of epic proportions.

We hadn't tested out our "coupledom" yet, that had been my fault. But I was positive that when it counted, we would bring it.

"You avoiding me?" His voice snapped me from my thoughts, which ironically enough had been about him.

"I've been avoiding everyone," I responded calmly, trying to stop the spike in my pulse as he looked at me. "I have so much work to do and not enough hours to do it in." I couldn't help but appreciate how incredibly good he looked, all rugged handsome, wearing jeans, black fitted T-shirt and a few days growth kissing his jaw. "Besides, I fear that if I see normal people flaunting their work/life balance it will be a jealousy I might not recover from."

He laughed, the light hitting his eyes as he focused on me. "Well, I wouldn't want to make you jealous. But I had hoped we could have hung out a bit more before . . . the *shoot*."

It was something I'd considered too, thinking it would be smart to get in a few more dates before having to play *couple* for an audience. There was still that kiss we had yet to reattempt. The memory of the first one still lingered on my lips even though it had lasted barely a second. I'm sure the attempted bodily harm probably made the memory less pleasant for him.

But weirdly, I was worried I might blur the lines. Scratch that, I *knew* that kissing him too soon would *definitely* blur the lines and didn't want to risk it. It had been a really long time since I'd been interested in a man beyond a casual acquaintance. And it figured that the first time I felt the spark, it was a man I was paying. Conflict of interest? Sexual harassment? Lord, it was a minefield of shit I couldn't even begin to decipher.

"I would have liked that too." I didn't even bother trying to lie. "But I've asked so much already. I know how precious your time is, and besides don't you have a script to study for your new part?"

The part I was referring to was not his starring role in my tragic love story, but the infamous script I'd dumped on Jeremy's desk weeks ago. I knew Dave would be perfect for it, and it seemed it had indeed been perfect. After an audition, he'd received an offer yesterday.

The urge to call him and congratulate him with the good news had been almost too much to bear. I'd lost count of the number of times I'd picked up the phone only to drop it again without dialing his number.

His brow rose. "Which is how I know you're avoiding me. Jeremy called me instead of you."

"He wanted the glory. Trust me, if you were getting a rejection, it would have been me on the other end of that phone. So, really, it was a good thing he was the one to call."

I hadn't *totally* been avoiding him.

We'd texted and sent a few emails. Plans needed to be made, airline tickets and the like needed to be booked, so I communicated as necessary. But I kept all those conversations completely professional, giving him the information, being as polite as I could, and then disengaging immediately. There were even a couple of times I'd almost cut him off saying goodbye, so intent of keeping it short, sharp and concise because I didn't want to give him the opportunity to distract me from my mission.

Because I was smart.

"What about the three calls I've made to you that weren't returned?"

Well that had been another story.

Those calls had ended up in my voicemail, replayed from time to time so I could dissect the tone and nuances of his voice. They hadn't been avoided so much as horded, enjoyed at a private moment when I didn't have to worry about being on my best behavior. And I fully intended to call him back sooner or later, I just hadn't gotten around to it yet.

"I emailed, I was trying to be more time efficient," I joked, trying to laugh it off like it was no big deal. "And did you miss the part when I said I was avoiding everyone? I'm very fragile these days."

He leaned in closer, bringing his sexiness up close and personal in case I'd missed it when he walked in. Newsflash: I hadn't. His silent seduction lingered in the air a beat as he looked at me. "I'll believe a lot of things, but that you are *fragile,* isn't one of them."

"Dave." Jeremy walked out, saving me from having to respond. "Come into my office and let's go over your contract. I want to get it squared away as soon as possible."

"Sure," Dave responded, keeping his eyes locked on me before casually stepping away. He didn't say anything else, slowly peeling

away his glance before heading into Jeremy's office, the door closing behind them.

My phone beeped while my gaze was still on the door, the
screen lighting up with an incoming message.

I'll meet you at the airport tomorrow.
Bring your A game because I'll be bringing mine.
D

Well then.

I hoped he was prepared, because while only one of us had
formal training, I wasn't going to be the one to let down the team.

I was going to need to give the performance of my life.

CHAPTER #9

WE ARRIVED AT Shreveport just before four.

I was a bundle of excited nerves leaving LAX. It was like we were on a covert operation or sharing the most awesome of private jokes.

While my mom and dad had offered to pick us up at the airport, I assured them we were renting a car and their welcome party wasn't necessary. Besides, I wanted to get to the hotel, check in, and drink a daiquiri, or five, before we headed over to the house.

Dave was already in character, hefting both our suitcases off the luggage carousel and barely breaking a sweat in a display of superior manliness. I swore I heard two college-aged girls behind us moan when he helped a mother who was wrestling with a toddler. The kid, who couldn't have been more than five, was trying to do a runner, Dave grabbing him before he was able to get too far from his mom. I might have moaned myself; it was pretty hot.

He grinned, hearing the appreciation either from the sorority sisters or me as he came to stand by my side. "Where to next, *babe?*" The last word accompanied by a wink.

"Not babe." I shook my head, the generic endearment making me want to puke. "I guess pet names was something we should have discussed."

I didn't mind terms of endearment if they were genuine and organic. Not *babe* obviously, which was terrible. But forced mentions of "baby" and "sweetie" just cheapened something that should be special. There were just some things I couldn't do.

He shrugged, like it was no big deal. "Well, I did try to tell you we needed more time together. But whatever, I can work on the fly. You have something in mind or do I need to just keep tossing them out until we find one you like?"

"No, it will sound forced. Maybe we just stick to our regular names."

"Whatever you want, *sweet pea*." He chuckled, looking pleased with himself.

"Didn't we just agree to regular names?" I was sure it hadn't been more than a few seconds since we'd decided. No one's memory was that short.

He grinned as he shook his head. "I didn't agree to anything, there's no fun in normal names. I'll find one you like, but until then, *honey*, let's get out of here."

"We just have to pick up the rental." I motioned to the sign for the Enterprise counter, trying to ignore the *sweet pea* and *honey*.

Dave lowered our suitcases as the lady behind the counter gave us a bright smile. "Hi there. Do you have a reservation?"

My hand dove into my bag, pulling out my printout. "Yes, Jessica Dawson."

She tapped on her keyboard and smiled. "Ah yes, four days and I have you down for a Hyundai Elantra."

I nodded, grabbing my license and credit card when Dave grabbed my arm.

"I'm meeting your family for the first time and we're showing up in a Hyundai?"

I forced a smile, the words coming out of the side of my mouth as I tried to reassure him and not attract any attention. "It's just a rental, Dave, trust me, no one is even going to look at the car."

His brow furrowed, shaking his head as his hand rested on the counter. "You show up in a shitty car, they notice the car. Show up in an awesome car, they notice the man. We're not taking a Hyundai." He looked over at the woman, his eyes dropping to her nametag. "Shelia. You have anything else available? Something with a little more flash?"

Her eyes lit up, her fingers getting busy on the keyboard. "I have a brand new Mustang convertible. It's red."

A mustang? Really? Um, no. The whole idea was to fly in, convince my family I was in a relationship and then fly out, attracting as little attention to myself as possible. Driving a freaking red muscle car was the opposite of that.

"We don't need a convertible. We'll take the Hyundai." I waved my card hoping she'd just process the thing, give us the keys and we could get out of there.

"*Sweetheart.*" Dave wrapped his fingers around my hand and pulled the credit card out of my grasp. His other hand found its way around my waist as he twisted me around. He looked at me with so much intensity that I had no choice but to look back. "I'm meeting your parents, and it's important to me that I make a good impression. You can understand that, right?"

"I guess," I squeaked out, not sure if I really understood or not.

"Which is why we're taking the Mustang." He planted a soft, chaste kiss on my nose before pulling out his wallet. "Here Shelia, charge it to this and if we can add me as a driver that would be great too."

Shelia looked to me with a smile, waiting for my approval before taking the card. "The Mustang is a beautiful car, and it does make quite the impression."

Screw it; I huffed out a breath, not willing to argue about a car.

"Fine, we'll take the Mustang. But you can use my card."

He went for my hand, taking out my credit card before bringing my fingers to his lips. "Please let me, darling," his voice dripping with charm.

"Sure." I didn't have it in me to stop him. Even though I knew he was acting—a dress rehearsal almost—it had been so incredibly sweet, I just let it happen.

The lady behind the counter looked at us and smiled. "Awww, y'all are adorable."

I did my best to adequately swoon, but sadly didn't have the ability to blush on cue. So instead I smiled, giving Dave gaga eyes and hoping I didn't look deranged. I wasn't sure I'd ever *swooned* before, and trying it with an audience for a first time wasn't easy.

Thankfully she processed our rental, handing over the keys before any additional smiling or acting like an idiot was required.

"I'll add the car rental to your fee," I said, walking out to the lot. It wasn't hard to find ours; there was only one red Mustang convertible on the lot.

Dave shook his head, "Nope, my choice in car and I'm paying it." He hit the keyless entry; the door locks popping open at his command.

The argument was fresh in my throat before he stopped me. "Relax, I'll give the receipt to my accountant and tell him it was a business-related expense. The guy literally gets off on deductions. So think of it as our gift to him if it makes you feel better."

Not sure that it did. Him spending his own money on my gig made me uncomfortable, but getting into an argument in the rental parking lot at the airport wasn't smart either.

While Shreveport wasn't small, it sure as hell wasn't L.A. There always seemed to be a neighbor, cousin, friend, teacher who taught you in third grade, ready at every turn. I couldn't get three feet without hitting someone I knew, and the chance of running into someone seemed to be multiplied the longer I stood in one place. Like being hit by lightning in a storm, I was flying a kite with a key attached.

"Fine," I relented, figuring we could worry about it later. "Let's go to the hotel first."

He nodded, dropping the suitcases by the trunk and shook the key fob between his fingers. "You going to direct me?"

"You know, it would just be easier if I drove considering I'm the one who knows where to go." I leaned over against the side of the car. As much as I hated to admit it, it was a hell of a lot nicer than a Hyundai.

The edges of his lips twitched. "Or you just want to drive the fast car now we have it."

"I've driven fast cars before. Jeremy has a Jag. I picked it up from the dealer," I countered, not willing to concede that he was possibly correct in his assessment.

He pressed against me—unfairly using his delicious body as a weapon—smirking as he whispered in my ear. "I'm not so insecure in my manhood that I can't let a woman drive. But make no mistake, the next time we take her out, she's all mine."

A nervous shiver ran through my body, holding out my palm as I waited for the key. "Deal."

He didn't hesitate, a satisfied chuckle passing through his lips as he popped the trunk and then dropped the key into my hand. He loaded our luggage into the back while I went around to the driver's side.

I'd already started the car when he slid into the passenger seat, pulling across his seatbelt before flicking through the stereo presets. "We're not doing country." He smirked, settling on a classic rock station as we pulled out of the lot.

The drive to the hotel wasn't long. Then again, it was less than eight miles to downtown, and even in the worst traffic didn't take more than thirty minutes. Nowhere long enough to appreciate the car or his company, our ride coming to a quick end as I pulled up to the front of the hotel.

The Hilton was one of the few fancy hotels that wasn't attached to a gambling facility. The Red River was lined with riverboat casinos filled with rednecks and high rollers alike. It didn't have the sparkle of Vegas or the nostalgia of Atlantic City, but there were less retirees than Branson. And trust me, that was a positive. Just try standing between them, a slot machine and a four thirty dinner special. I'd seen gangsters in L.A. with less aggression.

We left the car parked out front while we went inside to check in, the front desk attended by only a couple of staff.

"Shit," I muttered under my breath, looking over at the bright-eyed brunette finishing up with a guest.

"What?" Dave whispered back, his eyes scanning the area for the source of my irritation.

"The woman behind the counter. She's like my father's cousin's daughter." I tried to mentally calculate the family connection. Was that second cousin? Third? Ugh. Related was enough. "And she has a big mouth." I did my best to explain while not making direct eye contact and keeping my voice low. "No, don't look." I yanked on his arm trying to stop him from turning toward her.

I assumed over the course of the next few days we'd see people from my past. And I'd been prepared for that; I'd just not planned on it happening so fast. And knowing someone at the hotel added drama we didn't need, especially someone who had a mouth on her like Darla.

"Oh my goodness," she squealed from behind the counter, the guest she'd been helping disappearing. Lucky us—her attention was all ours. "Jessica Dawson, how wonderful to see you. You must be here for Lana's wedding. Oh, she is going to make the most amazing bride." Her eyes flicked over to Dave, her smile getting wider. "And hello to you too."

While Darla was friendly, she wasn't flirting. Or at least, I didn't *think* she was flirting. That enthusiastic smile of hers was hard to read, but I assumed it was her eagerness to gain information. Gossip, which she could later disperse to the family and town folk who reveled in that shit.

Or she could be flirting.

I wasn't sure which I preferred.

"Darla. How nice to see you," I lied, stepping forward and holding out my hand. It felt too formal, but reaching across and hugging her wasn't happening, so a handshake was the best she was getting.

"The pleasure's mine." She grinned, accepting my hand as she looked between Dave and I waiting for an introduction. "And who might you be?" she asked with a giggle, her eyes spending a little too much time lingering over his chest.

Flirting. She'd been flirting.

"This is Dave." My hand moved from my side to rest possessively on the chest she'd yet to stop staring at. "He's my boyfriend."

Her eyes and smile widened as she focused on me. "Well, how wonderful." Her taffy-laced voice rose an octave. "I'm Darla." She threw out her hand more enthusiastically than she had with me and offered it to him. "I'm Jessica's cousin."

Despite the complexity of our family tree, she declared she was kin with such pride, making it sound like we'd been tight when really we hadn't.

"Well, it's nice to meet you." Dave took her hand, bewitching her with his charming smile.

It was a quick shake, extracting his hand and then placing it around my waist. He pulled me in tighter, dropping a soft kiss on the top of my head. "It's a real treat for me to be able to meet Jessica's family, especially when she has met most of mine."

That was not a lie.

With three of the Larsson brothers all signed with Levin Murphy, I'd had the chance to meet not only Nick and Eric, but also the other two non-acting brothers, Roman and Alex. I'd even seen Dave's mother and father at one of Eric's premieres and spoken to Eric's wife. Not that I'd say any of us were BFFs, but I could pick them out of a lineup and have an easy conversation with most of them.

"Well, *honey*," I squeezed him back, deciding if I had to suffer a pet name so could he. "It's a little hard when we live in L.A. and all my family live out here."

Darla's eyes lit up with a mischief I was positive I wanted no part of. "But you're here now. And I can't remember the last time you brought a guy home." She focused back on Dave. "I'm sure everyone is going to want to meet you."

Or at least they would as soon as she got on the phone and gave everyone her detailed report. The FBI had nothing on her; I was positive there would be people in Arkansas who'd be hearing soon too.

"Great." I forced another fake smile, the moment hanging between us in an awkward silence. "So, we're checking in."

Darla caught herself, giggling before waving her hand. "Yes, of course, of course. Let me get you guys situated." Her busy fingers tapped on the keyboard.

"Oh." She stopped mid stroke. "So, we have you down for a double with two queen beds, is that right?" She looked over at me with renewed interest.

Shit

While I had agreed Dave and I would share a room, sharing a bed was not even a consideration. How could I even sleep while his big body was within touching distance? It was waaaaaaay too much temptation.

I shrugged, playing it off like it was no big deal. "I booked the room online, I didn't really look and we're happy to take whatever."

"Nonsense." She waved her hand again before returning back to her computer. "We have plenty of king rooms free. Actually." She looked at her co-worker who was distracted with his own customer. "I have a suite available, let me upgrade you."

"That won't be necessary," I tried to argue. "I wouldn't want to get you into any trouble."

I didn't give a rat's ass what kind of trouble she'd get into, but Dave and I sleeping in the same bed hadn't been part of the plan.

"It's no trouble. We're family. Just give me one second." She threw off the argument and continued with her tap-tap. "All done. Let me just get your key."

With efficiency I couldn't help but admire, she had swiped my card, gotten our paperwork ready to sign and produced a couple of keycards for us. She even arranged for the Mustang still parked out front to be moved to the garage at no extra cost, a bellboy instructed to bring up our luggage to the suite.

As we waved goodbye I was positive her plan was to stop and interrogate us later when she had proper time to dedicate to the cause. Then I'd have to regurgitate the story we'd concocted of how we'd come to be. She would sit on the edge of her seat, mentally taking notes, while asking twenty questions like a Louisianan version of Ann Curry.

And Lord knows she had easy access; she'd given me my room number for God's sake. So I had that added stress for the next four days too, the risk of seeing her more than just a slim possibility. At least thinking about Darla and her potential unannounced visits kept my mind off our new sleeping arrangements. Dave hadn't said anything about it so I was trying to play it cool. Besides, it was a king. We could lie beside each other and still have room between us.

As Dave shut the door of our suite, he looked over at me with an amused look on his face. "Well, that was interesting. Was that the southern hospitality I've heard so much about?"

"No." I shook my head. "That was her gathering currency to spend later. She likes to trade secrets for favors. Her sister, Marla, is worse."

He laughed, his eyes lighting up with animation. "Darla and Marla? Seriously, who'd do that to their kids?"

"It's a *thing*. Not a good one, but a thing nonetheless. My mom and her sisters all have Ann in their names," I said before glancing across to the bedroom, the corner of our bed just visible from my vantage point. "So, I guess we're sleeping together."

"That bother you?" He raised an eyebrow, clearly not bothered himself.

There weren't a lot of women who would be disappointed sleeping beside Dave Larsson, and it was more than his good looks.

He was respectful and kind, and was the last person I could imagine taking advantage of a situation. If anything, *he* was the one I worried about, people seeing his easy going, trusting nature, and using it for their own benefit.

"No, as long as you're okay with it, but I already feel like I'm asking a lot."

"Relax, it's just a job, right? Think of our time in the hotel room as our rehearsal, building the chemistry." He strolled over and looked into my eyes. "Trust me, Jess. By the time this weekend is over there won't be a single doubt we're desperately in love."

His words made my stomach flutter, my skin tingle without even being touched. "Oh, you are good," my smile automatic. "I think everyone else is going to fall in love with you too."

"Good." He wrapped his hands around my waist. "Look at me."

I did, my eyes snapped up to his on command like I didn't have a choice.

"From the detailed itinerary you sent me, we have dinner in an hour."

"Yes." I nodded slowly. It was our first big test and one I wasn't looking forward to.

"Now, don't freak out and don't hit me this time. I'm going to kiss you."

Was he kidding?

I'd been dying for a chance to kiss him again, only stopping it from happening because I didn't trust myself. I didn't want to seem over eager and fuse my lips to his throat like a deviant, so he was right to tell me not to freak out.

"Okay," I said, surprising myself with my calm. "Do you want to do it right now?"

Why the hell was I asking him? He wanted to kiss me, I wanted to kiss him—albeit for different reasons I'm sure—so we should kiss.

Now.

Before he had any stupid ideas like waiting until later, or even worse—never.

After all, we weren't going to have to deep throat each other in front of my parents. He could very politely kiss me on the forehead and cheek like a gentleman and earn a bucket load of ohhing and ahhing. But if he wanted to authenticate it, then I commended his commitment to the cause.

His eyes fell to my mouth, my tongue automatically sliding across my lips like they'd been preprogramed with his visual cue. My body was more than willing for it, even if it was under false pretenses.

"Yes, now," he responded, pulling me closer while his eyes moved to mine. "Consider it an icebreaker."

He lowered his mouth and brushed it gently against my lips, the barest of touches that had me questioning whether it even happened. And as I opened my mouth, ready to ask exactly that, he brought his back in rush that almost knocked me off my feet.

It was like being in a dark tunnel, in silence, as slowly the rumbled vibrations of a train started to build. And before you knew it, those rumbles were shaking your whole body, consuming you with the noise and excitement that you couldn't out run if you tried.

It was a perfect first kiss. The kind you would write about in your journal if you were that way inclined—which I wasn't. So instead I would catalogue it and compare it to every other first kiss I'd had.

With the right amount of tongue and pressure, it wasn't so much an invasion as it was an occupation. Like a general from a visiting army who'd been invited in and decided he didn't want to leave for a while. And I had rolled out the welcome mat, giving him full access.

His hands slid lower, skimming the edges of suggestion as he pulled me closer and deepened his intentions with his mouth.

Holy hell, the man could kiss.

My hands rose completely of their own accord and threaded through his hair as my lips stayed melded against him.

Anyone watching us would have believed we were into it.

Hell, I didn't know where he sat on the issue, but I *was* into it.

And then just as suddenly, he pulled away, keeping his hands on me as he smiled. "You didn't hit me this time."

"No, no I didn't." My head nodded, and then shook, not sure which was more appropriate while tingles moved through my body as I took a step back.

I knew it was pretend.

I knew it meant nothing.

But right now, I was happy to live in that fantasy.

CHAPTER #10

"SO, WE MET at work. Let's not over complicate things." I sat in the passenger side, my fingers knotted in my lap.

The agreement when we left the airport was that he could drive next, which meant it was him who got to be behind the wheel after we left the hotel.

We'd been over our backstory a million times, but the closer we got to my parents' house, the greater I felt the need for us to go over it again.

"I know, Jess. We stick to as much of the truth as we can." He gave me a sideways glance taking his eyes off the road briefly as he kept driving.

I'm glad he was confident, because I had left my self-assurance back in L.A. In my head there were a million reasons to panic, most of them ending up with someone in my family discovering my sham and outing me for the fraud that I was. It had been easier to believe we could pull it off when it was just a hypothetical. Or when I'd been under his spell in the hotel room and he was kissing me. His mouth was magic, able to dissolve panic and educe calmness with a single press of his lips. Like kryptonite but in reverse.

Maybe we should do that again?

Purely for research purposes.

Science was important and I'd happily give my lips up for the cause. That I might enjoy it, well . . . that was just a bonus.

"And try and steer clear of mentioning your brother, Eric. Hopefully they won't make the connection."

I had effectively avoided the topic of Dave's last name up until this point. Because I knew it was only a matter of time before they'd take that information and do some old fashioned digging. You know the kind, ask the Sherriff for a favor and run his name through the system to make sure he didn't have any outstanding warrants or a wife he'd abandoned in Albuquerque.

And while it made sense just to give him a fake last name— considering everything else about us was—I was worried the pesky detail would be the one thing that would undo us. Too many loose ends would be the rope that I'd probably hang myself with. Ironic that I was more concerned about them finding out he had a famous older brother than me paying him to be with me.

"If they ask, we segue into something, or say you're related and leave it at that. They don't have to know how closely related you are. There could be a million Larssons in the United States. Or it could be a stage name," I rattled off nervously, wondering if it was too late to drive to Baton Rouge and find a guy I knew named Catfish who made fake IDs. It wouldn't stand up to real scrutiny, but I'd take the risk if I thought it would help.

He laughed, his hand casually resting on the wheel. "You know that person you emailed all that stuff to was me, right? Like literally all these things have been discussed."

"I know, but we need to be prepared." I white-knuckled the car door in an effort to stop wringing my hands in my lap. "My mother has built-in radar, and we need to have our story tight if we want to get anything past her."

He rested his hand on my knee and gave me a smile. "Jess,

I've got this. Seriously, don't worry."

"Oh, and my mother's assistant, Tammy, is going to be there tonight too." She wasn't an unusual addition to family dinners but I had hoped she wouldn't be joining us. Not because I didn't like her, she was lovely, and I firmly believed she would take a bullet for my mother. But the fewer eyes we had on us, the better. Besides, she was a little friendlier than I would have liked. "You need to watch out for her, though. She's just come back from some Christian camp so she's either going to be preaching the Good Word or end up face first in your lap."

His brow scrunched in confusion. "Excuse me?"

"You know." My voice lowered as my eyes widened. I wasn't expecting to spell it out for him.

He laughed, looking at me like I was a crazy person. "I assure you, I don't."

"So, she loves Jesus but she also likes to suck cock."

"Okay, that, *that* is new information," he choked out before adding, "So tell me, do *you* love Jesus?"

I rolled my eyes, trying not to laugh as I shook my head. "Oh shut up and keep driving."

The drive wasn't far with us arriving at my parents' home quicker than I expected.

A huge double story on a spacious block, it was the largest and most elegant house on the street, and my mother's pride and joy. As we traveled up the long coral-colored driveway, we were greeted by the smooth white exterior and green roof of the grand house my father had built. The lawns were immaculate of course, every hedge and bush trimmed with not one leaf daring to be out of place.

"Nice house." Dave parked, tilting his head to get a better view as he cut the engine.

Shit . . . it felt so real.

I'd brought boys home before, but the key word was *boys*. High school, college—boyfriends I'd really just been killing time with. Most of them had grown up in the same neighborhood or even gone to the same church. But that had all stopped when I moved to L.A.

Suddenly bringing someone home with me had connotations they hadn't before, like smuggling a man across state lines meant I was going to end up taking his last name and start procreating. It was not an undertaking to be accepted lightly.

"You know, maybe we could come back tomorrow. Say our flight was delayed." I glanced at the window, the undisturbed drapes hopefully indicating our arrival hadn't been noticed.

"Not sure that would work considering Darla has seen us. Surely she's already worked her way through the greater Shreveport area. And the sooner we get it over with, the better you will feel." He popped open his door and got out before I had time to argue.

He was around my side of the car, opening my door while I'd made no effort to move. "Besides, it will be easier tonight with just your family than at the wedding on Saturday, *sweetness*."

Ugh, we were back to the names again. "Sweetness?" I stepped out of the car and joined him on the driveway. "What's next? Baby cakes?"

"It distracted you, didn't it?" He locked the car with a smirk. "And no, next was doll."

I grabbed his hand awkwardly and led him to the large wooden front door. It was too late now; we—or at least I—had passed the point of no return. With hesitation I pressed the doorbell, its distinguished and baritone ring echoing as we waited.

"They don't trust you with a key?" Dave chuckled as he leaned into me. "Did they think you joined a gang when you moved to L.A.?"

"I thought it would look better if we rang the bell, wiseass."

I jabbed him in the ribs. "Make a big entrance so they can stare at us like zoo animals all at once. They'll appreciate my efficiency."

"We're visiting your parents, how bad can it be?"

Oh, honey. I almost felt sorry for him.

"Hold onto that optimism," I whispered.

The door flew open, my sister's seven-month pregnant belly hurtled toward me as her arms tried to wrap around me in a hug. "Jessica, why the hell are you ringing the bell? We were beginning to think your flight got delayed."

See, I knew it could have been a valid excuse.

"Nope, we're here." I tried to sound enthusiastic as I squeezed her as best I could. "Just wanted to check in to the hotel first."

She pulled away, looking at me and then to Dave. "I can certainly understand that. Well aren't you just a tall glass of water. So nice to *finally* meet you." She held out her hand, her smile not in any way discreet.

"Thank you." He accepted her shake, wrapping his other hand around my waist. "It's nice to finally meet you too."

"Just look at you two." She stood back, examining us like we were a bunch of carolers showing up on the doorstep on Christmas Eve. "I don't ever think I've seen anything so adorable."

"You've got the whole weekend, Melanie," I warned her. "Pace yourself."

"Oh hush." She waved me off, tipping her head to the open doorway. "Come inside, the family has been dying for you to get here."

Dave brought me closer, kissing my temple as we walked in together. We hadn't even planned it that way, the man proving how proficient he was and adlibbing on our loosely drawn up script.

We followed Melanie down the hall where the noise grew louder, everyone had gathered in the living room with different voices fighting for position.

"All I'm saying." My older brother Dalton was in a heated debate with my younger brother Travis. "If you're going to eat Mexican, you should go to Miguel's. That other place near Pierre Bossier is a Texas steakhouse with sombreros and watered-down margaritas."

My sister stepped into the room ahead of us, clearing her throat dramatically before she announced, "Jessica and Dave are here."

The talking abruptly stopped as every set of eyes focused on us.

Wow, who knew all I had to do was walk in with a man to get them all to go quiet. I was going to have to remember that party trick for later.

"Look what the cat dragged in." My older brother smiled, his interest in arguing over Mexican eateries clearly shelved. "About time too, I was getting hungry and we were about to eat without you."

His wife Lisa jabbed him in the ribs. "Don't mind him, Jessica, dinner isn't even ready yet."

"Hey, everyone." I waved awkwardly, the room so quiet you could hear a pin drop.

"Oh quit staring, it's rude." My mother walked in from the adjoining dining room, swatting my younger brother, Travis, with a tea towel as she made her way over. "Welcome home, baby." She wrapped her arms around me and squeezed.

"You too, young man." She turned her attention to Dave, his turn for a hug. "If you come into this house you can expect to be hugged and fed, exactly in that order."

Dave didn't falter, accepting the affection without batting an eye as he greeted my mom. "You will get no complaints from me. It's a pleasure to meet you, Mrs. Dawson."

My father laughed, earning him a sharp sideways look from my mother. "You can go ahead and stop the formality as well. We don't subscribe to those city conventions. LeeAnn is perfectly acceptable." She smiled, eyeing Dave up and down despite telling everyone it had been rude to stare not two minutes before.

"LeeAnn, give the kid a break." My dad joined the fray, holding out his hand to Dave. "I'm Arlo Dawson, Jessica's father and we're glad you made it out."

It was like my soul had left my body, watching in earnest as the scene played out in front of me while I sat on the sidelines like a spectator.

"Pleased to meet you, sir." Dave grabbed my dad's hand and gave it a firm and respectable shake, completely unaffected while I stood next him like a taxidermied pig.

"Come here, sweetheart." My dad engulfed me in a hug that only a daddy could give. "I've missed the hell out of you."

Travis rolled his eyes, shooting me a grin. "You just saw her a couple of months ago." He'd moved off the sofa and managed to avoid another tea towel swat from Mom. "I'm Travis, Jessica's younger and favorite brother. Oh, I'm the better looking one too."

"Bullshit," Dalton added, slinging his arm around his wife. "Everyone knows I'm her favorite."

"Can we keep the cussing until *after* dessert?" Mom chided. "Anyone would think I raised you boys in a barn."

"Soooooooo." I rediscovered my voice and my confidence. "Let's do introductions one at a time."

Wrapping my hand around Dave's arm, I went to every member of my family and introduced them properly. My older brother, Dalton and his wife Lisa, my sister, Melanie, her husband Sam and my niece Anna, my younger brother, Travis and his girlfriend Amy, and of course Tammy, my mother's assistant, who looked at Dave like she was on a diet and he was a slice of cake.

My mom went back into the kitchen to check on dinner while my dad grabbed Dave a beer, the conversation kept fairly normal considering it felt like there were a hundred people in the room.

"So how'd y'all meet?" Melanie predictably asked.

"At work, Dave is one of Jeremy's clients and we just kind of clicked." I squeezed Dave's hand trying to look adequately in love.

Dave squeezed back and grinned. "We've actually known each other for a few years."

"Well isn't that sweet," Amy added. "It's amazing what's just under our noses."

I didn't even need to elaborate, Amy going on to tell Dave how she'd been friends with my younger brother since kindergarten but they hadn't fallen in love till after she turned fifteen. Amazing how quickly my brother went from seeing her as his *friend* to a *girl* as soon as she grew a pair of boobs. No big mystery in what happened there.

Mom called us to the dining room where we sat in front of enough food to feed the whole of Caddo Parish. My ass gained about ten pounds as I looked at the mountain of brisket, homemade Mac N Cheese and cornbread, not even counting the lemon icebox pie Mom had hidden away in the refrigerator.

"Larsson, Scandinavian, right?" my dad asked as we tucked into dinner.

I cringed at the mention, hoping the origin of it would be the last we'd talk about it. "Yep, originally," I answered for him. "Mmmm this brisket is delicious." I tried to turn the conversation back into safe territory.

"Thank you, baby." My mom glowed in appreciation. "I bet you can't get food like this in California."

I didn't bother arguing with the grunts of approval from around the table, letting them believe there wasn't anything decent to eat in my adopted home state.

"Larsson, like that other actor Eric Larsson?" Amy giggled, smiling a little too much for my liking. "His latest movie was amazing, too bad he got married recently."

I coughed, swallowing hard as I tried to shove the mouthful of cornbread down my throat and still be able to breathe. Dave passed me a glass of water while placing his hand on my thigh and giving it a reassuring squeeze.

"You okay, baby?" He rubbed my back in concern—either for my inability to get oxygen or for the topic of conversation, I hadn't decided which—as I tried to not die in front of my family. Still, a resuscitation call to 9-1-1 would make sure all talk of Dave's brother ended. It was a sad state of affairs, but I had considered it.

"Sweetheart, take it easy." My mom rose out of her chair, itching to get involved even though Dave seemed to have it handled. "Take another sip of water."

Travis barked out a laugh, ignoring my possible impending suffocation as he shot a glance at his girlfriend. "Now what do you care if he got married? You got a man right here."

Oh thank you, Jesus. My silent prayer of gratitude offered up to the heavens as for the first time my younger brother's arrogance paid off for me.

"Funny, I don't see a ring." Amy held up her hand, displaying her wiggling fingers.

Travis rolled his eyes. "Ring or no ring, we're getting married. So you can stop looking at movie stars."

My lungs burned as I slowly regained a regular breathing pattern, Dave's hand still on my thigh as I reassured him I was okay.

"Sorry," I wheezed out. "Must have gone down the wrong pipe."

"So." Amy ignored my brother and his assumptions of marriage, forking her cheese-covered mound of elbow macaroni. "Do you know him? Eric, I mean."

The hand on my leg squeezed, my heart drumming so hard in my chest I was positive I was going to crack a rib as Dave cleared his throat. "Yeah, I do know him. He's my brother."

What?

WHAT?

My body twitched in what I could only describe as an internal seizure while my eyes tried to not bug out of my skull. My full-body spasm and mental freak out only increased by the sound of silverware dropping onto china.

"Brother?" my sister Melanie asked, her eyes peeled so wide they resembled saucers. "Are you kidding?"

Yeah, Dave, are you fucking kidding? I mentally screamed as I recalled the conversation in the car where I told him, verbatim, not to mention his brother. He was supposed to segue, redirect the conversation or cause a freaking diversion. Not admit the fucking truth.

"He's my older brother." Dave shrugged like it was no big deal. "I'll let him know you liked his latest movie." He winked at Amy, which earned him a smile.

"Hey, hey, hey." Travis waved his hands in the air, all the amusement from before completely gone. "Don't be telling nobody nothing. And no winking at my girl either, she is spoken for."

He was completely serious, like Dave telling Eric about Amy would somehow jeopardize his relationship, and a stranger on the other side of the country would leave his wife to steal his girlfriend. Meanwhile, I was wondering if it was too late to throw myself on the floor and fake an aneurysm, although given the current amount of pressure in my head, faking was not going to be required.

"Relax, dumbass." Dalton punched Travis in the arm. "Did you not hear the part where the other guy was married? He's no threat to you."

"Wow, Eric Larsson's brother. We're eating dinner with some-one famous," Lisa repeated in case anyone had missed it the first time, reminding me any hope of salvaging the conversation was slim.

"I'm not famous," Dave answered with zero acrimony. "He is, but we're still just a normal family." He nodded his head and smiled. "Like you guys."

Firstly, he clearly did not read my notes as thoroughly as he claimed if he was categorizing my family as normal. We were a lot of things, *normal* wasn't on the list.

And secondly, I still wasn't sure why the hell he'd decided to go off script and throw in a bootleg play.

The truth was not our friend.

I cleared my throat, taking a sip from my wineglass—the time for water had well and truly passed. "Besides, Dave's his own man and a talented actor in his own right."

"Oh, I wasn't implying." Lisa had the decency to blush. "Sorry, I didn't mean to offend."

Dave shook his head with a warm grin. "No offense taken."

"Hey, baby." My hand gently draped across his shoulder. "You want to go down to the cellar and help me choose another bottle of wine?"

There was still at least a glass in the one sitting on the table, but I needed an excuse to confer privately. I didn't think asking him to join me in the bathroom would look good in front of my parents.

"Oh, Travis can go get that, can't you?" My mom shot him a look of warning.

Crap, if my brother went, then my excuse for leaving the table would be gone. I tried not to choke again as I stood up quick. "Really, I've got this."

He frowned, making no effort to move from the table as he continued to shovel food down his throat. "Why do I have to go? If she wants to drink that fancy stuff, then she can go get it. And besides, she said she'd do it and I'm still eating."

"Because your sister is visiting and I asked you to," Mom said through a tight smile, the ice from her glare and her tone, unmistakable.

"It's fine, Momma. I am happy to go. Come on, Dave." I silently thanked my brother for his lack of apathy, yanking lightly on Dave's arm. "I'd love your input."

He took the hint, rising from his chair as he dabbed his mouth with a napkin. "Sure, lead the way."

"Don't be long," Dalton warned, eyeing Dave hard. "We wouldn't want your food to get cold." I was positive my brother had little concern about the temperature of our dinner and more about us making out in the basement.

I nodded, looping my arm through Dave's as I dragged him away from the table. "Mh-hmm. We'll be right back."

We didn't speak, smiling silently like we were under surveillance as we made it to the stairs that led down to the cellar.

"What the hell were you thinking?" I closed the door behind us and flicked on the light. "I thought we agreed."

He laughed, pulling me closer. "Relax. I decided avoiding it would only make it worse, so I went with the truth."

I felt myself get lightheaded, wishing there was somewhere to sit down. "The truth? You don't think that giving them information like that isn't going to send my whole story unraveling? You think that I'd be dating the brother of someone famous but fail to mention that part?"

My brain tried to reconcile it but still came up empty. I was in deep, deep shit.

"I'm my *own man*, remember, and *talented in my own right*." He grinned, regurgitating the same line I had given at the table. "Besides, ten seconds online is all it would take to find the family connection. It's not exactly a state secret that we're family. I don't wear a sign saying I'm *Eric Larsson's brother*, but lying about it wasn't going to fly."

He was right of course; their other brother Roman had

deliberately used his mother's maiden name to avoid the attention. Not that any of that was helpful, the truth complicating the plan with the extra degree of intricacy.

"We don't know that," I tried to argue. "And what if someone talks to the press, tipping them off that Eric Larsson's brother is down in Shreveport dating his agent's assistant?"

He laughed, the genuine body shaking rumble escaping his throat as he threw his head back. "You *know* nobody gives a shit about my love life. I have been dating for years and not once has it ever ended up in a tabloid. I am not famous, remember? So unless Eric is planning on flying down and joining us for this wedding, no one is going to give a rat's ass about what I'm doing or who I'm doing it with."

While he might not be in the same league as his brother, he wasn't the no one he was claiming to be either. "That's not true. I've seen people notice you all the time. You are very pop—"

"I think it's adorable that you are trying to stroke my ego, but I'm fine with things the way they are." He stilled me, placing his hands around my waist as he looked into my eyes. "I'm not disappointed that I can go and have a regular life. I don't want photographers hiding in my bushes or chasing me down a street. And I love that I can be with someone and not have to worry about a reporter going through their trash. So thanks for the words of encouragement, but they aren't necessary."

I guess I hadn't really thought of it that way. There weren't many artists who walked through the doors at Levin Murphy that didn't want to be hugely successful, and with that, came the fame—the paparazzi not far behind.

"I just meant." I closed my mouth wondering exactly what I *had* meant. "I meant that you really are talented and even though you aren't famous now, they are going to care very soon."

It wasn't a line, or a half-hearted effort to inflate his sense of worth; I genuinely believed it. He worked hard, he turned up to every audition we sent him to, and even did the occasional shitty dog food commercial even though it was a waste of his talent. He was the real deal; he just needed that right role, that right movie, that right *something,* for everyone else to see it. And I didn't doubt for a second he didn't have what it took to be an even bigger success than his brother.

"It's really sweet that you think so." He grinned. "But right now, I'm not on anyone's radar so you don't need to worry about what we're doing ending up in the press."

I shook my head, worried less about TMZ and more about my relatives. Not necessarily the members of my family, but Darla would spill everything she knew if she thought there was anything in it for her. "But people in this town have big mouths."

"So let them talk." He tipped his head to the closed door with a smirk. "And think about how much worse would it have been if I made up some bullshit and then they found out the truth later?"

Of course that made sense and he had a very valid point. Which would have been rational if we were dealing with a situation that had any semblance of logic. But I had paid an *actor* to come home with me to pretend to be my *boyfriend* and we were currently in the cellar while my family ate dinner upstairs. Nothing about the situation was close to logical.

"You want to grab a bottle of wine before my family thinks we're down here making out?" I refused to admit he was right, instead avoiding the question entirely as my head tipped to the racks of wine bottles on the side of the wall.

He grabbed a bottle, not bothering to look at the label as he slid it out from its place on the shelf. "Them believing we're making out probably helps our cause, so maybe we should wait down here longer. You wanna make out just to be authentic?" His grin huge.

Tempted to say yes—because who in their right mind would

say no—I shook my head.

"Yeah, let's not do that." I pulled the wine from his hand and checked it was acceptable.

Oh for God's sake, he'd picked a Shiraz.

The night was not going well for me.

"Then after you." He stretched his arm out toward the door and waited. "Try not to choke for the rest of the night, I'm looking forward to dessert."

I shook my head, climbing the stairs with the bottle in my hand. "Then try not giving me a heart attack."

I was convinced I was asking too much.

CHAPTER

#11

"SO, ARE YOU excited about tomorrow's shopping trip?"

Dinner was over and we moved to the living room for dessert. It meant Melanie could put my niece Anna down for a nap, and the men could watch whatever game was being broadcasted on television.

Tammy, who had largely been quiet during dinner, had secured a spot right next to me on the sofa, daintily dipping her spoon into the icebox pie like I didn't know she was making eyes at Dave. She might be my mother's assistant but her loyalty did not extend to me.

"Sure," I lied, the thought of spending the day elbow deep in diapers and nursery items not my idea of a good time. Still, I loved my sister and was happy she was giving me another niece, so if had to suffer through a few hours at Babies-R-Us to make her happy, then that's what I'd do.

I was more concerned with leaving Dave unattended, his plans for the day not yet secured.

"I'd be happy to take Dave through Shreveport and give him a tour while you're gone," she offered, batting her eyelashes like she was doing me a favor.

"Thanks for the offer, Tammy, but I think he might be doing

something with either Dalton or Travis."

I had no personal feelings against Tammy per se; she was a beautiful twenty-year-old redhead who looked at my mother like she'd hung the moon. She didn't have family of her own, her drunk momma kicking her out of the house when she was sixteen. And while she did end up living with a wealthy aunt who gave her food and shelter, Tammy got less than zero emotional support or love. It was no wonder she ended up getting validation in other ways. My mom had hired her right out of high school, hoping that not only would she give the poor girl a job but also a sense of family, but old habits die hard and she spent more time on her knees giving blow jobs than she did praising the Lord.

"Well the offer is there." Her words trailed off as her eyes wandered to where the men were huddled together.

The lure of the large flat screen had proven too much for both Travis and Dalton, my brothers demanding Dave sit with them like they were the T-Birds while they had an in-depth discussion over which college kid was going to be the next NBA superstar. It was equal parts cute and frightening that they wanted to get to know him better, no doubt looking for an opportunity to question him about his intentions.

My mom had decided we needed another curveball thrown into the mix, asking my dad to go pick up my Gran Shelly and bring her to the house to visit. Because it would have been too easy to just wait until tomorrow night or until the wedding on Saturday. No, we needed to parade Dave around like a prized bull for all the family to see. *And they wondered why I didn't usually bring men home with me.* My mother was either on to me, and was trying to smoke me out, or she genuinely believed the ruse. I couldn't confidently guess which yet.

Amy sat on the other side of me, enjoying her pie while she smiled. "He's *really* good looking." The *he* in the sentence not needing to be clarified. "I can't believe you have kept him to your-self for so long. Just think, if Gran Shelly hadn't almost died, we wouldn't have even known about him."

Truer words had never been spoken.

"It was new, and kind of still is. I didn't want to jinx it." The rote answer fell from my lips with almost no effort.

"Honey, there's no guarantees in love. Look at me, I've been following your brother for who knows how long and I'm still wait-ing for him to get down on one knee," she said with a tired sigh. "I know he loves me, and there's no question I love him. But I really wish he'd stop assuming I'm going to wait around forever. Maybe having Dave around might light a fire under his ass, did you see how jealous he was at dinner?" She laughed.

"Well, anything I can do to help, just let me know." I wasn't exactly sure what help I could possibly offer other than hiring a fake boyfriend for her too. Chances were it wouldn't work a second time around.

The sound of the front door opening tied a knot in my stom-ach. I knew who it was and what it meant. I hated the deceit, and the subsequent elaborate breakup I knew was in my future. It stung more than it did before. But I reminded myself my intentions were honorable even if shit was about to get real.

Gran Shelly walked into the room followed by a cloud of Chanel No. 5. Her silver hair was set into perfect finger waves while her cheeks were stained a little too pink to be natural. She didn't care though, slathering on her face every day despite what people thought.

"Gran." I rose from my seat, excited she was up and about and no longer knocking on death's door. She'd come a long way since the last time I'd seen her, her pale blue eyes twinkling with mischief.

"Come here and give me a hug." She shuffled in on her walk-ing frame, her jeweled fingers reaching out as I got closer. "I've missed you, dear girl."

Her thin arms squeezed me as I leaned down to meet her, a waft of her perfume tickling my nose as I squeezed back. She was so small but strong, her heart beating defiantly underneath her tailored blue dress. I couldn't believe how close we'd come to losing her, the tears welling in my eyes at how lucky we'd been to be granted more time. If the lie or two I'd told made me uncomfortable, I'd gladly bear it, just so grateful to still have her around.

"Oh, stop with the fuss." She gave me a shake, the laugh bubbling up her throat. "I didn't get up out of my chair and come out at this time of night to see y'all crying."

"I'm not crying; it's allergies." I wiped away the tears from the corners of my eyes as I stood straight.

A hand replaced the warmth of Gran's hug, with Dave's arm finding its way around me while his fingers pressed against my hip. I hadn't even noticed him leaving his seat, almost startled to see him beside me.

"You okay?" he asked, without the tacky pet name on the end. It was clear the question was sincere and not for the benefit of the show.

I nodded, swallowing the emotion. "Gran, there's someone I'd like you to meet. This is Dave."

The introduction felt weird, everyone watching while I awkwardly waved at him like he was a toaster on the *Price is Right*. The moment not made easier as my gran narrowed her eyes in suspicion. "What are you doing here?"

My heart stopped as the she shuffled closer, her hand going to the chain around her neck and lifting the glasses attached to it to bring them to her eyes. Blinking she looked again, her smile widening as she proclaimed, "I *know* you.

A nervous laugh escaped my mouth as I grabbed Dave's hand. "You don't know him, Gran, you've never met. This is the man I told you about, remember? My boyfriend," I added, wondering if Gran hadn't decided to self-medicate with a couple glasses of Chardonnay before my dad picked her up.

"Boyfriend?" She looked even more confused. "No, no, I've seen this man on television. He travels house to house with an apparent allergy to wearing a shirt. I've seen the way those ladies smile as they hand him their money. If he disrobes, we'll know for sure."

Mortified.

A collected echo of gasps could be heard through the room as she shuffled closer, her shaking finger crooked, beckoning him to come closer.

"Don't be shy, son. I'm eighty-six years old and I'm not afraid of seeing a little skin. I think I have a rolled up twenty in my purse."

"Momma," my mother warned. "It's not polite to be asking the company to take off their clothes, especially not in the living room."

Really? It wasn't polite? That was the best she could come up with?

My gran had offered to throw my boyfriend—sure, he wasn't technically, but semantics—a twenty to get naked like she was at a strip show. And my mother was worried about it happening in the living room? As if it wouldn't have been as horrible if we'd been in the dining room. Because location mattered.

Now would be a good time to reconnect with religion.

Oh help me, Lord Jesus.

Dave smiled, ignoring he'd been propositioned by a woman pushing ninety. "Ahh, a fan of my work, I see."

"Gran." I wasn't sure if the situation was hysterical or horrifying, the blood draining from my head. "Dave is an *actor*. He acts. That was a pet food commercial for Doggie Chow. Dave plays the delivery guy, and the women were smiling because he's bringing their pets their food."

Well, not *really*. I am almost positive some dumbass in marketing had intended for the misconception, sex sells and all that shit. I guess the tagline hadn't helped—*Doggie Chow, bargain price but twice as nice.* No wonder she assumed he was the town gigolo.

"Oooooh." Amy snapped her fingers and laughed. "I know the one, I almost didn't recognize him with a shirt on."

Cue a lot of throat clearing and my brother Travis cursing under his breath.

Gran played with the strand of pearls that flirted across her collarbone. "See, I'm not the only one. I have seen that commercial at least a hundred times and not noticed any mention of dog food."

That fucking commercial had a lot to answer for.

"I'll pass on the feedback," I offered. "So . . ." And here I thought Dave being related to Eric was going to be our biggest problem. "This is my boyfriend, Dave." I tried again with the introduction, hoping this time around she didn't ask him to take off his pants.

"Hi, Gran Shelly." He stooped down, lowering himself to give her a gentle hug.

"Well." She smiled, tapping his back like he was a well-behaved Golden Retriever. "That's nice, I wasn't aware Jessica was dating anyone."

"I'm sorry, what did you say?" Another nervous laugh, beads of sweat forming at my brow.

I know I didn't imagine the time I sat beside her in my grandfather's old rocking chair as she struggled to keep her eyes open and told her about a man who didn't exist.

"Gran, remember last time I was here and you said that your greatest regret was that you hadn't met all your grandchildren's significant others? So I told you about my boyfriend and hoped you would get to meet him through my words?"

"Honey, I had so much morphine in me you could have told

me that little green men had come to earth in their spaceship and I wouldn't remember." She looked over at Dave with appreciation. "But him, *him* I promise you I will not forget."

It was like I had been run over by an eighteen-wheeler with my brains strewn all over the interstate. All the worry, avoiding the calls from my family, the initial lie and the guilt I had experienced after the fact, had all been for . . . nothing?

"Come on, Momma." My mother led Gran over to a chair where she could be more comfortable. "Let's get you situated so you can visit for a bit. I know you get tired easily. Jessica can tell you all about it, just think how lovely it will be hearing it all again."

"How exciting." I desperately tried to hide the panic in my voice. "I can't wait."

My legs felt like pudding as I wandered back to the sofa. Dave's hand was still glued to my side and helped keep me upright so I didn't fold like a two-dollar lawn chair as I took a deep breath.

"Just breathe," he whispered. "It's just a day at work and you're pitching an actor to a director. You've done this a million times."

His words of encouragement eased me as I sat beside her, making me feel a strange sense of calm and reassurance as Dave took the seat beside me.

"Now tell me," her bright pink lips spread into a grin, "tell me all about your man." She nodded to Dave.

"Well . . ." *Breathe. Breathe. I've done this a million times.* "As you know, Dave is an actor and the talent agency I work for represents him. So we met at work, went out on a date and fell in love. It's pretty standard."

If that was my pitch, I wouldn't have only passed on the project but I would have fired my ass. I shook my head, disappointed in myself.

You are a confident, successful woman, Jessica Dawson. Now, we might not like the corner we're backed into, but we sure as hell ain't going to sit cowering in it. Own it, sell it—or pack up your shit and go home.

"The first time I noticed him was a Tuesday," I started, relaxing against the cushions. "I'd seen him before but I'd been so busy trying to make a good impression with Jeremy that I barely looked up from my desk when someone came in. But that day, I looked up."

"Awwww. It's like a real life romance novel," Lisa—my overly romantic sister-in-law—cooed, settling in and giving me her full attention.

Dave put his arm around me, kissing my shoulder as he grinned. "No matter how many times I hear this, it's always like I'm hearing it for the first time."

I gave him a subtle glare, playfully jabbing him in the ribs as I coughed out "asshole," under my breath.

"It was his eyes," I continued, my audience enthralled as I wove my tales of finding love. "I'd lost a contract earlier in the day and hadn't gotten around to telling Jeremy. I was stalling, trying to think of everywhere it could be before I walked into his office and admitted I'd misplaced it. But when I looked up there were the kindest, warmest chocolate brown eyes I'd ever seen. They stopped me in my tracks, and then he asked me why I looked so upset. For three hours I had been tearing up my desk and not one person asked me if I was okay. But *he* did."

Dave's handed tightened and I didn't need to ask him why.

My little scenario of how we started dating probably wasn't as *fictional* as he'd expected. It was in fact the first day I'd really paid attention to him, deciding that unlike so many assholes who walked through our door, he wasn't one of them.

In order to not lose my nerve, I ignored him, putting whatever he had going through his mind out of mine, determined to finish what I'd started.

"And then he told me that whatever I was looking for would turn up, and if it didn't then I wasn't meant to find it in the first place. And of course, he was right, the contract was sitting right in front of me the whole time. I guess I took his words to heart, and he has made mine stop ever since."

My older brother groaned. "I think I'm going to puke."

"Hush, Dalton. Some women want more romance than to be taken out to the local Denny's for a midnight dinner after being picked up at a bar." His wife stared him down, silencing him with a look.

I ignored my brothers, and hoping I wasn't freaking Dave out as I went on to elaborate about how we started as friends at first and then moved to dating. We'd decided to keep it low-key so people around the office didn't find out, but now we were both deliriously happy and looking forward to the future.

Blah, blah, blah—happily ever after—the end.

Gran tapped my hand gently and smiled. "Well, I am really glad I got to hear that again. And I'm glad you're happy. Maybe the two of you can come sit with me on Sunday before you fly home and I can hear more."

"Sure, no problem," I agreed, glad the inquisition had stopped for the night. "We'd love it."

Sunday was a lifetime away so making plans to sit at her round kitchen table sipping on iced tea and telling more stories was an easy promise to make. Hopefully by then she would have forgotten—like she had the first time—and we could go back to talking about the Catholics instead.

I casually yawned, making a show of checking the time and saying we should get back to our hotel. Dad was going to take Gran back home and Melanie and Sam wanted to get Anna to bed so it seemed like we should make a move too. Besides, it had been our first big outing, and like any team, we needed to go back and look at the game tapes, debrief and formulate the strategy for the rest of the weekend. Oh, and I was going to have to find a way to go to sleep with Dave lying right beside me. Because *that* was going to be easy.

We said our goodbyes, thanking my mom for the amazing dinner, and followed Dad, Gran, Melanie, Sam and Anna out the front door.

"Nice ride." Travis tipped his head to our shiny red rental, following us out to the convertible. "You can tell a lot about a man by the car he drives."

Dave's eyebrow rose in a silent I-told-you-so as he opened the passenger door for me, not bothering to ask if I wanted to drive. "Thanks, she handles like a dream too."

He didn't gloat for too long, sliding into the driver's seat and starting the ignition, peeling out of the driveway before Dad had even gotten Gran into the car.

"That went well." He laughed, finding his own way back onto the road.

I pointed to the sign up ahead. "Get on 49, and *that* was a mess."

"It wasn't that bad, you're too critical. Think of it as the dress rehearsal, a chance for us to get all the kinks out before opening night." He tapped on the steering wheel in time to the radio, completely calm.

I guess it was easy to be calm when it wasn't your ass on the line; they weren't going to want *his* head on a spike if they found out it was all just some elaborate sham.

"You're right, it can only get easier from here on out." I didn't bother arguing, looking out the windshield at the passing lights.

Shreveport had always seemed so small town, my ambitions bigger than what the city could give me. But I loved it, and it would always hold a place in my heart. There was a certain comfort to being back. Like sliding on an old pair of jeans or a worn in pair of shoes, everything moved slower and a day just seemed to last longer.

"What are you thinking about?" Dave asked, breaking the silence.

I sighed, stretching my arms in front of me as we pulled into the hotel. "Just about the city. It feels different this time around."

"Good different or bad different?" He stopped, putting the car into park.

"I'll let you know when I've decided."

Oh, I had decided, and nothing about being with him could ever be bad.

Nothing.

CHAPTER #12

IT HAD BEEN an hour and a half and I was still holed up in the bathroom.

I'd showered, shaved my legs, moisturized, brushed my teeth, blow dried my hair and reorganized the hotel-provided toiletries. It was utterly ridiculous that I was hiding out like a fugitive.

It was usually a month or more before I slept with a man, and even longer before I stayed the night—if ever—but my concern wasn't about him seeing me when I woke up.

No, my anxiety was all my own, my nerves jangling as I looked in the mirror and gave myself a pep talk so I could go out there and face him.

It would have been a hell of a lot easier if I had taken a shower the minute we'd gotten to the room, gone through my routine and gotten my ass into bed. But instead, I offered the first shower to Dave.

I was attempting to be considerate, accommodating even— hoping my *good* and *considerate* behavior would help work off some of the sin-debt I had accumulated by lying my ass off.

He accepted happily, disappearing into the bathroom only to emerge twenty short minutes later clean, damp, and with a towel slung low around his waist.

No good deed goes unpunished.

Words got stuck in my throat as he waltzed out of the steam-filled room, rivulets of waters clinging to his chest as they snaked their way down his torso. I was hypnotized by their descent, following each dip and curl of their journey across his extraordinary muscles.

It was obscene, watching the strong cords across his shoulders flex as he twisted, using a small towel to dry off his hair. I was positive he could feel me staring, but as much as I wanted to—okay, that was a lie, I didn't want to—I couldn't look away. My eyes stayed glued to his body, following his every move like I was documenting it for prosperity.

"You good?"

He'd moved closer, bringing his mostly naked, clean smelling man body inches away from mine, the urge to reach out and touch him proving almost too much.

It took every ounce of willpower to stop myself, muttering like a crazy person that I needed a shower before locking myself in the bathroom.

Which was where I still was.

Hopefully during that time he'd put on some clothes, saving me from the hormone explosion I'd barely escaped when I ran into the bathroom like a loser. Although, given what I'd seen *before* I walked away, I was sure a full body Hazmat suit still wouldn't be enough.

Shit.

I looked at the door handle like it was covered with spiders, repelling from it. My reflection fell back to the mirror, glancing at myself wearing what I had packed to sleep in, the cotton boxer shorts and plain cotton tank—not a good choice. I'd never given much thought to my sleep attire before, my nipples poking against the thin fabric. Of course it was too late now to travel back in time and pack something less suggestive, like, I don't know, a freaking nun's habit.

"Open the goddamn door you coward." I willed my hand to move, whispering to myself like an idiot. "You're acting like a moron."

With a decisive jerk and a deep breath, I pulled open the door and emerged into the bedroom, the air conditioning hitting my skin and instantly making my nipples pebble.

And if it wasn't bad enough, the thermostat had declared war on my body while Dave's had decided to mount its own assault, the glow of the television screen lighting his pecs in what could only be described as spectacular.

Without words I slipped between the sheets, feeling the temperature across my skin rise by a hundred degrees as I plumped up my pillow like I wasn't aroused.

Obviously he hadn't found that shirt, the allergy Gran had spoken of earlier still afflicting him. I had to wonder if his lack of clothing extended to the bottom half and I was tempted to look. He wouldn't sleep naked, would he? I wasn't even decent enough to be ashamed that I hoped he would, and was.

"Plans for tomorrow?" My eyes stared dead ahead as I kept my voice low, watching the animal documentary with intensity even though I had no idea what the hell was going on.

"Travis needs to work, but Dalton wants to take me out to one of the casinos for lunch." I felt him shift beside me. "I need to run lines in the morning but everyone needs to eat."

My head nodded, careful not to expand my field of vision. "Sure. Everyone needs to eat."

My voice sounded foreign, devoid of tone as I focused on the elephants on the screen. I couldn't allow myself to think too much about him, concerned my body would betray me.

He stopped shuffling, and I felt the weight of his stare. "Is there something else you would rather me be doing tomorrow?"

How about me?

No, you cannot say that.

"No, of course not." I tried to laugh, but didn't sound convincing. "You should go. Have a good time."

My recovery wasn't great, but at least I no longer sounded deranged.

"If you're worried about me flying solo, you don't need to be. I'm rock solid."

Really? Mind if I reach down there and check for myself?

Goddamn it, Jessica.

It was adorable that he thought the reason I hadn't made eye contact was because I was worried about his ability to complete the mission. I had to wonder if he knew what kind of firepower he wielded with that body of his, or if he knew how his little half-naked display had worked me up into a state.

"I'm not worried. Just don't offer any additional information and we'll be fine."

He wasn't the only one who needed to be concerned with adding additional information. I took my own advice, saying as little as possible as I continued my passionate viewing of The Discovery Channel.

"If it makes you feel better." He threw off the blankets and jumped out of bed. "I'll go over the notes one last time so they're fresh for tomorrow."

My narrow field of vision didn't do shit as he walked from his side of the bed to his suitcase by the closet and pulled out an iPad.

His ass was encased in a pair of Calvin Klein boxer briefs that looked like they'd been sprayed on. I didn't even need to use my imagination, the reality far better than anything I could have dreamed up. The bulge in the front was substantial, straining against the cotton in the protest of being contained. I didn't blame it, his penis having my full support of being freed as well.

I hadn't meant to look, but it wasn't like something I could avoid either. The height of his man parts had been exactly level with my line of sight. It was a conspiracy of the highest order.

I'd tried to avert my eyes, begging my head not to turn or for my retinas to look elsewhere, but it was too late. My optical nerve won the war with my brain, tracking him like prey as he strode casually back to the bed and slid in.

The relief that he'd covered himself was short-lived, his leg brushing mine as he shuffled on the mattress. If he was looking for a comfortable spot to lie, I could help him with that, namely the space between my legs.

OH. MY. GOD.

Please do not let me suggest that.

I shut my eyes, pretending I was home alone. Or at the Vatican staring at Michelangelo's fresco with all those judgy Catholic fat angels glaring down. My skin burned, prickling, and I just knew he was watching me.

"What is it?" I asked, keeping my eyes shut and my mind on the Virgin Mary.

"You like to sleep naked," he said casually, like he'd announced I didn't like polyester.

"Yeah, so?"

"You're not naked now." I could hear the smile in his voice.

My eyes squinted tighter hoping the darkness might cleanse my dirty thoughts. Lord knows the fat judgy angels hadn't done shit. "I'm also not in bed alone and I was trying to be considerate. You're welcome."

He coughed, a low rumble traveling up his throat. "Don't go to any trouble on my behalf."

I was hearing things, or misinterpreted it, because surely he wasn't inviting me to . . .

"I could say the same for you, you know? I remember reading something similar on your notes." I went on the offensive.

"You're right. You did."

At some point I must have blacked out, or had a moment of stupidity, because the next thing out of my mouth could only be described as dumbness of the highest order.

"It's fine, Dave. If you want to get comfortable, you can go ahead. It's a big bed." My effort to sound all fine and dandy with the situation volunteered me for something I was positive I would not be able to ignore.

"Are you sure? I don't want to—"

"Please, we're both adults. Knock yourself out."

I was insane.

Certifiable and in need of serious help, my breath held as I waited for his response.

The words I expected to hear didn't come, with the mattress compressing beside me. My eyes flung open and focused on the ceiling not daring to turn to the side while my lungs burned for air as I lay still. Every single sound was put together like a puzzle, my mind building a picture for me in my head.

He shuffled, moving across the bed as he peeled off the only layer between him and nudity. All I had to do was turn around and reach out and . . .

"You should do it too." His voice broke through my silent dirty thoughts.

My eyes widened as I took a sharp gasp of air.

He wanted me to touch him?

I wasn't sure if I'd spoken out loud or he could read my mind, but even with his permission I had to remind myself it was not a good idea. Or at least I tried to remind myself, the argument unable to form in my scrambled brain.

"Are you sure?" The words came out of my mouth before I

had a chance to stop them.

Oh my God, I couldn't be seriously considering this?

I had barely kissed the man and even *that* had been under false pretenses, the whole relationship was a sham and I was paying him to be with me. He wasn't a plaything, and it didn't matter how sexually frustrated I was, it would be wrong.

So wrong.

The wrongest.

W.R.O.N.G.

God, why did I still want to?

The seconds seemed to stretch out for an hour, his response coming with a chuckle. "Of course I'm sure. You said it yourself, we're both adults."

I slowly turned, my skin tingling as I tried to keep my movements unhurried and relaxed. Not sure I was doing so great, flipping over to face him with no grace or coordination.

"Hi." He smiled, his biceps bulging, resting on the pillow with his hands anchored around his neck.

Not smiling was impossible, my eyes following the curves of his amazing body up to his perfect face. "Hi yourself."

He laughed. "I'm glad you turned around, you know I love attention and it was starting to feel weird."

It was starting *to?*

We'd already left *weird*. It was a distant memory of when I still had a conscience and wasn't considering molesting him. Now we were in a whole other realm, and I wasn't sure I felt bad about it.

"I'm glad I turned around too."

He turned to his side, facing me and bringing temptation closer. "So are you going to do it? Or you are you all talk?"

"I'm not all talk," I fired back.

It was a question of honor now. Even if I didn't want to touch him—which I did—I would have to. I was compelled.

My hand inched further while mentally I prepared myself to feel all that beautiful tanned skin. His smile widened as if he too was anticipating it, opening his mouth to speak. "So lose the sleep clothes and get naked."

Wait a second.

What?

"Me? Get naked?" I coughed out, my hand rearing back like it had been electrocuted.

"Yes *you*. Isn't that what we've been discussing?" His brow furrowed in genuine confusion, not having read my mind like previously thought.

"Yes, of course." *Lord help me.* "Me. Naked." The panic kept out of my voice by sheer force of will.

His mouth dropped the smile like it was on fire, the apology coming soon after. "Jess, I was only playing around. I don't want you to do anything you don't want to do. I just thought . . ." He waved his hand to me. "You sounded like you wanted to."

"No, I want to," I started to protest. "You're right, I hate sleeping in clothes."

Besides, we were both under the covers and you could have parked a Buick in the space between us. Before I lost my nerve, my fingers curled around the hem of my tank top and pulled it up over my head. Thankfully the comforter stayed in position, saving me from flashing my boobs. My naked collarbone and arms were as scandalous as it got, my top getting tossed to the floor.

He watched with interest as I continued my undercover dance, my attention shifting to my boxer shorts.

It felt illicit, his eyes on me as I slid the thin cotton down my legs. I kicked them off, using my foot to toss them out of the bed, my fingers gripping the top of the sheet.

"Better?" he asked, an amused look on his face.

"Much," I answered, feeling a tug in my lower belly with the sheets against my naked skin.

He breathed deeply, a long exhale passing through his lips. "I want to ask you something. That story you told, about us in the office?"

Shit, I cursed under my breath. I'd hoped he'd forgotten about it or somehow had missed it. Or at the very least decided not to mention it. But that would be asking too much as I took my own gasp of air and tried to explain.

"I needed a story, something that I could talk about and not worry about being caught in the lie. What I said about meeting you that day was true, it was the first time I really noticed you." I swallowed, feeling exposed, and it had nothing to do with the fact I was naked in the bed beside him.

"I embellished," I quickly added, hoping he wouldn't think I was a psycho who was really in love with him and this was some elaborate plan to get him to date me. "You know . . . made it sound more romantic than it was. So that it sounded convincing."

His eyes narrowed, not seeming to be convinced. "That's all it was? A *story*."

"Yes, yes of course." I laughed, trying to sound casual. "Just a story."

He opened his mouth like he was about to say something but then closed it again, looking at me for what seemed like an eternity before he spoke. "I remember that day too."

I didn't move, my body tingling as we looked at each other. "We should get some sleep."

My suggestion was complete bullshit and I knew it. I had a greater chance of digging a tunnel to China than I did actually being able to get to sleep. How was it even possible? Was I supposed to forget there was an incredibly gorgeous naked man in the bed with me? Unless I could somehow hypnotize myself, it wasn't going to be likely.

Meanwhile, there was a pair of cheetahs fucking on the television, the previously safe Discovery Channel had degraded into animal porn.

Everything was literally conspiring against me.

"Yep, big day tomorrow." He ignored the sex on the screen, his lips edging into a grin. "Goodnight."

Just like that.

Goodnight.

Forcing my eyes shut and keeping my breathing level, I tried to will myself to sleep. When willing didn't work, I moved to bargaining, promising to pamper myself tomorrow with a pedicure and a massage if my body agreed to shut down. Whatever it took.

I turned on my side, grabbing blindly for the remote control and shutting off the television, hoping the darkness would make it easier—it didn't.

Instead of getting sleepy I was confronted by the stark fluorescent numbers of the hotel clock ticking by one agonizing minute at a time every single time I opened my eyes.

At some point either my body had given out or my bargaining with Jesus had been successful, because when I woke up it was five a.m. It was still dark in the room, the glow of that obnoxious digital clock the only illumination there was.

My body was stiff, tight as I uncoiled myself from the weird curled-up position I'd slept in. Pins and needles tingled as my limbs regained circulation, stretching myself out as I breathed a sigh of relief.

Carefully, trying to make my movements as casual as possible, I angled my head to the other side of the bed. By some miracle last night, I had managed to forget about the naked hottie, but I didn't have the same blessing in the early hours of the morning.

The limited light gave me just enough illumination to see that he was blissfully still asleep. His face was relaxed, his eyes closed while his lips slightly parted.

He'd pushed down the covers, the most spectacular torso I'd seen in a long time disappearing into bunched sheets that pooled at his hips.

Without any of the shame I should have had, I ogled him. Floated over his fit muscular body with my eyes like my hands were dying to do. It was like I was suspended in the moment, watching from the sidelines like a spectator, and I couldn't look away.

I blinked a couple of times, making sure I was really conscious and this wasn't a dream, my finger nails digging into my palm, confirming I was in fact awake.

A barely audible groan passed through his lips, his hands pushing the covers lower. My eyes widened as it exposed more flesh, hovering only an inch or so before becoming indecent.

"Shit," I cursed under my breath, wondering when I'd become a creepy voyeur. I should have been horrified with my behavior and pray for forgiveness for objectifying the man like a piece of meat. But instead of seeking penance like I ought to, my mind was trying to Jedi mind trick the covers to slip just a little bit lower.

This is not the body you were looking to cover.

I whispered it again and again, stopping short of waving my hand like an Obi-Wan Kenobi version of Jesus.

That was what it had come to; I was summoning the Force in an effort to do my depraved bidding. And the fact I wasn't ashamed of myself could only mean bad things.

I needed to get out of bed, get a cold shower and get dressed. It didn't matter that it was ridiculously early in the morning and I had nowhere to be for the next five hours, I would find a way to occupy my time that wouldn't result in a stalking charge.

Reading the Bible might be a good place to start.

Before I could change my mind, I lifted the covers strategically—with as little noise as possible—and slipped out of the bed. I dropped to the floor like a possum falling out of a tree but thankfully he didn't move, his eyes and his breathing remained the same as I commando crawled on the floor, picking up my discarded bedclothes.

I needed to get them on, get into the bathroom and—

There was another soft groan, my eyes widening as I rose from my place on the floor. My discarded clothes forgotten as I left them where they were and peered over the edge of the mattress. His hand had disappeared under the covers, resting where I assumed his cock was.

Watching him touch himself was the biggest turn-on ever, my body flushing hot all over as I felt myself get wet. If I had thought last night had been difficult, it was nothing compared to dealing with the morning. I dropped any pretense of getting dressed, forgetting why I was even out of bed in the first place as I kneeled beside the mattress and stared. Arm muscles flexed as he gave himself one long stroke, his legs kicking apart to give himself more room.

If I had been a decent person I would have left, allowed him to have his moment in private and pretend I hadn't seen what I had. The key word was *decent*, and I was almost positive I wasn't. At least I didn't want to be, and I didn't want to miss what was probably the sexiest thing I'd seen in a long time.

There was another heavy breath and another long stroke, my place from the floor no longer adequate as I felt myself stand. All rational thought stopped, my mind unable to think about anything else other than what was going on in front of me.

Slow and steady his hand moved, pumping against his shaft while his jaw tightened. I wasn't sure whether I should go over there and give him a hand or touch myself like I was dying to do, both options more appealing than standing around doing nothing.

God it was hot, so freaking erotic that I could feel myself wanting to come even though I wasn't involved. His eyes slid open, freezing me in my place as his hand stopped what it was doing. No words were spoken, lowering his gaze from my eyes to my body, stopping at my breasts.

He licked his lips, my nipples stiffening like they'd been the ones tongued as he continued his visual tour down. I didn't try and hide, standing still as he looked at me.

"You like watching me?" he asked, his eyes moving back to mine.

I nodded, the "yes" coming out almost immediately. My honesty was startling, yet there wasn't a thing I wanted to do to stop it.

"Do you want me to stop?"

"No."

"Then come back to bed."

There was no argument, my body getting back in between the sheets. I had no idea what was going to happen next, but I knew I wanted it.

There was no thought process, no weighing up whether or not it would be a good idea, my body on autopilot as I moved closer and stretched out my hand.

Under the covers I reached for him, feeling his fingers curled around his hard cock. I didn't even ask, my hand covering the top of his as I guided him up toward the crown.

"Are you wet?" His eyes blazed, letting me lead him with each pump.

I squeezed hard, moving a little faster with each pass. "Yes."

"Let me touch you."

It was both a question and a statement, his hand stopping under mine.

With his other hand he pulled down the sheets, exposing us both. And while he had already seen me naked, it was the first time I was being treated to what was under the covers.

One finger at a time he lifted, my hand coming away as he

unwrapped from his shaft, the large hard cock underneath begging for attention.

The hand he'd been jerking off with slid up my thigh, the weight of his palm getting me hotter the closer it got to my center.

It shouldn't have been happening, the sex almost too intimate. The statement in itself was ridiculous for a one-night-stand, and yet it felt so right.

Him touching me—felt right.

I no longer questioned or cared if it was wrong, and how no man had ever made me feel this good.

"What do you want, Jessica?"

His finger dipped lower, teasing me, driving me crazier with each pass.

My hips bucked, forcing more contact as my hand went back to his cock. "I want to see you come."

"Just me?" He tilted his head, his wet fingers circling my clit.

My hand curled around his length, tightening on the upstroke. "No, not just you."

"Good, because I won't come until you do." He smiled, his fingers plunging into me.

I gasped, "Yes," lifting my ass off the bed and felt him go deeper. My hand moving faster as it twisted up and down his erection.

He groaned, getting harder in my hand as I jerked him, and I could feel he was close, his body tensing as he fought the urge to come.

"Fuck I want you," he whispered against my lips, bringing his mouth to mine and kissing me hard as he added another finger. I kissed him back, rocking my hips while he did the same, fucking my fist as I gripped him tight.

It was impossible to tell which felt better, what he was doing to my body or the control I had over his, but I felt myself go over in a sudden, heated rush.

"Yes, yes, yes," I panted, my body shaking as he continued to thumb my clit. His finish wasn't far behind, his cock pulsing in my hand before exploding all over his stomach.

The pleasure echoed in my body, my grip around him loosening as I kept my gaze locked with his. He watched me as I rolled to my side, bringing my mouth to his abs and then licked the mess he'd made off his skin.

"I want to be inside of you," he growled, his eyes narrowing as I lapped. "Making you come on my hand isn't even close to how good I can make you feel."

"That goes both ways." I laughed, kissing and nipping my way up his chest.

There was no stopping me; the seal had been broken and I wanted more of what he'd just given me. I wanted to feel him deep inside, thrusting and pulsing while I rode the hell out him.

It would probably be my only chance and I was sure as hell going to make it count.

He pulled me back to his mouth, kissing me while he palmed my breast, squeezing hard as I moved my body to straddle him. I could already feel him getting hard, lengthening between my legs as I rubbed against him.

"I want to be on top." I moaned as he took my nipple in his mouth and sucked.

He smiled against my skin, biting gently before moving to the other breast. "We can start there, we'll just have to leave it up to fate where we finish."

I wasn't about to argue, closing my eyes as he tongued my nipple, so close already to an orgasm I was almost embarrassed.

His erection was ready for round two as I reached down between us and gripped him. He hissed, inhaling sharply as I pumped him twice and then held him upright.

He shuffled a little on the bed, forcing me to lose my grip on him as he paid special attention to my breasts. My mind blacked out, closing my eyes tight as I got lost in the sensation, only barely being aware he'd gone back to touching himself too. Or at least that's what I assumed he was doing, his hard-on brushing against my wet core as he tugged between his legs.

Shifting me into position, his hands gave up on himself and concentrated on me. Our eyes connected as he positioned himself at my entrance, my hips pushing down as I impaled myself on his length. A moan escaped from my lips as I took him all the way to the root.

"Fuck me," he demanded, circling my hips with his hands as he encouraged me to move. "Fuck me, Jess, like I can feel you want to."

He was right; I was desperate to. Anchoring myself, I gripped his shoulders as I started to move, taking him in and out of my body with fast urgent thrusts.

I was a woman possessed, no longer in control of my mind or my body, and I didn't care how irrational it seemed.

"Yes." He drove in deeper, rocking with me and increasing the friction.

Harder and faster I bucked, desperately chasing the high as I kissed him. "God, you feel so good," I moaned. "This feels so good."

"I'll make it better." His back jerked off the bed, pulling out of me in a rush. He lifted us both, flipped me onto my back before covering me with his body. I barely had time to register the change in position, his cock reentering me the minute my back hit the mattress. He pulled my knees up, getting himself in deeper with each drive of his hard length until I couldn't hold out any longer.

"Dave," I screamed, my body feeling like it was splintering into a million pieces. "Dave."

Every muscle in his body tightened, primed for his own explosion as he hissed out my name, every part of me shuddering as he came with a shout. He pulsed inside of me, my eyes closing as I absorbed every single minute of it.

It was amazing, my fingers automatically pinching myself again just to be sure I was actually awake and this wasn't some elaborate sex dream I was having. The sting of my fingernails and the two orgasms he'd given me were proof that it wasn't.

It was better than I could have ever imagined, my body hoping it wouldn't be the last time. I wasn't sure if it was because my brain was sleep logged or the orgasms had me off kilter but the awkwardness of a first time wasn't there with him. Or maybe it was because I wasn't trying to impress him and overthink every single thing I did. It was liberating and exciting and I wanted more of it.

All those reasons I had to not have sex with him were stupid, and there was no reason we couldn't have sex if we both wanted to. As long as we were both on the same page, which I was sure we would be.

He lowered himself, covering me like a blanket, as I breathed in his scent. I loved feeling him heavy against me, the weight of him making me sleepy.

"I wear you out?" He chuckled against my ear, licking my neck. "You have a few more hours before we have to get up, why don't you get some more sleep."

I nodded, making my mouth say the words seemed to take too much effort as I felt him lift off me and roll onto his side of the bed.

"Sleep, beautiful." He kissed my mouth, the pet name sounding more sincere than the other ones he'd used, and for the first time, I liked it. "I'll wake you when it's time."

My lips parted into an O, yawning as I nestled into the pillow. I knew what we'd done was going to need a conversation, and I had every intention of talking about it.

Later.

It could wait until later.

CHAPTER #13

OH.

My.

God.

I woke up in a rush, my body jerking from the bed.

What the hell did I do?

What the HELL did I do?

The memory of the early morning came back to me as the panic set in. I'd not only had sex with Dave—a man who was my make-believe boyfriend—but I'd had UNPROTECTED sex with him.

My head whipped around, looking to his side of the bed and finding it empty. The sheets were mussed, so at least he'd been there at some point, but the body of the hot dude I'd had irresponsible sex with was MIA.

Perfect.

So not only was I the dumbest person of all time—unprotected sex with a man who wasn't even my boyfriend—but he'd obviously been so fucking horrified that he'd left right after.

Like a fucking drive by.

Oh my God, I hope he didn't go back to L.A.

I kicked off the covers, ignoring my nakedness and the soreness in my muscles, and immediately started investigating my surroundings. My cellphone was still beside the clock on the nightstand, the time displayed just before nine. Well, at least I hadn't slept till noon.

Next I checked the bathroom, my body sagging against the wall as I found it too—empty. Nothing else was out of place, the wet shower stall and a towel hanging on a hook the only evidence he'd even been in there. So if nothing else, I knew he had good hygiene practices, washing the sex off before he hit the door.

Pulling on one of the hotel-provided robes, I wandered out into the living area, finding no Dave and/or clues.

Thankfully his luggage was right where he'd left it, so if nothing else he'd eventually have to come back, which only made the situation slightly better than it was. My body collapsed into one of the sofas as my head fell into my hands. How—and I do mean *how*—could I have been so fucking stupid?

Thank God I hadn't paid him yet, a voice in my head whispered, like *that* fucking silver lining was helpful at this point. Not to mention that I had to figure out how to tell my goddamn family that he'd split. Oh, and then get freaking tested for every disease known to man. God I hoped he didn't give me something that was going to kill me or make my uterus drop out.

OH. FUCK.

What if I was pregnant?

Was it worse to be dying or to be carrying his bastard child?

I felt my vision get wavy, my breath coming out in fast short bursts. It didn't take a brain surgeon to work out that I was hyperventilating. At least I was sitting down, the chances of me hitting my head on the coffee table and killing myself were dramatically reduced by the fact I was no longer on my feet.

Instinctively I put my head down to my knees, trying to not black out. There was nothing good about the situation. My hormones—the traitors, that they were—had taken my otherwise perfect life and flushed it down the toilet, turning it into the nightmare it was now.

"Are you okay?"

The door of the suite slammed, making me jump as Dave walked toward me.

He looked concerned, pulling his shades from his face and sinking to his knees in front of me. "Jess, you don't look well."

You think? I would have yelled if I'd had enough oxygen in my lungs in order to talk and remain conscious. I was choosing straight breathing for now, at least until I could be somewhat sure I wasn't going to pass out.

"Breathe." He rubbed my back, his fresh man scent invading my nose as he leaned closer. "Breathe."

While I was glad he was back—that he didn't screw me and leave was certainly a victory for the day—I was still a long way from celebrating.

"What did we do?" I coughed out, my eyes so wide I was surprised they didn't drop out.

He stopped rubbing my back, his thumb moving to my chin as he looked me in the eyes. "Please tell me you're fucking with me and you remember what we did this morning." His concern deepened.

"I know we had sex, of course I remember that." The words felt raw in my throat, my voice hoarse. The best sex of my life wasn't something I was going to forget in a hurry, especially if I was carrying his child. There was one hell of a souvenir; I would have preferred a commemorative T-shirt.

He nodded, reassuring me that no, it hadn't been an extremely explicit dream and I had been completely irresponsible. Did I ever dare wonder what it meant for us? Lord, there was a conversation I could barely have with myself, let alone speak it out loud.

"Okay, so I didn't plan that." I wasn't sure if it was apology or pity in his eyes. "Honestly, Jess. I woke up and you were standing beside me naked."

"We had sex," I repeated. "*Without* a condom."

He pulled away, his face screwed up in confusion. "What? Of course I used a condom."

"No, no." I replayed it in my head, the moments of our sordid morning. "I jerked you off, then we made out and then I fucked you."

I was positive I hadn't missed anything, although to be quite honest it was dark and after the first orgasm my brain had been sort of scrambled.

"Yeah, all of that happened except in between jerking me off and the sex, I put on a condom."

"Are you sure?"

The edges of his lips twitched as he rubbed his hands over my arms. "Jess, it's not something I'd forget. It's still in the trashcan in the bathroom if you want to check."

"Oh thank you, Jesus." I threw myself onto my knees, a huge weight lifted off my shoulders.

Of course it still didn't deal with the fact I had sex with a man I was paying, which unwittingly made him a prostitute. But at least I wasn't going to keel over and die, or end up rocking a baby nine months from now.

He watched my thanks and worship with curiosity, shifting onto the sofa beside me. "So, you're okay now?" The hesitation still in his voice.

"We had sex." I cringed every time I said it.

Not because I didn't enjoy it, or hell, not even because I regretted it. But because only one of us had been using our heads and it *hadn't* been me. I should have been the responsible one.

He was an amazing man. He was funny and smart and

extremely good-looking, and if we didn't have all the extra baggage I'd probably be high-fiving myself. He was waaaaaay more considerate than any man I'd ever dated, and as for what he did between the sheets—Lord Jesus, there were no words. Any woman would count herself lucky to be with him.

But things were complicated.

There were blurred lines where there shouldn't be, and not to mention even after all of this, we were going to have to work together.

There was no way I could read his emotions, his eyes betraying nothing as he sat beside me. I wasn't sure if he was the one with regrets, or if he didn't feel somewhat coerced into to sleeping with me. Did he feel obligated? Like it had been part of the package?

Oh God.

I was going to throw up.

Trying to stop myself from another panic attack or vomiting all over his clean clothes, I shoved my messy emotions and thoughts out of the way, leaving them to be dealt with another time. Like later, when I grew a brain and stopped trying to sabotage my life. My priority was to try and salvage the situation and sound like I had a handle on it.

If he didn't have a problem with it, then I would not have a problem with it.

There would be *no* problem.

"This doesn't have to be weird." I was positive I was convincing myself more than I was him.

But the truth was, it didn't *have* to be weird.

People had sex all the time *and* were still able to be friends. Not me, of course, but other people. *Sensible people.*

And yes, there were times we all made poor choices, but surely we weren't going to be crucified for them. Pfft, we'd just move on, like nothing ever happened. Or not.

Maybe he didn't want to forget.

Did he want to forget? I should probably ask.

Great, I was not doing a good job of making it not fucking *weird*.

He tilted his head, wordlessly watching my internal debate, which was sort of freaking me the hell out. "Why would it be weird?" he asked, like he honestly didn't know. "We had sex, Jess, and while it might not be what either of us planned, it doesn't have to be a bad thing."

I shrugged, not entirely convinced but not wanting to be the one who was freaking out either. Newsflash: it was a little late for that.

"You're right, it doesn't." *Ha, you are such a liar!* I desperately tried to salvage the situation, not able to keep with the it's-all-cool vibe while needing to take responsibility as well. "I guess, I woke up and you were gone, and I thought . . . I just don't want you to do stuff that you maybe didn't want to."

Ugh.

So much for not acting weird.

Still, it needed to be said, if for no other reason than to be sure I hadn't accidentally sexually harassed him, and he was biding his time until he was able to file charges against me.

"You think I didn't want to?" He laughed, the light hitting his eyes. "Trust me, I wanted to. You're fucking beautiful, of course I wanted to. And at the risk of making myself look like a dick, the only reason I left this morning was to go buy these." He reached into his pocket and pulled out a box of condoms. "We used one, but I only had the *one*."

My eyes went wide, staring at the box in his hands. "You left to go get condoms?"

"Look, I'm not assuming anything, so don't think that." He tossed the box onto the coffee table, the edges of his lips twitching.

"I just wanted to be prepared, and there's no reason why we can't have a little fun while we're here. Assuming that is what you want?"

A thrill ran through my body as my cup overflowed with gratitude.

One. I had *not* had unprotected sex.

Two. I had not sexually harassed him, with all sexual activity being consensual. There was still that gray area because of my agreement with him and the exchange of money, but hey, I would not let that bullshit rain on my happy party.

Three. He hadn't had sex with me and then left—and/or hightailed it back home without saying goodbye—Praise Jesus.

And four, he was considering—rather seriously judging by his condom purchase—a repeat performance.

"Well, it's always good to be prepared." I stared at the box on the table, wanting nothing more than to rip it open. "But, we probably shouldn't."

There were lots of things we *probably* shouldn't do. Having the conversation before coffee was a start, but having casual hot sex with each other didn't have to be on that list. Unless I wanted to be responsible, which clearly was what I was attempting.

"Then we won't," he said with a smile. "We'll keep it just for the audience."

I was just about to agree—or open it up to further discussion, I hadn't decided which—when there was a knock. My eyes darted to the door as I shot to my feet and tightened the bathrobe, expecting the door to fly open at any minute like the police would on a drug raid. "Who the hell is that?"

"Probably room service." He glanced at his watch. "I ordered breakfast."

He strode over to the door, opening it—not the slightest bit worried about who was on the other side—to a man in a hotel uniform standing in the hall holding a tray.

"You can leave it on the table." Dave pulled out some money and tipped the guy as he lowered the tray. "Thanks."

Breakfast was a surprise I hadn't dared to hope for. Apart from my rather manic morning of freaking out and general neurotic behavior, I hadn't expected more than to run downstairs to the coffee shop and snag something on my way out the door. But an actual meal, delivered to my door—well that required the kind of preplanning that clearly I currently lacked. I mourned the loss of my usual organized self while simultaneously being curious as to what he chose.

I strolled over to where he was standing beside the food, the metal domes covering the plates giving me no clues. "How did you know what I wanted to order?"

"I'd tell you but you made me agree not to discuss." He lowered his voice to a whisper. "Your detailed email." He grinned removing one of the covers.

Underneath were two eggs over easy, hash browns and a couple of slices of bacon. It was my greasy guilty pleasure, and what I usually ordered for myself.

My stomach growled, the smell of the food wafting up and making me feel hungry. "Thank you."

He took a seat, uncovering his plate covered with waffles as he smiled. "Don't mention it."

Oh, I wouldn't, but only because I had no idea what I was actually thanking him for.

CHAPTER #14

I DIDN'T SO much as eat as inhale breakfast, alternating between shoveling food in my mouth and swallowing coffee and juice. And while my hurried way of eating didn't leave a lot of time for conversation, there was an easy silence that stretched between us.

It was ignorant bliss, willing to bury my head in the sand rather than deal with the obvious mess. Not that I was capable of forgetting, the memories from earlier in the morning burned permanently in my mind.

Besides, I didn't have a lot of time, needing to shower, dress and be ready for when my brother's girlfriend arrived. Or at least that's what I told myself as I left any further discussion on whether or not we would have sex again sidelined.

Dave cleared the breakfast dishes, letting Amy into the room while I finished up. "Hey, just need to grab my purse." I strolled out to the living room, Amy barely having had time to sit down.

The smile widened across her face as she looked between us. "We're in no rush." Her eyes dropped to the box of condoms that were conspicuously left on the table. "No rush at all."

That, of course, was bullshit. My sister Melanie didn't do late. She had been born two weeks premature, and the only time she'd been five minutes late—due to a flat tire—we'd been on the brink of calling 9-1-1 to file a missing person's report. She took after my mother, both of them believing being *on time* was running late, and punctuality was one of the forgotten commandments.

I not so subtly gestured toward the door. "We might as well get going. I'm ready."

"Of course." Her smirk stayed in place. "Enjoy your day, Dave."

He followed us out, walking us to the door where we both stopped.

We had kissed when he first arrived at the hotel under the guise of "practicing," and then in the morning for an entirely different reason. Both times had been hotter than hell, with neither feeling pretend. But as I stood there wondering if I should do it again, I hesitated.

But he didn't.

Taking my head in his hands, he brushed his lips against mine. There was no tongue, just lips, but it didn't feel any less electric. My eyes closed of their own accord, leaning into him as Amy cleared her throat.

Under protest, I tore my mouth away from his, not sure how much of it had been for performance. The butterflies in my belly sure felt real. "I should go."

"Have fun." He kissed my nose, tipping his chin to Amy as he said goodbye. "I'll see you when you get back."

My fingers tightened around the strap of my purse, nodding to Amy we were good to go. Staying any longer would be dangerous, and I was going to leave even if I had to throw myself out.

She looped her arm into mine and pulled me into the hall, her infectious laugh bubbling the minute we had made it to the elevator. "Wow," she fanned herself, "you might want to take extra precautions, girl. A kiss like that will get you pregnant."

"Oh ha-ha." I smirked, my skin still tingling as we rode the elevator. "You're hilarious."

She giggled, the metal doors opening out into the foyer. "You know, I bet y'all would make the cutest babies too. We've got time to go to the courthouse and get an extra license. I'm sure Lana won't mind sharing her big day with you."

"Yeah, that is not happening. I'm not even considering marriage until I'm at least thirty. Besides, it's your turn next, not mine."

We walked out to her Chevy Malibu, the sun blinding me as it reflected off the silver paint. "Yeah, here's hoping," She shrugged, hopping into the driver's seat as I got into the car.

Unlike the rental, Amy's stereo was blaring country tunes like it was its job, both of us laughing as we made our way to my mom's.

The plan was for Melanie to drop off Anna with her in-laws, and then meet us at Momma's house. Anna was going through separation anxiety and would scream the house down every time Mel disappeared. It didn't matter if it was in a bathroom or she was headed to the store, unless that child was asleep she wanted to be on my sister's hip 24/7. Not conducive to a day of shopping which was why we were leaving my niece behind.

Lisa greeted us at the door with a cup of coffee in her hand. "What are you two smirking about?"

"Jessica's man gave her quite the sendoff," Amy volunteered. "I might need to change my panties before we head out."

I rolled my eyes, usually on the other end of the good-natured teasing. "You guys going to be at it all day? I'm not supposed to be the center of attention."

"What was I thinking having two kids? I swear I need my head examined." Melanie looked tired, walking in from the front door and giving me a hug.

I rubbed her bulging belly, feeling the soft kicks of my niece. "It's a little late for that."

She sighed, following us into the living room where my mom

was. There had been some kind of emergency at the office and she was trying to get it sorted before we left.

"Now listen here." She planted a hand on her hip as she paced. "The contract has already been signed. We can't just go ahead and change everything now. It would take hours if not days contacting all the relevant parties."

Mom didn't look pleased, her pointed-toe shoe tapping on the floor impatiently as the person on the other end of the line answered.

"Are you kidding me? The client had no idea what they wanted, we sold them on that design, you can't tell me that the change of heart hasn't come from that two-bit architect from Baton Rouge putting their nose where it doesn't belong."

"Sounds serious," Amy whispered. "It won't fair well for them if they get LeeAnn in a mood."

She was right about that, and judging from my mother's huffing and puffing, our plans didn't sound as sure as they did last night.

"Steve, stop." She held up her hand. "I'll be in the office in twenty minutes, I suggest you use that time to decide whether you want to continue working for me or if you want to go pave roads for the Parish. Don't disappoint me." She hung up the phone in a huff.

"Bad news?" I asked, not really needing the confirmation.

She shook her head, silently seething as she gave me a hug. "I'm so sorry ladies, but y'all are going to have to go on without me. This contract has taken too much time and too much money for me to walk away from it. And if we don't finalize today there is going to be hell to pay. I'm sorry, Melanie, I promise I'll make it up to you."

If Melanie was disappointed, she didn't look it, her lips spreading into the first grin since she walked through the door. "It's okay, Momma. I understand."

Mom fussed a little more, looking at her eldest daughter with suspicion before turning to me. "Oh, before I forget, there's a BBQ dinner at your aunt and uncle's after Lana's rehearsal. I've told them that you and Dave will be there, it's time for him to meet the rest of the family."

"Mom, he is seeing everyone at the wedding tomorrow, why the hell do we have to go to dinner tonight?"

I knew that the chances of a quiet night were probably slim. My parents would probably expect us to come over for dinner again, the opportunities to grill us before we headed back to L.A. limited. I'd accepted that and figured it was a good way to psyche myself up for the main event. Because if I thought dinner with my parents had been a challenge, that was nothing on what it would be like with my *whole* family.

My mom didn't even bother looking sorry, straightening her row of pearls. "Because tomorrow is Lana's day, and everyone is going to want a proper opportunity to fuss over you. Besides, you love your cousin, I would have thought you would be dying to see her."

A proper opportunity to fuss over me? I had brought a boyfriend home; I hadn't won a Nobel Peace Prize.

"Mom, I don't want to bombard him. I know everyone and sometimes it's even too much for me. And there is no reason for everyone to fuss, we're here just like any other guests"

Lisa snorted, not buying my excuse. "Are you kidding? Gran Shelly has been on the phone telling everyone about him. I'll be surprised if the mayor doesn't offer him a key to the city. Oh, and he's coming too, along with about a hundred other people."

"Oh Lord." My hand flew up to my mouth, the thought of one hundred or more people greeting us like visiting heads of state enough to throw me into a panic.

"Jessica, you know I don't like when you take the Lord's name in vain. Anyway, it's done. And you know the mayor is one of our oldest dearest friends, it would only make sense that he be there. I'll expect you there at seven, and make sure you dress nice. Now, I better get to the office before the whole deal collapses. Have fun." She kissed us all, grabbed her keys, reveling in the carnage she'd left behind.

"This is out of control. He's going to see all those people there tonight and run a mile." I shook my head wondering whether or not to tell him the truth or spring it on him last minute. Neither was appealing, the thought of jumping on a plane and saying I had my own business emergency in L.A. extremely tempting.

"Be grateful there's not going to be any reporters. I heard Darla was already trying to sell her feel-good piece. I swear, she wouldn't know the definition of discretion if it bit her on the ass." Amy sat on the edge of the armchair.

Well, I guess that was something to be thankful for. That, and the fact that even if we did get a mention, *The Shreveport Times* didn't exactly have an earthshattering readership.

"Okay, let's get out of here before I get any other surprise invitations. We're going to take Lisa's car, right? It's going to be tight in Amy's Chevy."

Melanie looked at us, her eyes brimming with excitement. "I say we call this whole thing off and head to a bar instead."

"You're overlooking the fact you can't drink," Lisa pointed out, which was a shame because heading to a bar sounded a hell of a lot better than going to the mall. Especially now.

"So, they can put a cocktail umbrella in it and I can make believe. Besides, how often does Jessica come to town? We going to waste the opportunity shopping in Target? Or are we going to ply her with malt liquor and make her tell us all her dirty dark secrets?" She raised her eyebrows, taunting me.

I waved my hands, dismissing the idea of sharing my secrets. "I'm not kissing and telling, and I thought you *wanted* to go shopping?"

Her face fell, her eyes starting to water. "I thought I did, but my feet feel like two hams stuffed into shoes and I need to pee every five minutes. And I'm worried I'm turning into one of those women who all they ever talk about is babies and being pregnant. Oh, God." Her lip began to quiver. "I'm one of them, aren't I? I'm going to continue wearing elastic pants even after the baby is born and only ever wash my hair on Tuesday."

"Okay, we're *not* going to the mall," I declared. "And if you want to go to a bar, then that's exactly what we'll do."

"The Creole Crab on Texas opens at eleven." Amy looked at her phone. "By the time we get there we could be ordering cocktails."

"Sounds good to me." I nodded, slinging my arm around my sister, hoping to curb the waterworks.

She wiped her eyes, failing miserably as she tried to manage a smile. "And me."

"Fine, but if I'm driving, no one is allowed to throw up in my car," Lisa warned. "And no one tells LeeAnn. We're supposed to be shopping, not drinking."

"She'll never know. We'll order some things on the internet and have them delivered. It will be like an instant baby shower," I suggested, knowing we could build an impressive inventory without even stepping foot in a store.

Amy rubbed her hands together in anticipation "Oh, that sounds like fun."

"It's going to be amazing," Melanie agreed, no longer thinking about her ham feet or visiting the mall.

While it was probably a recipe for disaster, we piled into Lisa's SUV and drove to the bar. Its tacky neon OPEN sign was flashing, as was its promise of a good time.

We got ourselves situated in a booth, ordering a round of rum and Cokes—Melanie's minus rum—and a bunch of appetizers so we didn't look like a bunch of alcoholics. We laughed, eating fried food I knew I was going to regret, and continued to drink. Lisa and Melanie switched to iced tea, while Amy and I took one for the team and stayed with the rum. We were in a bar after all, it only made sense that some of us needed to continue drinking.

"So," Amy giggled. "Is he as hot in bed as he is a kisser? Because, girl." She bit her lip suggestively. "That goodbye at the door was smoking."

I pressed my mouth together pretending to zip them and then throw away the key. "A lady never tells."

"Come on, you need to tell us and let us live vicariously through your exciting life." Amy shoved me, sloshing her drink on the table.

I might not be sober, but I hadn't lost all my faculties. Instead I pegged them with a sharp look and prayed my mouth did what I told it to. "How come I'm the only one who needs to be volunteering personal information? You want the goods, you need to offer something in return."

"Dalton and I are trying for a baby," Lisa tossed out without too much cajoling.

Melanie sipped her iced tea, giving Lisa a shove. "Pfft, we already know that. Something else, but nothing gross. I'm sober and I don't want to hear about my brother in that way."

She bit her lip like she was contemplating, leaning in closer as she dropped her voice to a whisper. "Okay, Tammy and I went to Dallas three weeks ago. She had to run an errand for LeeAnn, but we decided to stay the night rather than driving there and back."

"So scandalous." I laughed, wiggling my eyebrows for effect.

Lisa rolled her eyes. "I'm getting there, don't be so impatient. Okay, so you know how good and innocent she acts."

I scoffed, trying hard to keep a straight face at my sister-in-law's claim of Tammy's virtuous behavior. "Please, she claims she's a virgin because she hasn't had penetration." I wiggled my finger for effect. "And I'm sorry, an intact hymen doesn't qualify if you've done everything else. I'm not trying to slut shame, I'm just saying don't be preaching abstinence on Sunday and doing anal on Monday."

The table erupted into laughter, Melanie choking on her tea. "Oh my God, Jessica!"

"It's true." I laughed, finishing what was left in my glass and feeling the warmth spread through my body.

"Anyway." Lisa ignored us, continuing with her story. "So while we were in Dallas, she took me to this club apparently she hangs out at sometimes. You guys, it was a *sex* club."

"Wait a minute. You cheated on my brother?" My eyes widened, wondering if I wanted to hear the rest of the story. I mean, sex club in Dallas sounded interesting. But then having to be sworn to secrecy in what could potentially ruin my brother's marriage—no bueno. I already had my own lies and secrets, any more and I might as well be running for office.

"We were just watching, not participating. People on trapezes and stuff, having sex behind glass—that kind of thing." She lowered her head, looking around at the almost empty bar. "It was the biggest turn-on. I came home and had the best sex I ever had. The next day I felt guilty so I told Dalton all about it. He was so excited I was willing to try new stuff, he wasn't even mad. We're taking a trip out there together next weekend."

"Ewww, too far." Melanie groaned, shuddering as she locked eyes on me. "I'm going to be having nightmares for weeks."

"Me too." I laughed, trying to scrub the thought of my brother having kinky sex with my sister-in-law out of my mind.

"So I've told you mine, now you tell me yours." Lisa waved

her finger at me, the blush rising up her cheeks.

I shook my head, not sure what to say. While the morning had provided me with more than enough material that I didn't have to lie, it felt too personal to share. And I knew that it had just been sex.

We weren't entangled in a deep and emotional relationship where we *made love* and then fell asleep in each other's embrace. But for some reason, those private moments we'd shared didn't feel as cheap and sordid as they probably were. Maybe I just didn't want to admit to myself that the best sex I'd ever had was with some guy who I'd probably never sleep with again.

And he wasn't my boyfriend.

And I'd had to pay him to go out with me in the first place.

Yeah, that didn't exactly make me feel warm and fuzzy inside.

"I don't know." My eyes dropped to my empty glass, suddenly wishing we were in Target scanning aisles of diapers and breast pumps instead of having that conversation.

Melanie tugged at my arm. "What do you mean, *you don't know*. Three months ago you said he was your soul mate and that you were in *love* with him. You're adorable together, and he's obviously head over heels with you. He's so caring, so attentive—you just have to look at him to see he's smitten."

Her words made me more uncomfortable than they should have. And not just because of my deceit. The only reason they believed he was smitten was because he was a very good and convincing *actor*.

I, on the other hand, wasn't.

"Yeah, you're right. Of course he's my soul mate, I love him." I forced the smile, unable to admit to anyone how empty it all felt.

Not because Dave wasn't in love with me, but because I couldn't remember a time where any man had felt that way about me. Or where *I'd* felt that way about a man. I'd always seen relationships as a means to an end, believing that I'd settle down later in life when everything else was worked out. But what if I'd already met my soul mate and dismissed him, missing the opportunity because the timing wasn't right.

What had started as a good idea suddenly felt wrong, that I could possibly end up alone because I was too selfish made my stomach churn. That was putting aside the conflicted feelings I was already having about Dave. Who knew I'd have to come all the way home just to put my life under a microscope.

"Hey, we should stop drinking or I'm not going to be able to stand tonight." I pushed away the rum and Coke the waitress had delivered and vowed to sober up. "Why don't we swing by the mall on the way home, pick up some stuff and get our hair blown out."

"Yes." Amy clapped. "I've been itching to get my nails done too."

And while Melanie didn't seem too enthused about leaving her comfy seat and dragging her ass from store to store, she agreed a pedicure might be nice. I hoped it would make her feet seem less ham-like than when she began her day because I wasn't sure I could handle any more tears.

All I had to do was shut my mouth and pretend to be blissfully happy.

Piece of cake, right?

Yeah, not so much.

CHAPTER #15

WHEN I ARRIVED back at the hotel, Dave was in the shower. I hadn't had the opportunity to ask him about his day but I assumed it went great. Probably better than great, with no doubt he'd charmed everyone. Of course he had, he was a professional. It was *literally* his job.

"How was baby shopping?" He emerged from the bathroom wearing the obligatory towel. It was too much to expect he put clothes on, using that body of his as a weapon every opportunity he got.

Don't look at him. You slept with him once, be satisfied you went there, now move on.

My eyes flipped off my subconscious, ignoring the compelling internal debate I had going on and feasting on his beautiful naked torso.

"Great." A one-word answer tested the waters before I committed to letting my mouth say more. "How was your day? Which casino did you go to?"

He sat on the bed—still wearing the towel, clothes obviously too much effort—and looked at me. "I like your hair like that." He smiled before changing the subject. "We went to the Horseshoe;

I won five hundred bucks on the tables."

"Wow, how lucky." I feigned excitement as I got up and went to the closet. Sitting on the bed with him in a towel was only marginally better than being in bed with him naked. And while I had already decided we probably shouldn't sleep together, I wasn't all that confident in my own willpower.

He followed me off the bed, not giving me the distance I had wanted. "You seem off. Everything okay?"

"Yep, all good." My fingers skirted along the dress I'd decided to wear.

"Yeah, now I know you're not telling the truth. Something happen at the mall?"

Part of me wanted to tell him, to be honest with him and admit what was going on in my head. But he didn't sign up to be a therapist and the last thing I wanted was to show him a vulnerability I wasn't even comfortable showing my family.

It wasn't his problem.

Me, and my stupidity, were not his problem.

"No, I just don't want to go to this stupid dinner. Have people stare at me like I'm in a fishbowl."

Gently, he tugged at my arm, turning me around to face him as he looked at me with genuine concern. He tilted his head to the side as he asked, "So why are we going?"

"Because my family—"

"Jess, if you'd done what your family wanted you to do, you'd have never left Louisiana. It's obvious you love them or you wouldn't have wanted to go through with this crazy charade. And even to an outsider, I can see they care about you. But you need to make yourself happy. Now, what do we need to do to make that happen?"

His words had been so incredibly sweet and had been exactly the right thing to say. And I wasn't sure if he'd read some secret boyfriend manual especially for the role or if he was genuinely perceptive. And at that moment, I didn't care. Without thinking, I threw my arms around him, allowing myself to get up close and personal with the chest I'd been trying to avoid. He laughed, accepting my weight as he returned my hug.

"What's it going to be, beautiful? A dinner you don't want to go to? Or . . ." He raised an eyebrow. "I have it on good authority there's an interesting club we should check out in Dallas."

I laughed, burying my head against his pecs. "This interesting place in Dallas wouldn't be a sex club, would it?"

"A sex club?" He pretended to look horrified. "Is that even a thing?"

I pulled away, pushing him playfully while I shook my head. "Oh hush, Dave Larsson. Don't pretend that wasn't exactly what you were talking about. I wouldn't be surprised if you've already been to one. I've heard rumors about all you Larsson boys."

"All lies, I'm a fucking saint. Can't you see my halo?" He pointed to the top of his head.

"We are not driving to Dallas." I sighed, wondering if now I had taken my hands off him if I could think of a legitimate reason to put them back. "But maybe we *could* be a little bit late."

"The traffic was terrible." He circled his hands around my hips.

"And we lost track of time," I added.

"That car trouble didn't help either. I'll be having words with the rental company the minute we get back to the airport." He pretended to look annoyed.

"Let me get dressed and then we can get out of here. I know exactly where to go. You might want to put on some pants as well. We wouldn't want to scandalize the good folk of Shreveport." My eyes dipped to the towel.

He grinned, his hands moving from my waist to his. "Oh, I'm only here to scandalize one person, and lucky for her she's the only one in the room."

And with that, he dropped the towel.

AS MUCH AS I would have loved to allow myself to be scandalized, we had to get out of the hotel and get MIA before anyone wised up. I wouldn't put it past my well-meaning family to drop in unannounced and "remind us" about our dinner plans. So while I enjoyed the view—the first time seeing him naked in proper light—I stored that away in my mental filing cabinet and got dressed. I was hoping it wouldn't be the last time—his gorgeous body defying all definition of perfection—but if it was, I was fairly confident I'd still be able to describe it in detail for a police sketch.

The fancy dress I had planned to wear stayed in the closet. Instead I pulled on a pair of denim cut offs, a tank top and pair of strappy sandals. Dave dressed down too, slipping into a pair of worn jeans and a T-shirt. Both of us sneaking down to the lobby like we were teenagers avoiding curfew.

"Aren't you heading to the BBQ?" Darla stopped us before we'd made it to the door, eyeing my choice of outfit like I was wearing a pair of stripper heels and a thong. I'd hoped she was done for the day, but it seemed there would be no such luck.

"Ahhh, yes," Dave answered, putting his arm around my waist. "We just have some stuff we wanted to do first. BBQ isn't until seven and we wanted to take advantage of our time while we're here."

A quick glance of the wall clock said it was five, which didn't give us much leeway. And judging by the skeptical look on her face, I'd say she didn't believe us. "Like what?" she had the nerve to ask.

"Like the Elvis Statue," I offered, mentioning the bronze likeness of the King sitting in front of the Municipal Auditorium. "And no visit to Shreveport would be complete without seeing the air force base." I turned to Dave, biting my lip as I filled him in. "Did you know the President landed at Barksdale on his way to Washington D.C after 9/11?"

"Wow, I did not know that." Dave nodded, looking fascinated. "We can't be this close and *not* see it."

Darla narrowed her eyes, not buying it for a second. "The two of you are just going to waltz onto a military installation?"

It was astounding to me that someone who barely classed as a relative was giving me the third degree. And why the hell was she so interested in what we were doing anyway? I didn't owe her or anyone else a freaking explanation

"We'll go to the gate, show our ID and see if we can't check out the main buildings. It's not like we're going anywhere restricted," I answered coolly before making a show of checking out the clock again. "We better get going, we wouldn't want to be late."

"Wait." She grabbed my arm stopping me from leaving. "You're still coming tonight, right?"

"Why do you ask?" My limit for being polite expired as I put my hands on my hips. She had always been nosey, but this level of interest was new even for her.

She fidgeted, shifting her weight between her feet, looking uncomfortable. "Well, now you know I'm not one to gossip." Her preamble was so ridiculous I almost laughed out loud. "But one of my best friends in the whole wide world is an extra on that movie they're shooting out near Cross Lake. And I happened to mention that you were dating Eric Larsson's brother, and well, she's a big fan."

"Of me?" Dave asked, looking genuinely surprised.

Darla's smile tightened as she looked at his chest. "Well, you know that dog food commercial got a lot of airtime."

I cleared my throat in case she forgot I was standing right beside him. "Anyway, I obviously can't bring her here because it's against hotel policy to harass the guests, but I figured . . . well just about everyone is going to be at the BBQ." She smiled nervously as she shrugged.

"We will just have to wait and see how the night pans out." I wrapped my arm around Dave protectively.

Dave took the hint and pulled me closer. "We should probably get out of here, sweetheart. That Elvis statue isn't going to see itself."

I stifled the laugh, trying to be serious as we waved goodbye and walked out the door. The effort proved too much, barely making it to the car before I erupted into giggles. "That Elvis statue isn't going to see itself?" I sucked in a breath. "Oh my God, how could you say that and keep a straight face?"

Dave shook his head, fighting his own grin. "Hello? Did you not see the commercial that apparently everyone in this goddamn city has seen? You think it's easy to stand around with no shirt on and not look as ridiculous as you feel? That's real talent there. Also, this place is doing wonders for my ego."

"Give me the keys, wiseass. Let's get out of here before the paparazzi show up." I held my hand out and waited for the keys.

He didn't argue, tossing the key fob to me as he walked over to the passenger side door. "No country," he said, giving me the sexiest smile as he slid into his seat.

"No country," I agreed, getting into the car. Hell, with a smile like that he could have put on the Christian rock channel and I wouldn't have cared.

We pulled out of the parking garage and got on the main road, driving a little faster than the speed limit. With the top down and the wind blowing in our hair it felt good as we drove, no one watching us and not needing to worry about what I said or did. We didn't even talk, not feeling the pressure to fill the silence.

It wasn't until we stopped that Dave spoke, looking at the building with interest. "A trampoline park?"

"You scared to get a little sweaty?" I cut the engine and grabbed my purse. "I figured I'd put you through your paces and make you jump through hoops . . . literally."

He laughed, getting out of the car and walking to the driver's side. "I'm not scared of anything. Let's see what you've got."

The excitement traveled up my spine as we made our way to the front desk. We purchased the special socks, paid our admission and then moved into the jumping area like a pair of teenagers on a date.

He dragged me on the trampoline, bouncing wildly as he held my hand. I couldn't stop laughing, each of my jumps slightly out of time. He didn't seem to mind, grinning at me while we moved across the black mats, jumping like lunatics.

With the skill of an Olympic gymnast he tucked into a perfect frontward roll, diving into the sponge pit. I followed him in with a less graceful dive of my own, sinking into the green and blue squares.

He grabbed me, pulling me onto him as I fought against the spongy quicksand, hugging me tightly around the waist as he helped me out. "Sweaty enough for you?" he whispered in my ear, his hot breath tickling my skin.

"Maybe." I breathed against him. "You want to go get something to eat? I'm worried if you get any hotter you're going to need to take off your shirt and our cover will be blown." I looked around suspiciously.

He rolled his eyes, putting his hands on my waist as he guided me off the trampolines. "We wouldn't want that now, would we? And I have definitely worked up an appetite."

We put our shoes on and got back into the car only this time there was no silence, both of us laughing and chatting until we pulled up to a restaurant that looked more like a rundown old shack. The tables were covered in cheap, brightly colored plastic tablecloths, with candles stuffed into empty beer bottles as centerpieces.

Most out-of-towners wouldn't have even stopped at Jax Corner, let alone eaten at it. But there was nowhere in town better to get a Po' Boy, and I'd missed them since I'd left.

"Oh my goodness, Jessica Dawson." Miss Holly wiped her hands on her apron before leaning down to give me a hug. "I'd have thought you'd be at your cousin's BBQ dinner. I hear even the mayor got invited."

"We decided to skip it." I smiled at Dave. "Dave, this is Miss Holly, she runs the place with her husband, Mr. Jackson. Miss Holly, I'd like you to meet my friend, Dave."

Miss Holly was in her fifties but hadn't missed a day of work in almost a decade. It was her secret family recipes that made the place a success, and even though the restaurant had been profitable for years, they hadn't changed a thing since the day it opened. They were firm believers of *if it ain't broke, don't fix it*, the worn inside décor a testimony to their theory.

"Well, it's a pleasure to meet you." She held out her hand but didn't give him any undue attention. "I haven't seen you here before, are you new in town?"

I smiled at him, looking at how comfortable he'd fit into my world. There weren't many guys I knew who could have integrated so seamlessly, and who wouldn't have complained at least once. "No, Dave lives in L.A, it's his first visit here."

"Oh, well welcome. Big change from L.A. I bet." Miss Holly's smile widened, glancing at our interlocked fingers across the table. I hadn't even noticed he'd been holding my hand. "So y'all ready to order?"

I nodded, ordering our Po' Boys and beer as zydeco music played through the speakers. My hand stayed right where it was, comfortable with the contact and more importantly, liking it.

"It's like a sandwich." Dave looked at his basket of food, inspecting it with a smile after Miss Holly brought our order.

I shook my head, lowering my head and allowed the amazing smell to waft up my nose. "It's like a sandwich but a million times better."

He took a bite, his eyes rolling back as he savored the mouthful. "Oh my God, this is amazing."

"Yep," I agreed taking a bite of my own. "I'm pretty sure Miss Holly adds crack to her secret spice mix. I ate so many of these my first year of college, I gained like twenty pounds."

"Only twenty pounds? I'd have gained at least fifty, these are so good." He took another bite. "Wonder if there is some way we can get these delivered back home? I'd seriously pay whatever they asked."

We finished our dinner and ordered another beer, Miss Holly bringing out some peach cobbler with ice cream before we could decline her offer of dessert.

It was almost nine by the time we walked back out to the car, the night air crackling between us. "Tonight was fun." He pulled me closer and brushed his lips against mine. "Thanks for taking me out."

My eyes fixed on his, my body heating with him being so close. "It was my pleasure. I just didn't have it in me to pretend tonight."

"So don't pretend."

He kissed me, not softly like he had that morning before I'd left for the day, but deeper, more intense. His hands moved over me, bringing me closer as one curled around my neck and locked me in place. He didn't have to bother; I wasn't going anywhere.

It was hot, yet unhurried, his lips on a quest to discover every inch of mine as he pressed me against the driver's side door. My body melded to his, loving the feel of him as we devoured each other.

"No one was watching." The words came out in a breathless whisper. "You didn't have to kiss me."

He shook his head, nibbling my lips. "No one was watching us this morning in bed either."

Earlier I had chosen ignorance, not wanting to question or even deal with what us having sex had meant. We were in a strange situation, both of us red-blooded adults who had found ourselves naked in bed together. It wasn't shocking that we'd slept together. In fact, I'd have been more surprised if we hadn't. He was gorgeous and I wasn't unattractive, so of course if you put gasoline next to a fire it was going to burn.

I wasn't even sorry, the release it had given me far out weighing the confusion that came after.

But the kiss had been different.

We weren't naked, alone in the dark and fighting against the primal urges of our human sexual nature. The kiss had been a choice.

One where he *chose* to kiss me.

And I'd *chosen* to kiss him back.

God.

What the hell did that mean?

"Dave . . ." I couldn't finish the sentence, not even sure I knew what was going on in my head let alone able to say it out loud.

He kissed me again, slower as he leaned against me. He was hard, pressing the ridge of his cock along my body and leaving no confusion as to what he was feeling. "Don't think about it, Jess," he breathed against my mouth. "Just be here now, and don't think."

I didn't argue, letting myself get lost with him as my body responded, arching against him with an urgency I had no hope of controlling. My fingernails clawed at him, wanting him closer as I fused my lips to his, his tongue stroking mine.

"You're so fucking beautiful," he groaned, moving his mouth to my neck as his hands grabbed my ass. His control seemed as desperately unhinged as mine was, our bodies dry humping each other against the side of the car.

My skin was on fire, the ache between my legs almost unbearable as I swallowed a groan. I wanted him, wanted him to invade every single part of me, and screw the consequences.

"Get a room," someone shouted, followed by a laugh that pulled us back to the present.

He lifted his body, the sweet friction of his weight stolen from me as my eyes stared at his beautiful mouth stained with my lipstick. "Sound advice," I panted.

"Is that where you want to go? Back to our room?" he asked, bringing his lips as close as they could get without touching me.

Yes!

At least that was what I wanted to say, beg him to take me back to our room and make love to me fifty different ways. I wanted it to be more than just one time, to prove it hadn't been a fluke, but as I looked at him I shook my head.

"We should go make an appearance at this BBQ. As much as I would rather go back to the hotel, we're only here until Sunday afternoon and then who knows when I'll be back."

I'd told myself it was because I was really in a good mood so putting up with the third degree didn't seem so bad. If we'd played our cards right, by the time we got to my uncle and aunt's house everyone would be drinking and not even notice us. But part of me knew it was a cop out.

I was confused about my feelings, and was worried about our new intimacy. I had no idea if he felt the same way, or if I was just another girl he occasionally had sex with. And I had absolutely no clue as to what we were actually doing.

It was good to be cautious, to have a good time but not get in too deep.

At least not yet.

He chuckled, wrapping his arms around me as he kissed me

one last time. "BBQ it is then. But I'm driving."

There wasn't an argument, dropping the keys into his hands as I kissed him back. "She's all yours."

He winked popping open the door. "Just the way I like it."

It was the way *I* liked it too.

"JESSICA!" MY COUSIN Lana screamed, throwing herself at me the minute we'd walked in the door. "I was beginning to think you weren't coming, we tried calling you but you didn't pick up."

I frowned, pretending to be surprised that the phone I'd put on silent hadn't delivered any of her calls. "I must be having issues with the service. You think if they can put a rover on Mars we should at least be able to get decent cell reception."

"Right? It's just the worst." She hugged me again before turning to Dave. "And *you*, we have heard so much about you."

The glassy eyes were the first clue Lana had been drinking, as was her relaxed posture and overenthusiastic smile. She wasn't drunk by any means, but she was well and truly relaxed.

He grinned, ignoring how creepy it sounded as he pulled me closer. "I've heard a lot about you too. Where's the lucky guy?"

"Getting last minute warnings to treat me right by every member of our family, he'll be glad you're here to take some of the heat." She blushed, giggling as she pulled us into the house. There were people in every room, the house looking like it had been invaded by an army of human ants.

"Wow, there are a lot of people here." Waving to the many

hellos we got, not stopping as we pushed through the crowd to the backyard.

Lana shouted over her shoulder, her voice having difficulty carrying over the noise. "Yeah, Mom got a little carried away with the guest list. Tomorrow is insane, I'm not even sure I'm going to know half the people at my own wedding."

While my dad's family hadn't come from money, my mom's family was a different story. And while each of my aunts—my mother was one of four girls—had married and continued to add to their wealth, they had been given an incredibly generous helping hand by my grandparents.

"Do you know all the people here?" I looked around, a few faces looking familiar. "It's like the whole neighborhood is inside your house.

My mom was sipping wine with her sisters, MaryAnn—Lana's mom, KerriAnn, and JoAnn. There was a theme in case anyone missed it.

"There she is!" Aunt MaryAnn quickly put down her wine and rushed over to us. "Look at you. You just keep getting more stunning every time I see you."

I cringed, feeling far from stunning. My hair was a mess from bouncing, my make up half worn off from sweat, and my lipstick was history from the making out we'd done after dinner.

"Thanks, Aunt MaryAnn, I'm sorry we're late. We got tied up and lost track of time."

She waved her hand dismissively. "Psh, now don't worry about that, I'm just glad you came. Terry," she hollered for my uncle, "get Jessica and her man a drink."

Uncle Terry was at the opposite end of the yard, holding court with a bunch of men who looked like they were probably important. He owned a group of car dealerships so he loved being in the middle of the crowd. Even in the hottest part of summer he wore his uniform of Wranglers, checked shirts and cowboy boots, and tonight was no exception. He tipped his head to his wife, excusing himself before grabbing drinks out of the cooler and making his way over to us.

"Jessie." He nodded, the deep lines of his face cracking as he smiled. "It's so good to have you home."

He was the only person who was able to get away with calling me Jessie. Anyone else would have got the stink eye followed by a string of expletives, but with him I didn't mind it so much. And he was too sweet to be mad at.

"Thanks, Uncle Terry, this is my boyfriend Dave." I introduced them as we accepted our beers. "He's an actor."

My uncle looked skeptical, sizing him up as he took a step back. "You're from California?"

"Yes, sir." Dave nodded, extending his hand.

Uncle Terry returned the handshake, wrapping his fingers around tight. "Well, you're a pleasant surprise."

Oh God.

What the hell did that mean?

Ignorance seemed to be the best course of action so I pretended I hadn't heard. I widened my grin, hoping I didn't look crazy as I stared at the table of desserts. "Wow, look at all that pie, there must be at least ten different types."

Dave hadn't gotten the memo, ignoring my change of conversation as he volleyed back. "You were expecting something else?"

"Yeah, a skinny guy with blond hair who says *dude* a lot." Uncle Terry sunk his hands into his jeans. "You don't surf do you, son?"

"Uncle Terry, I keep telling you California isn't like that." I laughed nervously.

Just like everyone in the South wasn't screwing their cousin in the back of their pickup truck while chewing tobacco, not everyone in California was a scrawny surfer dude with blond hair.

"Yeah, well you can never be too sure." He hitched up his pants, looking pleased. "Oh, and I'm glad you aren't one of those metrosexual types either. I don't trust a man when he takes more time in the bathroom than a woman."

Wow, okay then.

Dave laughed, taking it all in stride. "I think we're good on that front too."

Hoping to be done with awkward, I took the opportunity to introduce Dave to my other aunts, both of them looking impressed.

"You sure are handsome." Aunt JoAnn squeezed his arm. "You're like one of those big lumberjacks." She laughed.

Aunt KerriAnn nodded. "Very handsome."

"We're going to go say hello to everyone." I looped my arm around Dave's arm wondering how much weirder it might get. "We'll catch up with you later."

"Not so fast, missy." My mom tapped her foot, stopping me with just a look. It was something she'd perfected when we were kids and even as a grown up, I had a hard time not succumbing to its power.

"I know I told you dinner was at seven and for you to dress nice." She glanced down at my denim cut offs. "You could have at least worn a complete pair of pants."

"There's nothing wrong with my pants." I rolled my eyes. "It's hot and we're at a BBQ. And we're late because I wanted to show Dave around. I was out all day with the girls and didn't get a chance. Besides, it doesn't look like we've missed anything important."

She might not have liked my sass but she wasn't surprised by it either. I'd always been the most headstrong of her children, pushing her limits whenever I could.

"Well." She straightened her pearls. "Make sure you say hello to everyone. Gran Shelly has had a few too many fruit punches so just be mindful anything you say tonight might not be remembered tomorrow."

"Thanks, Mom." I gave her a smile, waving her goodbye as I dragged Dave away. At least this time I would *know* Gran Shelly might not remember stuff, a tip-off that could have saved me the last time.

As directed, I made sure I said hello to everyone even if half the time I didn't know who they were. Most everyone was polite, treating Dave like he was the shiny new toy. There were appreciative smiles and subtle nods, and about five million questions. Where we'd met, how long we'd been dating, did he have a brother who was single—it went on and on. There were more than a few who recognized him either from the commercial or his family connection, but for the most part they were respectful.

Satisfied we'd been seen enough, we pulled up a chair next to Travis and Amy. "If I have to shake one more hand I'm going to end up with a wrist injury." I massaged my muscles.

"Probably would have been easier if you'd been here earlier and didn't have to condense all your greetings into one hit." Travis hid the smirk behind his beer. "And they always said you were the smart one."

I laughed, flipping him off discreetly. "I am smart, which is why instead of being here eating BBQ, we went to Jax Corner and had Po' Boys."

Travis sat up straighter, suddenly more alert. "You went there and didn't bring me anything? I'd kill for some of Miss Holly's cobbler right now."

"It was excellent. The best I've ever had." Dave leaned in, grinning and baiting my brother.

Travis pegged him with a stare. "Listen here, Hollywood. I didn't say anything about you dating my sister but you best believe you start making moves on my cobbler and we're going to have words."

Dave put his arm around my shoulders pulling me closer, barely containing his laughter. "Anytime you get the itch, Travis, you let me know. But don't expect either of those things to stop anytime soon."

My heart stopped, his words making me shiver as my fingers linked with his. Even if it was all a lie, I was going to let myself believe it, wanting to live in the fantasy at least for now. Because I'd never had it before, and truthfully, wasn't sure I'd have it again.

"Aww," Amy sighed. "You guys are just too adorable for words and even sweeter than Miss Holly's cobbler."

Travis whipped around facing his girlfriend. "Ain't nothing sweeter than Miss Holly's cobbler. To even pretend is sacrilegious."

I was about to argue just to see how upset we could make Travis when I felt a tap on my shoulder, forcing me to turn around.

"Hi." Darla waved, a petite brunette standing beside her. "We missed out on saying hello before, so I figured I'd come on over now." She shot Dave a smile. "I hope you enjoyed Elvis."

"Elvis?" Travis asked, confused. "You been sniffing moonshine again, Darla?"

Her smile dropped, thinning her lips into a tight line. "The statue downtown, you idiot."

Darla wasn't a big fan of my brother. She'd once had a crush on him—yes, dating cousins, how fucking cliché—but he'd told her there'd be a cold day in Hell before he'd go out with her. It didn't matter how far removed, kin was still kin, and sleeping with someone you had to share holidays with wasn't a good plan. Since then, they have taken great pleasure in flinging verbal insults at each other, their current conversation no exception.

He shook his head and laughed. "Now, now, no need to be name calling. If I didn't know how much you liked me, I might take it personal."

"Anyway," she did her best to ignore him. "As I mentioned back at the hotel, my friend Suzie wanted to meet Dave." She gestured to the woman beside her. "She's a big fan."

"Darla." Suzie groaned, her cheeks flushing pink. "Don't embarrass me."

Darla patted Suzie's arm like a proud parent showing off her debutant. "Oh please, we're all friends here. There's nothing to be embarrassed about. Why, I bet Dave has women fawning over him all the time. Isn't that right?" She looked to him for confirmation.

"I wouldn't say that, but thanks for the compliment." He stood, extending his hand. "And always happy to meet new people."

Suzie almost combusted, her face flaming as she tried to compose herself. I had serious doubts the woman could act her way out of a paper bag let alone be in a movie, but I was probably just being bitchy.

"Hi, Suzie." I sidled up to Dave, staking my claim like the jealous girlfriend I had no right to be. "So, Darla tells us you're working on a movie? How exciting for you."

Suzie's eyes hit the floor, wincing as they lifted back to mine. "I'm just a walk on extra, I don't have any lines. But I'm taking classes, and my teacher thinks I have natural talent."

It was funny that in my line of work I'd heard those exact words a lot. *I'm taking classes, I'm a natural talent*—blah, blah, blah. None of it counted for shit. But I wasn't going to stomp on her dreams and be completely evil. That pleasure would belong to the hundreds if not thousands of agents and directors she would meet. Assuming her dream of being something other than window dressing was legit. I still wasn't sure to be honest. I'd once said I wanted to climb Mount Everest, but I'd gotten altitude sickness just from being in Denver, so it probably wasn't a good idea.

"What's the movie?" Dave asked, folding his arms around me

like it was the most natural thing in the world.

"*Blue Oasis*, Bill Casey is playing the lead." Suzie almost levitated, clearly so excited about being asked a question she had to contain a full body shimmer. Or she had a nervous twitch, her hands jerking at her side.

Must be all that natural talent, eye roll.

Dave's smile widened, this time showing real interest. "I know Bill. He made a movie with my brother a few years ago. When you see him make sure you tell him I said hello."

Let me be clear, Dave was being kind. Bill Casey was a solid A-lister and lived in a massive house in Bel Air. And while we didn't represent him, I'd met him at least a dozen times and had multiple conversations with him. Dave's brother, Eric, had not only starred with the man, but considered him a friend. So if Dave were so compelled to offer his greetings and salutations, he wouldn't need Suzie-I'm-a-walk-on-extra to deliver them.

But it seemed that fact was overlooked by Suzie. Her eyes illuminated, sitting up at attention like a well-trained retriever looking for a treat.

"I would be honored to," she crooned, acting like the responsibility of saying hello to Bill had given her life meaning. "Or you could come by the set and tell him yourself if you wanted to. There's security, but you could walk on with me. And they probably have exceptions to the rules for people who are already movie stars."

My head turned so quick it made the chick from the exorcist look like she'd been slacking.

"Thanks, but we're not in town for long. We're leaving Sunday afternoon and tomorrow we're tied up with the wedding." I smoothed down the front of Dave's shirt, the contact both deliberate and territorial. I liked it better when Suzie Q was all gosh-dah-gum, maybe she was a better actress than I gave her credit for.

Dave kissed the top of my head, and—hopefully

acting—sounded genuinely disappointed. "Thanks Suzie, I would have loved to but Jess is right, we're flying out Sunday afternoon."

"What about Sunday morning then?" She perked up, ignoring the slamming door and forcing open a window. "We start shooting at five a.m. because the director has a thing about catching the sun coming up. You could come see Bill and be back in time for breakfast."

Hope shone in her eyes, batting her mascaraed lashes as she stuck out her boobs. She wasn't ugly either, her lithe body probably appealing if you were into thin girls with perky breasts.

"Early shoot, huh?" He tilted his head like he was considering it.

The She-Devil—I mean, Suzie—bit her lip seductively. "It would only be for a little while, and I could introduce you to the whole crew. Kate West is there too, didn't you guys do a Calvin Klein campaign a year ago?"

"Yeah, we did." Dave folded his arms across his chest. "I had no idea she'd gone into acting."

"Well, it seems like the perfect opportunity." She smiled like it was a done deal. "I'm positive they'd love to see you, and I promise you'll have a good time."

You know what, Suzie, no. You do not invite a man you don't know to meet you for a rendezvous at five in the morning. It's actually the opposite of what you should do. So take your offer and shove it up your—

"Sure, why not," Dave agreed, the words making me tense beside him.

Why not?

I had a million reasons, how much time did he have?

My own acting skills were put to the test, laughing like I wasn't about to claw Suzie's eyes out. "Wow, five o'clock is so early. I'm not sure I could be convinced to leave my nice cozy bed."

It was a point I hoped he'd come to on his own, especially not knowing if once we were in that bed there'd be a repeat of last night. Not that I wanted him leaving me either way, I didn't even care how irrational it sounded.

"Oh, that's so great." She completely ignored me, beaming at his acceptance. "I can give you my number if you like."

He kept his hands on me the whole time, almost as if to reassure me that he knew I was there. "That's okay, why don't you just tell me where to meet you."

"Sure, I can do that." Her bubble deflated slightly, possibly disappointed she wasn't acquiring his number. "We're shooting at Cross Lake; they still have all the trailers set up so you can't miss it."

"I'll see you then." He tipped his chin goodbye before kissing my forehead.

She took the hint, backing away slowly like she was saying farewell to a king and couldn't turn her back. At least Darla left with her, both of them scampering off while the unsettled feeling inside of me remained.

"Well, that was fun," Travis announced, barely bothering to lower his voice. "Who even invited her? She's from Dad's family, not Mom's."

I looked at my brother and shook my head. "Lana and Darla were in the same year at high school. I'm assuming even the doctor who delivered her is going to be there tomorrow."

"Sounds like it's going to be quite the event. You want something else to drink?" Dave pointed to the empty glass sitting in front of me. "A beer, or another wine?"

"Maybe just a soda." I tried to smile, the restlessness churning in my gut. I wasn't feeling so festive now, but didn't want to dull the feeling with alcohol. I needed to keep myself sharp in order to process the bucket load of emotions that had been tossed in my lap.

Dave leaned across giving me a soft kiss on the lips. "Of course, anyone else?"

"Hey, if you're making the trip I'll take another beer." Travis held up his almost empty bottle.

"No problem." Dave nodded. "I'll be back soon."

Him leaving just stoked the feeling, my skin prickling in warning as I watched him walk away. I had no idea if it was all in my head or he'd sensed it too.

"That girl wants in his pants." Amy smiled, nodding to the direction they both disappeared.

Travis laughed, grabbing Amy and planting a big kiss on her lips. "I told you, baby, she can want all she wants. I wasn't interested in her then, and I'm sure as shit not interested in her now."

"Not *you*." Amy shoved him, rolling her eyes. "Dave, Suzie wants *Dave*."

A shallow victory bubbled inside me knowing I hadn't been imagining it and someone else had picked up on the vibe. I'd assumed my feelings of jealousy were irrational, brought on by a hormone imbalance or something. But no, the need for me to mark my territory had been for reasons that weren't in my own head.

Travis rubbed his jaw, his brow creased in confusion. "How do you figure? Just because she wants him to say hello to her friend?"

"God you can be dumb, Travis." Amy sighed. "If you think that invitation had anything to do with Dave saying hello to her friend, then there's no hope left for you."

He looked at Amy, then to me, finally the penny dropping. "Oooooh, I get it now. She's hoping that she gets him out there alone and he's going to give her an autograph of a different kind."

"Well, regardless of what she wants." I tried to not sound as insecure as I felt. "She's not going to get that, Dave wouldn't cheat on me."

That was complete bullshit of course, because in order for him to cheat, we'd have to be in a relationship—which we weren't. There was nothing stopping him from hooking up with Suzie, Kate—model come actress—or anyone else he wanted, and not feeling guilty about it. After all, in two days our little charade would be over and he'd be free to publically date five women at a time if that's what he chose to do. So I had no idea if her invitation was something he'd like to RSVP to, or if he was just trying to be friendly. Most of all I hated the uncertainty of it all, the thought of him even kissing her making me want to puke.

Travis held up his hand, his voice turning serious. "Look, Jess, I'm not saying you're wrong, but women here are different to how they are in L.A. They don't just flick their hair over their shoulder and hope you notice. Darla locked us in a closet when we were teenagers and tried to stick her tongue down my throat."

"Travis." I screwed up my face in disgust. "I did not need to know that."

He waved his hand, continuing with his story. "I'm just telling you so you see how it is. Now, if Suzie has feelings that are similar, I wouldn't put it past her to try something. I mean, it's Cross Lake, people go out there and make out all the time."

"I hate to admit it, but Travis is right," Amy agreed, wrapping her arm around my brother. "Especially if she thinks this is her one time to try something. Might as well go for broke, right?"

"I'm sure it will be fine," I reassured them, not willing to admit that I had concerns.

An uncomfortable silence stretched between us. The noise and the laughter from the party irked me while I sat with the thought hanging in the air.

"Maybe go with him," Travis offered, trying to be helpful. "She probably won't do anything if you're there."

Amy nodded. "Yes, go with him."

I shook my head, even though the thought of him going there alone made my skin crawl. "And what will that prove if I go? That he can only be faithful when I'm around? He won't do anything, Dave isn't like that."

My voice had been harsher than I'd intended it to be, saying words I knew I had no right to say.

Amy reached out, her hand sympathetically placed on my knee. "You're right. He's not like that, and he's totally devoted to you. Anyone with a pair of eyes can see how much he adores you, right Trav?"

Travis shrugged, using his mouth to finish the last of his beer rather than add anything to the commentary. Probably for the best because I imagined he wasn't convinced Amy *was* right.

"What did I miss?" Dave returned, his hands gripping a couple of sodas and a beer for my brother. "You guys look like you were discussing something serious."

"We were just debating whether or not Lana is going to stick with traditional vows tomorrow or if she wrote her own. She has been Pinteresting this wedding for at least twelve months," I lied, not willing to tell him we were debating his future fidelity.

A look of understanding passed between Amy and I as she added, "I think she is going to go completely traditional. Love, honor and obey. She's a crier, I bet she'll barely be able to choke out *I do*, let alone add anything else."

Dave sat next to me, enjoying his soda as we continued the stupid conversation. His hand rested on my back, listening as we changed the subject to something else, and watched the crowd thin out.

"We should probably go." Amy yawned, checking the time. "I have a hair and makeup appointment early in the morning and I promised to help Melanie get Anna ready."

I stood up, giving her a hug. "Drive carefully and call me if Melanie needs an extra pair of hands."

"Bye, sis." Travis grabbed me in a one-arm tackle. "Let me know if you need *anything*." His eyes conveying exactly what he meant.

The undertone was subtle considering the source, and I was thankful my brother was acting so sweet. I didn't doubt that if I'd ask him to, he would wake up early Sunday, tail Dave, and then report back any suspicious activity. But I wouldn't do that, even if the offer was tempting.

Amy and Travis said goodbye to Dave and then went to go find my parents. It was probably something we should do too, the fatigue from the day making me feel tired.

"You want to go?" he asked, reading my mind.

I wrapped my arms around him and kissed him gently on the mouth. "Yeah, I want to go."

He grinned, kissing me back. "Good, I think we both have unfinished business back at the hotel."

"Sounds good to me." I looped my arm around his. "Let's say our goodbyes, you just have to keep looking devoted for a little while longer."

He frowned but didn't say anything, dutifully guiding me through the guests that were left as we hugged, kissed and smiled our way out the door. He didn't ask, popping open the passenger's side and waiting for me to get in.

"Are you sure you are okay to drive?" I hesitated at the door. He'd only had three beers over the course of a few hours, there was no way he was anywhere close to being over the limit. I was just looking for a distraction, and being the one behind the wheel seemed like a good one.

He grinned, kissing me again even though there was no one to see. "I'm more than okay, stop trying to usurp the car and get in."

Closing my eyes, I pressed my lips against his, loving the way they felt. He was a great kisser and I could easily spend the night lip locked with him. Which is what I'd decided in that moment to do.

"Let's get back to the hotel." I gripped his shirt tighter. "I hope you aren't sleepy, I have plans that involve you being awake."

He leaned closer, the ridge of his hard-on pressing against me. "Sleep is for the weak and I'm not even close to being done for the night."

I wasn't sure if I was ever going to be done.

Shit.

That was so *not* how I'd planned it.

CHAPTER #17

WE'D BARELY GOTTEN into the room when he pressed me up against the wall and kissed me. I dropped my purse as he tossed the keys, our hands finding better purposes as they explored each other.

"I've been thinking about this since the trampoline park." He pulled off his shirt before helping me out of mine. "I want you naked and underneath me. I'm so glad you revised your decision on us not having sex again."

It was probably for the wrong reasons, wanting the connection with him to validate feelings he had no idea about was probably not helping my cause. But I didn't care, willing to take him anyway I could get him, while ignoring he probably didn't see me the same way.

I laughed, arching against him as his fingers flicked off my bra, his hands circling my breasts as his lips moved across my neck.

"These are fucking perfect." His mouth moved to my nipple, sucking it into a firm peak. "I was barely able to see them in the dark this morning, and I wasn't about to make the same mistake tonight."

My fingernails dug into his back, closing my eyes as I absorbed the sensation. His tongue lavished me, sucking and kissing before moving to the other breast, his hands constantly on me.

"That feels so good," I moaned, rubbing myself against him. "Take off my shorts. Please."

He chuckled, keeping his mouth busy while he reached down and freed me from my cut offs, the denim dropped to the floor as I kicked off my sandals.

His hand cupped my pussy, pressing his palm against the cotton of my underwear, the thin barrier not enough to disguise how wet I was getting. "You're driving me insane, Jessica. I want to taste you, lick you until you come on my mouth and you forget your own name."

That sounded like a perfect idea, my hands getting busy on his jeans as I encouraged him to strip.

Our tongues tangoed, kissing and licking each other as he peeled off layers and dumped them on the floor. We walked blindly back through our suite, not breaking the contact. Dave stopped briefly at the coffee table, collecting the box of condoms he'd bought earlier before picking me up off the floor and carrying me into the bedroom. "Glad I wasn't a gentleman this morning and stocked up on protection. I'm going to attempt to use every last one of them tonight."

He tossed me onto the mattress, flicking on a lamp and then slowly climbed on himself. A satisfied smile spread across his lips as he admired his handiwork from above, my body naked and strewn across the bed like a panting rag doll.

His body was perfection, every inch of it toned and hard in all the right places. I hadn't had a chance to appreciate it properly before, but—watching his muscles flex—it was difficult not to stare. My eyes traveled across his body with greed, stopping when they reached his impressive cock. I had seen it and felt it but it was no less spectacular the second time around. My legs squeezed together in anticipation, desperate for the friction that would get me off. If

I wasn't so distracted by how beautiful he was, I'd have reached down there and made myself come.

"Let me kiss you." He parted my knees, lowering himself between my thighs. "I want to see you come for me while I fuck you with my tongue."

His hot words were nothing compared to the way he was looking at me, my body rising off the bed as he dropped his mouth to my heat and locked his eyes with mine.

"Yes." My fingers fisted his hair as his tongue flattened against me, slowly lapping to the top of my cleft, circling my clit and then down again.

I forced my eyes to stay open, watching his slow steady movements against my skin, his gaze not breaking as he thrust his tongue inside of me, making me cry out.

Encouraged by my moan, he did it again, moving his thumb to circle my clit while he continued to penetrate me. I bucked against him, his other hand steadying my hips, but he didn't stop, over and over again slowly making me insane.

Every part of me tightened, my body at his complete will as I pushed out ragged breaths. I moaned, restlessly rocking my hips against his mouth, torn between wanting to live in the suspended pleasure forever and desperate for the release.

"Dave." My hands went either side of me, gripping the sheets as my body arched, the explosion shooting up through my spine and fracturing me into a million pieces. The wave washed over me again and again as I felt myself pulse, my limbs reduced to jelly as the tremors continued.

He slowly lifted his head, lapping me leisurely as he smiled with satisfaction. "You taste so sweet." He kissed my thigh, moving his lips to my belly and then flattening his body against mine. "And watching you come made me so hard my balls ache."

He pressed his erection against me, sliding his length up and down my slick center, watching me as he circled his hips.

"I want to taste you too," I panted, letting go of the sheets and planting my hands on his ass.

He gave me a wicked grin, continuing his slow and deliberate rock. "Really? And what part of me do you want to taste?"

"Your cock," I said without embarrassment, the heat in my body rising again.

My fingers locked around his hips holding him still as I pressed against him. "I want to suck your cock."

Heat flared in his eyes, blowing out a breath as he lifted off me and rolled to his side, giving me full access to his body.

"This." I took his length in my hand and gave it a firm, tight stroke. "Is mine."

Feelings of possession surged through my body without a hint of apology. I didn't care what happened tomorrow, or next week, or even in the next hour. At that moment he belonged to me and sharing him wasn't up for negotiation.

"All yours." He kicked out his legs, his arms folding behind his neck as he propped himself up to watch.

With our gazes locked, I lowered my mouth, letting the tip of my tongue circle the head of his cock slowly.

He breathed deeper, watching me intensely as I teased him with my mouth. Alternating between kisses and nibbles against his length—tasting myself on him—as my tight grip held him in place.

"Suck me," he groaned, his muscles locked tight as I deprived him of what he wanted. "Suck me, Jessica." The tone in his voice raw with need.

My mouth hovered, cupping the crown before drawing him in deep, his eyes rolling back as I sucked in urgent pulls.

"Fuck," he growled, moving his hands to cradle my head. "That feels so fucking good." His hips lifted, trying to find a rhythm as I sucked and licked.

The hand I had wrapped around his girth tightened as I pulled it up to meet my lips, fisting him as I jerked him off.

"I am not coming in your mouth." The warning so raw it tore at his throat.

My eyes bulged as I took him in deeper, taking as much of his length as I could without gagging and defying his resolve not to come.

"I said." He yanked on my hair, pulling himself free from my lips with a pop. "I am *not* coming in your mouth."

"Where do you want to come?" I asked, lowering my lips to his balls, drawing one of them into my mouth and sucking hard.

His body shifted on the mattress before I had time to react, freeing himself from my mouth and kissing me hard on the lips.

"Inside of you." He pulled me against him, flipping my back onto the mattress and then covering my body with his. "I want to be buried deep inside of you when I come. I want to feel you come with me, pulsing around my cock while I thrust into you over and over again."

A whimper escaped from between my lips, my body heating to his suggestion as I writhed underneath him.

His body lifted, balancing his weight on his elbow as he reached down and grabbed the box of condoms he'd tossed on the mattress, and tore the lid off with his teeth.

Oh. My. God.

That was so freaking hot.

He didn't waste time, pulling one out and opening the packet. My eyes dropped to his hands as he pushed onto his knees and grabbed his cock firmly. He rolled the latex down his length, covering himself before rewarding his good work with a firm, tight pump. It was incredibly erotic, my body tingling all over as I watched, annoyed I had missed it in the dark the first time we'd had sex.

"I *want* you," he growled, positioning himself at my opening. "I *need* you."

It was too much to hear, the words rattling around in my brain.

Want.

Need.

You.

My heart hoping those words carried the same weight for him as they did for me. I knew it wasn't an act, but I had no idea how deep in it he was with me.

With a thrust of his hips he plunged into me, filling me completely as he pressed in deeper. My body accepted the invasion, adjusting to accommodate him, the warmth spreading across my skin.

"You feel so good." He pulled out and then pushed in again, the sensation making me tingle.

I lifted my legs, wrapping them around his hips and locking my ankles around his waist. "More," I begged as I circled my hips. "Give me more."

He cursed out a breath, his arms pushing him higher to give him more room to move. Deeper and deeper he drove into me; swinging his hips faster and harder as I panted underneath him.

My eyes closed, gripping his shoulders with my hands as want and lust overwhelmed me, my fingers struggling to maintain hold.

"Open them," he moaned, my eyes flinging open to see the passion in his. "I want to see you and I want you to see me, like this, when I'm buried inside of you."

I didn't argue, the lust in his eyes incredibly hot as I felt my body prime for another explosion. "Dave, I'm going to—" I couldn't get the word out, teetering on the edge as he pulled out again and sunk in deep, pushing me over.

"That's it, beautiful." He continued to move. "Come for me. Oh my God, that feels so good."

He rode out the wave, each drag of his cock sending me deeper and deeper into the spiral, the throb inside of me getting more urgent. "Fuck." All his muscles tensed, his torso tight as his own wave took him, pulsing hard as he too found his finish.

"Yes." He rocked, his lids lowering as he looked down on me. "Yes."

My pulse raced as I watched him, his beautiful perfection coming undone and it had all been because of me.

Our bodies spoke a truth neither of us had articulated with our mouths, the feelings it exposed almost overwhelming me.

My hands ran up his arms, feeling the strong muscles underneath my fingertips and I didn't want it to stop. As insane as it sounded I wanted to forget all about the wedding, my family and the fucking city, and spend a whole day just making love to him.

He panted against my skin, bringing his mouth back to mine before slowly pulling out. "Give me a second, I'll be right back." He disappeared into the bathroom, the faucet running for only a few minutes before he returned, gloriously naked.

My mind was a wasteland, acutely aware of how attractive he was, with everything about him more strikingly handsome than I remembered. I was seeing him with new eyes, and what I saw, I liked very, *very* much.

"You still with me?" He lowered his lips, kissing me gently before sliding back in between the sheets. His weight shifted, rolling onto his side as he studied me. "You look like you're deep in thought."

He was wrong about that; I wasn't thinking.

If I had been thinking, I wouldn't have slept with him again. I would have enjoyed the lapse in judgment made earlier in the day and moved forward, keeping it platonic. But I had been greedy, wanting him again and again and didn't give weight to the consequences. I still didn't, preferring to live in the suspended fantasy

I'd created.

And I knew it wouldn't last forever.

I rationalized that we were friends with benefits and tried to forget our monetary transaction. I assured myself that it wasn't prostitution, or worse, that he'd slept with me under duress. He'd seemed to want *it*—the sex—as much as I did, with no concerns for the consequences either. It was okay as long as we were both being irresponsible, right?

"Don't take this the wrong way, but you wanted to have sex with me, right?" I said in a moment of guilt.

"You're kidding? I thought we already covered that?" He laughed, pulling himself up onto his elbows. "Did you think I *faked* the hard-on? Twice? Or do you think that I generally sleep with women I'm not attracted to?"

I took a breath, shaking my head as he misunderstood what I was asking. "I didn't say you weren't attracted to me. I'm not fishing for compliments. I know I'm not hideous or anything like that."

He stopped me, placing his hand on my arm. "Jessica, you are *far* from hideous."

"Again," I reiterated, "this isn't about padding my ego. I'm talking about whether you would have slept with me if we weren't here."

He shook his head as if discounting the thought, his eyes were unreadable as he opened his mouth and then closed it again. A shiver shot up my spine when he didn't answer right away, and I guessed he was probably searching for a way to spare my feelings.

"It's okay," I reassured him, more angry at myself than I could ever be at him. "I'm not—"

"Yes, I wanted to sleep with you " He cut me off. "And not just because we're here. Given half a chance, I would have slept with you a year ago. My hesitation about taking this *job* wasn't whether or not I'd be able to pretend to be attracted to you, it was whether or not I was going to be able to keep my hands off you."

I couldn't breathe, my lungs feeling like they were paralyzed as my eyes widened. I had no idea what I expected to hear, but telling me that he'd wanted me from before wasn't even on my radar.

Of course, I wasn't sure if it was just a physical attraction or if it went deeper. I was confused, turned on and slightly worried this was some elaborate trick—the punch line imminent.

While I knew he loved a good laugh and acting like a wise-ass, he didn't look like he was joking; his face stone cold serious as he kissed my shoulder. "I tried, Jess. I'm just not very good at behaving."

"I-I had no idea." I struggled to find the words, completely floored by his admission as a thrill ran through me.

My lips widened of their accord, unable to stop the grin. I enjoyed the moment, rationalizing that it was because I was glad I hadn't sexually harassed him. Because my fucking delight couldn't be for other, more personal reasons like—I don't know—I liked him and he liked me.

His lips moved back up my neck. "Not sure Jeremy would have been too pleased if I tried to fuck his superstar assistant. So I assumed it wasn't going to happen."

He wasn't the only one who'd made assumptions.

"I don't sleep with clients," I added quickly before correcting myself. "I mean, I *usually* don't sleep with clients." Clearly there was a loophole, with Dave Larsson being the exception to the rule.

There weren't many rules I wouldn't break for him to be honest; the way he made feel worth any trouble it would cause.

His lips continued to kiss me, covering my mouth as he mumbled. "I know, which means one of us is the bad influence. Why don't we have some fun until we work out who that is."

"I like this plan." I wrapped my arms around him, pressing

my breasts against his chest. We needed to test the theory, right?

He chuckled, shifting on top of me and holding me hostage with his weight. He needn't have bothered; the four horsemen of the apocalypse couldn't have torn me away. "I hope you don't plan on sleeping tonight, because you're not getting any."

It wasn't a threat but a promise, a low growl bubbling up his throat as he dropped his mouth to my nipples. "There isn't a part of you I don't want to cover with my mouth."

I arched against him, widening my legs so he could settle between them. "You say that like it's a bad thing. I have a few things I want in my mouth too."

He didn't seem to mind.

We explored each other slowly, taking our time to kiss, lick, suck, and touch our way up and down each other's bodies. It was less hurried but five times more intense, every cell in my body feeling like a burst of electricity had just been pumped through it.

The teasing was without mercy, bringing me close to the brink with his mouth and hand and then backing off before I could finish. It was both frustrating and sexy as hell, my body in a constant state of arousal.

And not to be outdone by him, I implemented some torture of my own. I twisted around, giving him access to my body while I took him in my mouth. Cupping his balls, I drew him in between my lips in desperate pulls until he was harder than steel.

When he'd finally entered me, I orgasmed, thrashing against him as waves of pleasure rolled through my body until he came too. Our arms and legs tangled as we panted against each other.

It was late in the morning when we lost our battle against sleep, his arms wrapping around me as he brought me closer, his lips resting on my shoulder.

"I thought we weren't going to sleep." I yawned, barely being able to keep my eyes open.

"I said last night. It's now morning." He pulled me tighter. "Sleep."

It was another loophole.

CHAPTER #18

"YOU LOOK AMAZING." He grabbed me, circling his hands on my hips as I walked out of the bathroom. "It's a shame the bride is going to be pissed."

My fingers smoothed down the front of his charcoal grey suit, admiring some *amazing* of my own. "Why would Lana be pissed?" I asked, staring down at my dress.

"Because when you walk in the room, no one is going to be able to keep their eyes off of you." His eyes rolled over my body.

It was a nice touch and such a sweet thing to say.

If he'd been my boyfriend.

Which he wasn't.

"Oh please." I pushed his chest roughly. "I specifically chose this color so I wouldn't stand out."

My outfit was a stunning pale pink cocktail dress that fell to just above my knees. It was fitted but not too tight, tastefully dipping at the front to just tease at a hint of cleavage.

"It's not the color you should be worried about." His hands moved to the front of my dress, a finger trailing along the neckline. "It's your body. I'm already hard."

I laughed, finding it ridiculous that a dress I deemed conservative was turning him on. Not that the thought didn't excite me; turning around and grinding against his hard-on as I inspected myself in the mirror. "Well, I'll just have to do the best I can to remain inconspicuous. I'm sure I won't be too difficult to ignore."

He held me still, pressing the ridge of his cock against my ass. "That would be impossible."

It was tempting to be late, to take off my troublesome dress and let him prove how *impossible* it would be. But I knew if we started, we wouldn't stop, missing the wedding entirely which was the whole reason for my trip.

"We can argue about it later, let's get going, I'll even let you drive."

He didn't move, looking at me in the mirror. "In case I haven't told you enough, you look beautiful. And I'm really glad I got to come here with you."

"Thank you, I'm really glad too."

THE WEDDING AND reception was held on the rooftop of the Remington Suite Hotel. It was one of the few places in town that could accommodate the large guest list *and* was still classy enough for my aunt to approve. It was bad enough Lana hadn't wanted to get married in a church, there wasn't a chance in Hell they were going to have the service in some second-rate ballroom of a no-name hotel.

We were ushered to our seats, taking our place near my parents and siblings, my family taking up almost an entire row.

"Nice dress." Amy smiled, fanning herself with the wedding booklet. "I had to look twice to make sure you weren't nude."

"Maybe I'll save that party trick for the reception. I'll strip off and distract everyone so you'll have no competition for the tossing of the bouquet." I laughed, elbowing her playfully.

Amy grinned, looking at Dave who was standing on the other side of me and apparently oblivious to my plan to get naked. "Yeah, because you *aren't* going to push me out of the way and grab the damn thing for yourself."

My brow creased, the idea not having occurred to me before. Not because catching the bouquet was an outdated tradition that I thought was stupid. But because she assumed that Dave and I were going to be heading down our own aisle. The truth that we wouldn't, not something she or anyone else knew.

"Don't be silly." I tried to keep my voice low, hoping Dave didn't hear. "We haven't been going out long enough to even think about marriage, let alone for me to be next."

"What does it matter how long you've been together, if you love someone and it's right, why wait?" She sighed before looking at Travis who was talking to Dalton. "Unless you're me who will probably be eighty before I get to wear a wedding dress."

I tried to laugh, hoping she wouldn't see my panic. "I promise I won't get married before you."

She giggled. "Don't make promises you can't keep."

I didn't bother telling her it was probably one of the easiest promises I was ever going to make. Instead, I decided to change the direction of the conversation, asking her about the shade of lipstick she was wearing and pretending to be interested.

Dave put his arm around me as the crowd was brought to a hush with the change in music. Lana's brother Blake escorted Gran Shelly to her seat, followed by both sets of parents and the groom's party. Clay grinned as he waited, looking down the aisle with expectation, waiting for his bride.

Lana was a vision, covered head to toe in French lace and tulle. She cried, dabbing her eyes gently with a handkerchief while they said their vows and exchanged rings.

Both her and the service had been beautiful, the preacher

declaring them husband and wife to the sounds of cheers. And I breathed a sigh of relief that we had gotten through the ceremony without too many people staring at us.

There had been some over the shoulder glances and a few whispers in our direction, but mostly people smiled, with only a couple of wedding guests looking expectantly at Dave like he was going to be inspired and drop to his knee at any second.

"So what happens now?" Dave handed me a glass of champagne, the band starting to play as waiters circled with hors d'oeuvres.

"We stand around and judge people, talking about them behind their backs." I smiled as I took a sip.

My mother coughed loudly beside us. "Jessica Lynn, I'm not sure why you would say such a thing. She never used to be this jaded," she said to Dave before turning to a woman who looked like she'd been poured into a white dress. "But I will tell you while I might forgive Celia for wearing white on someone else's wedding day, those red shoes are not appropriate."

I leaned into Dave, grinning as I whispered, "Told you."

"Come on, LeeAnn." My dad winked at me as he took my mother's arm. "Let's leave the kids to socialize and see if we can't find me a decent glass of whiskey."

She agreed, affixing a smile on her lips as he led her away to the bar.

"Wonder what they're saying about us?" He lowered his head, looking around with a smirk.

I shrugged, surprisingly not really caring about their opinions at that moment. "It could be anything. I'm not wearing red shoes so at least I've got that going for me."

"Well, that is true." He glanced down at my nude-colored pumps, taking the champagne from my hand and placing it on a table beside us. "Maybe we should give them something worth talking about." He lowered his drink, leaving it near my abandoned glass.

"Oh really? What did you have in mind?" I looped my arms around his neck, tilting my head back to look in his eyes.

There was no hesitation there, no hint for concern—his calm washing over me like warm bathwater.

His nose brushed against mine. "I can think of a few things."

"You want to steal a bottle of wine and go make out?" I suggested, only half joking.

He cupped his hand to his mouth, looking shocked. "In front of your parents, you are a very naughty girl."

I laughed, picturing the horror on the face of my family if I did just that. "I do work for a heathen, you know. So they probably expect it."

He held out his hand like an invitation. "Dance with me."

"I thought you were still traumatized by your junior prom?"

"What do you know?" He looked at me with a smile. "Looks like I've been cured. Want to help me test out the theory, just to be sure?"

"Right here?" I looked around, people milling around the rooftop.

"Right here."

I dropped my hand into his and didn't question. I didn't want to. Instead, needing the moment to linger, letting him lead as we started to move to the music.

There was a dance floor but we weren't on it, choosing to sway in our own corner as people started to notice.

His hand tightened around my waist, bringing me in closer, keeping his eyes on me the entire time. It was as if we were in a bubble, and he was ignoring the outside world.

Ignoring it was eventually going to be over.

Ignoring that *we* would have to end.

The idea of *breaking up* with him weighed on me like an anchor tied to my ankle, pulling me down to the bottom of the ocean. Even though our relationship had been fictional, the pain of saying goodbye to him probably wasn't going to be.

"They're watching us." I felt the heavy gaze of the crowd around us.

He didn't stop, dipping his head as he smiled. "Let them watch."

I was used to being the one in control, to being the one with the plan, but as I stood there with him, I didn't care about any of that.

I had always liked him. And of course there was an attraction, but in the last few weeks, it had grown into more. In the last few days, it had grown again.

More than liking him, and lusting after him, I felt something else. An energy between us that was more pure and honest than anything I'd ever felt. It scared me a little, but calmed me at the same time, and in that, I felt truth. It was the reason why I was able to let go and let my feet move to wherever he wanted to take me.

I *trusted* him.

Wow.

Without any good reason, I felt it in my gut, and I knew he would never hurt me.

We might not be dating and I wasn't sure if he even felt the same way I did, but what I had with him was something very real and special. Something that I didn't think I'd ever had with any man.

And I knew that I was falling in love with him.

Why did I do this? Bring him here, and make him pretend?

The stupid *part* I'd made him play, stealing the chance that he might have fallen in love with me too.

But how could we go back?

Or how the hell was I going to pretend after?

And why couldn't I make myself stop?

"Is the offer to make out still good?" He chuckled in my ear.

I didn't hesitate, bringing my lips to his. "Always."

THE SUN SETTING lit up the sky in stunning ribbons of pinks, oranges and yellows. It was beautiful; fairy lights threaded through the trees making them glow like golden orbs while strings of bright bulbs hung around the periphery.

The happy couple kissed every time someone clicked their glasses while the rest of us sat and enjoyed the food and music.

Dave was the perfect date, mingling and spending time with my brothers without needing his hand held. And there was no shortage of people wanting to speak to him, waiting their turn before seeking an audience with *the new guy*. No one even cared that I had left his side and was sitting down, but he looked over at me constantly, checking in as he continued to engage the crowd.

"I know I don't remember the conversation." Gran Shelly shuffled herself into Dave's empty seat beside me. "But I really am glad we had it. I like him, Jessica. I like him a lot. I like the way he makes you smile, and I'm really glad I got to see that."

I glanced over at Dave and caught his smile. It felt like my heart had just expanded in my chest, and those feelings were more than just gratitude. "I know, and I'm glad too. He means a lot to me, Gran."

Maybe I'd said it so many times I had started to believe it myself, or maybe it was just no longer a lie. And as I reached for my grandmother's hand and squeezed, it felt like something I wasn't sure I could give up.

"It's not always going to be easy." Her voice turned serious.

"What Gran?" I turned to face her, wondering if I'd missed part of the conversation.

She tapped my hand, her brow furrowing in concern. "It's nice now when everything is good and you love each other, but real relationships take work. And it's important to remember both the good times and hard times—neither are going to last forever."

Her words confused me, and if she weren't so lucid I'd have dismissed it as the babbling of an old woman. But as someone who was usually focused on the silver living, her pragmatism was surprising. Even more so when discussing relationships. Her desire to see me with the perfect man, the catalyst for where I was now.

She shook her head, her warm hand giving mine a squeeze. "But if you love him like you say you do, then you will stick it out. Later, *later* is when the real reward comes."

There had always been a calmness in her pale blue eyes, a sense of coming home. I had stared into them so many times as a child and immediately felt at ease, but as I focused on them now there was a storm brewing.

"Are you feeling okay?" I asked, more concerned about her than the relationship advice. "Gran, do you need me to get you something?"

She shook her head and smiled, closing her eyes a beat before opening them again. "I know I'm old, child, but I know what I'm talking about."

While previously unnerved by her crystal ball styled rhetoric, I had now plunged into downright concern. Alarm bells rang and my skin prickled in a silent warning, hoping I wasn't hearing words of a woman who wasn't going to wake up tomorrow.

Maybe I had been wrong about all of this, the lie of me being happy and settled down giving her permission to finally leave. Dread filled me as I looked over at Dave and wondered if me and my stupidity would be what ultimately took her from me.

His face changed when he saw me, immediately excusing himself and leaving the crowd. He walked calmly but with purpose, his eyes staying on me the entire time.

"I've neglected you." He dropped a chaste kiss on my forehead, rubbing my shoulders in silent reassurance. He might not have known what was going on in my head, but obviously sensed something was wrong. "But I am glad to see you had someone worthwhile keeping you company." He lowered, sinking to his haunches beside Gran. "Thank you so much for sitting with her."

Her lips spread into a grin, her eyes crinkling as she laughed. "You don't ever have to thank me for that. But I am getting tired."

"We can take you home," I volunteered, already rising to a stand.

Dave nodded, reaching for his keys. "I'll go get the car and bring it out front."

"Don't be silly, they haven't even served the cake." Gran shook her head as she looked into the crowd. "I'll get your daddy to take me home."

I grabbed her hand, not willing to let her leave. "No, Gran. We'll do it."

She could try to argue if she wanted, but there would be no other outcome. She'd lived with my Aunt JoAnn since my grandfather died, and with everyone here for the wedding, there was no way I was sending her off into an empty house.

"Go get the car, Dave, we'll start saying our goodbyes."

He gave me a soft kiss and left while I helped Gran out of her seat. She shuffled with her walking frame, chiding me for making a fuss, but I didn't care. I smiled as I guided her out, ignoring the disappointed faces because we were leaving so early.

"Momma, are you okay?" my mother asked, her concern matching my own.

Gran straightened as best she could, looking my mother in her eyes. "LeeAnn, I will not have you hovering over me like a child. It's bad enough my granddaughter is doing it. Enjoy the rest of the wedding and I'll see you tomorrow."

I hoped her promise of seeing my mom tomorrow was one she intended to keep, the words not giving me the reassurance they should.

"I'm going to take her to our place, and I think I'll stay the night," I told my mother, an understanding passing between us. "It's been so long since I've slept in my old bed and I kind of miss it."

Mom dug in her purse and pulled out a set of keys, putting them in my hand before covering them with hers. "Call me if you have any trouble with the alarm." The urgency in her voice had nothing to do with the alarm. "We'll meet you at the house as soon as the bride and groom leave."

I forced a grin, my hand resting on my frail grandmother's back. "Let's get you home, Gran. I'm kind of tired myself."

Dave was out front waiting beside the still-idling Mustang. The passenger's side door was open and he stepped forward to help Gran into the car. I stood completely mesmerized as I watched them. He was so gentle, holding her hand as she eased into the seat, waiting until she was situated before closing the door and folding up her walker.

"Get in, beautiful." He kissed me, carrying the walker to the trunk.

I nodded, popping the driver's seat down so I could scoot into the backseat, watching Gran as I waited for him to come back.

"It's such a beautiful night." Gran smiled as Dave closed the door and put the car in drive. "Mind if we take a drive around the city before we head home?"

He pulled away from the hotel and merged into traffic, giving her a cheeky smile. "We'll go anywhere you want. Just no strip clubs though, okay? Giving other men attention will make me jealous."

She laughed, shaking her head as she agreed.

We drove through the streets without purpose or direction,

my fingers white from being knotted in my lap so tight. The top of the convertible was down with the wind blowing through our hair, touring most of the city until finally Gran asked to be brought home. She'd initially demanded to go to Aunt JoAnn's, but I dug my heels in and brought her to my family home instead. Once there, we helped her out of the car and got her settled into the guest room. She looked so tired, the color dropping from her cheeks as she took slow, steady breaths. I didn't need to have a medical degree to know that she wasn't doing too well, but she point blank refused for me to call a doctor. I pulled over a chair, wanting to sit for a bit but she insisted she didn't need watching and told me to leave. I hated it—the thought of walking out the door—but ultimately gave in to her wishes.

I went back to the kitchen and found Dave waiting, sitting at the table. He held out his hand and I grabbed it, squeezing it tightly as I took the chair next to him.

"This is the end." I felt my voice warble. "The things she was saying, it's like she knows that it's the end."

He put his arm around me, holding me as he kissed my forehead. "What can I do?" he asked. "Let me help you, just tell me what you need."

I shook my head, not knowing what to ask for and feeling the same pain in my chest I'd felt three months ago. "Just hold me, I have a feeling it's going to be a long night."

He pulled me out of my chair and into his lap, his body engulfing mine. "That's easy. I'll hold you for as long as you need."

As long as you need.

What I *needed* was for him to hold me *forever.*

And for everything to be okay.

I was almost positive I was going to get neither of those things.

CHAPTER
#19

MY PARENTS GOT home a little after midnight. They'd gone by my aunt's house and got Gran some pajamas and personal items, Mom going upstairs to check on her.

Dad looked over at me still perched in Dave's lap as we sat at the kitchen table. "Why don't you go back to the hotel, sweetheart, we'll call you if anything happens."

Just the suggestion was proof enough that my dad was worried. He wasn't a fan of me staying at a hotel, but unlike my mom, he kept his feelings to himself. Asking me to leave meant he probably thought the worst too.

"We're going to stay in my old room," I said, not bothering to ask Dave if he was okay with the sleeping arrangements. I guess he could always go back to the hotel if he wanted, but I wasn't leaving.

Dad sighed, knowing better than to argue. "Well then, go get some sleep. I'll have your mother wake you if anything changes. Whether Gran Shelly likes it or not, I have Dr. Bartlett coming in the morning."

Knowing a doctor was coming gave me some comfort, and with not much else I could do, I said goodnight to my dad and went upstairs to my old room with Dave.

"She's a fighter, Jess. I barely know her and I can see that in her."

We were curled up on the bed facing each other, neither of us bothering to get underneath the covers.

I couldn't speak, feelings of guilt overwhelming as I replayed all our conversations.

The last time I sat by her bedside, I'd told her my lie. In my head it had made sense, giving her comfort in what I thought were her final hours. Except I had been wrong and she hadn't remembered a thing. I wasn't even sure she'd heard my elaborate story. And maybe that was why she had kept fighting, not being able to rest until she was sure I'd found my significant other.

"We have to break up." I sat up in the bed suddenly, clinging to the slightest hope that maybe she would keep fighting if things went back to the way they were. After all, she couldn't die if I hadn't found my soul mate, and if Dave and I were no longer together, then obviously it hadn't been him.

He shuffled up to the headboard, looking at me like I was insane. "Jess, what are you talking about?"

I guess he had a point, I hadn't exactly told him what was going on in my head. "I know I said we'd do the breakup when we got back to L.A. but we need to do it now. It can't wait, so you need to ditch being sweet. You need to break my heart and leave me. The messier and more dramatic, the better, it is the only way."

He looked like he was going to argue, his brow rising in concern.

"Please, Dave. She didn't remember me telling her about you the last time, and the fact she fought her way back was a miracle. She'd always said that she didn't want to go until all of her grandkids were happy. If you break up with me, then maybe she'll keep fighting. Trust me, I *know* her."

He blew out a breath, putting his arms around me. "You honestly think the change in script is going to help? Yell out plot twist and move on? Jess, maybe it's time we just tell her the truth. That you lied, and now . . ." He left his sentence deliberately trailing.

I didn't ask what he was going to say, too terrified it was going to be *"and now you paid a man to pretend and you were stupid to fall in love with him."*

Because sleeping with him obviously wasn't bad enough.

"I just can't." My heartbeat raced as I looked into his eyes.

Deep down I knew I'd been falling in love with him, and I hoped those feelings would eventually be reciprocated. But I hadn't dared to even think about it, let alone speak about it out loud. I just assumed that when we got back to L.A. and the dust settled, I'd see if the connection was still there, hoping the spark I felt wasn't just one of circumstance. But I also knew there was a chance that I was in this alone.

He took my face in his hands, brushing his lips against mine. "Come on, Jess, you have to know she is going to love you anyway."

He had no idea what he meant to me, no clue that the act had been one sided and the lies I'd told everyone weren't even close to the one I'd told myself.

It was ironic that my heart was both blooming and breaking all at the same time, my body crumbling against his as I choked out a sob. "Please, Dave. I need you to follow through with the plan."

As much as I wanted to forget about Gran, her words rang in my ear. *There would be good times and hard times, and neither would last forever.* And if I had a chance to keep her with us just a little while longer, I had to try, even if it meant putting us on a collision course.

"I know it sounds crazy, and I know I am asking way too much of you, but please do this for me."

I felt the subtle shake of his body as he wrapped his arm around me and said words he probably didn't want to say. "What do you want me to do?"

There was a lump in my throat as I swallowed, gripping him

tight as I answered. "Find Suzie. Call her and tell her you couldn't wait. I'm sure Darla has her number and—"

"No." He shut me down, not letting me finish. "I'm not doing that. I only agreed to meet her tomorrow to be polite; I have zero interest in *anything* else. Jess, you realize what you are asking me to do is insane, right? I can't just go and fuck someone else."

"I'm not asking you to fuck her, just kiss her," I reasoned, even though the idea of his lips on another woman made me want to go on a rampage. "Just kiss her, tell me it's over—"

"No. I'm not kissing her either." He moved his lips to mine, his finger tracing my jaw. "I'll break up with you if that's what you want, but I'm not involving anyone else. No one else, Jess."

"Okay," I agreed, kissing him back. Our breakup didn't exactly feel like a breakup, but I knew it would probably be the last time I kissed him and I couldn't make myself stop. "But you need to leave me, and soon. How are we going to do this?"

He blew out a long breath and hugged me tighter. "You sure you really want to?"

No, I wasn't sure. In fact I was positive I didn't want him to break up with me even if it had been the plan all along. What I wanted was for him to tell me that he loved me, and that we'd work through this, but I seriously doubted that would happen.

I knew he cared about me, and yeah, he enjoyed sleeping with me, but that wasn't enough right now. I couldn't be his friend with benefits, and I was so tired of pretending, so maybe it was for the best anyway. Sparing me the humiliation later.

"Yes, this is what I want." It took every ounce of strength to look him in the eyes and spew out more lies. "It's what I'm paying you to do. We've had fun, but the plan was always to end it, and I need you to do that for me now. Like we agreed. Please."

I hated myself. The loathing of what I was asking him to do making my skin crawl, but I did it anyway.

"Wow. Okay then. Yep, can do." He shuffled away from me, his hand lifting off of me like my skin was repellant.

"What are you going to do?" I asked urgently, wanting to know if maybe he was considering my earlier suggestion and going to spend time with Suzie.

He shook his head, blowing out a slow breath. "Sorry, I forgot you needed creative approval. I was thinking we go a little old fashion, me saying I'm no longer interested and skipping town? Sound good?"

"Dave."

God, I wanted to tell him the truth. That I was petrified of what I was feeling and worried that the minute we got back to our real lives it would all end anyway. We'd been living an illusion, one that would shatter sooner or later, so there was no point trying to prolong the inevitable. And even so, I wanted to beg him to be gentle. Even though I probably didn't deserve it.

"Yes, Jessica, any lasts requests?"

The warmth that had been in his eyes was gone, and in its place the coolness of a stranger.

"No, say or do whatever you have to. It's okay, I can take it."

It was another lie. I wasn't sure that I could, but I didn't have a right to make him feel bad about it either.

He shook his head, running his hands through his hair as he looked at me. "I'm going to need to be a dick." The conflict flashed in his beautiful brown eyes.

"I know, but you're acting. I *know* you aren't a dick."

The mattress shifted under his weight as he pulled away, putting his shoes back on as he grabbed his jacket.

"Where are you going?" I asked, hoping we had few more hours before I had to say goodbye. Even if it was just one more night. And I realized how hypocritical I was being; wanting more time when it was my fault he was walking away to begin with.

"I'll be back in the morning." He leaned down on the bed, moving toward me like he was going to kiss me and then stopped.

He chuckled but there was no humor to his laugh. "Sorry. Habit."

"No, I'm sorry." I wanted to grip his shirt and kiss him one last time. "I'm so sorry I dragged you into this mess."

He tried to smile, but didn't quite manage it. "I'll see you soon."

Before I could stop him, he walked out of my bedroom and closed the door quickly behind him. I had no idea if my parents were up and asking questions, and I hated myself for leaving him to deal with that too.

There was no way of knowing if I'd made the right choice but ultimately it was the only one I had. After all, what kind of relationship could survive when it started out as a lie? Even taking Gran out of the equation, there would always be a small part of me that would wonder if he was with me for the right reasons. Because I was enough, and not because he owed me.

We had been in a bubble, and I didn't know if any of it had been real.

My hands covered my face but the darkness didn't make me feel better. It just amplified how big a mess it all was.

The lies.

The act.

The intricate story.

I'd take it all back in a heartbeat if I could, but it was too late for that.

I shucked off my dress and slipped in between my covers wearing only my underwear. The room where I'd spent my entire childhood didn't hold the same feelings of warmth and comfort it once did, my bed feeling empty despite me being in it.

My eyes squeezed closed and I tried to clear my mind, concentrating on the love I *knew* was real. For my gran. The reason why

I had put myself through this to begin with. There was nothing more I could do tonight, and I had to believe that tomorrow, it would all work out.

THE SMELL OF breakfast wafted up the stairs.

I had no idea what time it was or how long I'd slept, my brain and body feeling stiff and sluggish. I pushed off the covers and redressed in the same clothes I'd worn to the wedding. It wasn't like I had anything else to wear, and I didn't have the energy to raid my mother's closet.

Leaving my heels beside the bed, I padded down the stairs barefoot, walking into the kitchen where my family was assembled.

"Hey, baby." My mom was dressed—her hair and makeup perfect as always—cooking breakfast as I entered the room. "I'm glad you got some sleep. Dave awake?"

Well I guess that answered the question on whether or not they had seen him leave last night. His departure had gone unnoticed.

"He went back to the hotel last night," I said, offering as little information as I could. After all, I had no idea what we were going to use as a cover story, and I didn't want to complicate things by adding more lies to an already overwhelming load.

She stopped dishing up breakfast, giving me a sideways glance. "Oh, really? Well then, I guess he can bring you a change of clothes when he comes back this morning." The assumption made that he was returning.

I took a sip of juice, mumbling in the affirmative as Travis and Amy came through the door. "Hey, how is she?" Travis asked, tipping his chin hello before taking a seat at the kitchen table.

Mom slapped his hand, stopping him from stealing some bacon. "Wait until I've got it all on the table. I swear I taught you better manners than that." She shook her head as she continued to dish up. "And Gran Shelly seems to be doing okay. She slept most of the night, but is still really tired this morning. Dr. Bartlett is visiting in an hour or so, and hopefully we'll get some answers."

Travis grumbled about being hungry, helping himself to juice while he waited for the go ahead to eat. "What about you? How are you holding up?"

I shrugged, not really sure exactly what I was feeling. Scared, sad, out-of-my-mind-with-worry—any one of those could have been an answer. "I'm fine," I lied, deciding it was better to change the subject. "How was the rest of the wedding? Who ended up catching the bouquet?"

Travis and Amy looked at each, a smile passing between them.

"I'm glad you managed to tackle the crowd on your own." I smiled at Amy. "I'm sorry if I let down the team."

"Oh, I didn't catch it, someone else did." She shook her head looking smugly at my brother.

"You?" I asked, staring at Travis.

"Finally playing ball in school ended up being useful. And the throw was a thing of beauty, fell right into my hands like I was the greatest wide receiver of all time." He laughed, clearly proud of himself. "Helped that Lana knew exactly where to toss it. I still need to thank her for that."

"Which means, we're next." Amy lifted her left hand, flashing a diamond ring.

"Oh my God!" I grabbed her hand and examined the ring. It was beautiful, and completely unexpected.

"Congratulations." My mother smiled placing the rest of the plates on the table. "We'll have to start planning an engagement party soon, and I'm sure Gran Shelly is going to be over the moon about another family wedding."

I was sure Mom, like I did, just hoped she'd be around to see it.

Travis shrugged, looking over at Amy who couldn't stop

beaming. "It was the situation with Gran that kind of made me decide to man up. Who knows how long any of us have left?"

"Well, I'm really happy for you. It's the best news I've heard all morning." I willed myself not to cry, reaching across the table and giving his hand a squeeze.

"Thanks, sis. So where's the big guy? Don't tell me he's still sleeping?" He looked around as if waiting for Dave to appear.

I did my best to not look concerned, forcing the smile to show I wasn't worried. "He went back to the hotel last night. I think he's coming back later."

"Please tell me after everything that went down, he did not go to that film set this morning," Travis warned. "Because straight up, that is bullshit."

"No, he didn't," I answered with absolute certainty. Both he and Amy had made it clear that they had thought it was a bad idea and even I'd had my doubts. But even when I begged Dave to go—and to kiss her—he'd turned me down.

And Dave was right, infidelity was a cop out, something he would never do. "He just decided to go sleep at the hotel."

"Of course. It makes sense, Trav." Amy shoved his arm, throwing her support behind me. "All their stuff is back at the hotel, someone needed to go back and get their luggage, and there's no way Jessica would have left."

It was a flimsy excuse at best, but I was glad to have her on my side. My nerves prickled with the uncertainty, it was like falling and waiting to hit the ground. Just because you knew it was coming didn't mean it wasn't going to suck.

The doorbell rang breaking the tension, my dad leaving the table to answer it.

The voices carried into the kitchen, but we couldn't hear the words exchanged, Dad returning shortly after followed by Dave who looked like hell.

"Hey." He waved to everyone but didn't smile, the temperature of the room dropping a few degrees with his frosty glare landing on me. "Check out was at ten, so I brought your bags. I've left them beside the door."

I swallowed. "Thank you."

His demeanor was at odds with the man I knew. He was so cold, so distant, and even though I assumed it was an act, it was hard to be in the line of fire.

"No problem." The lack of warmth in his voice was almost jarring. "I'm on an earlier flight so I'll take the rental car back. I'm assuming you can get a ride to the airport later?"

I swallowed, unsure if he'd actually booked an earlier flight or if it was part of his performance. As selfish as it sounded, I didn't want him to leave. "Yes, thanks, I'll be fine."

"Good. Well," his mouth thinned to a tight line, "I guess I'll see you around. Take care." He turned, not bothering to say a proper goodbye.

I couldn't move, invisible bands holding me in place as I watched him stride toward the door.

When I had originally asked him to do this, breaking up had always been the end game. I assumed we'd fall back into some kind of friendship and maybe even become closer having shared the experience. But I hadn't counted on having actual feelings for him.

"What the fuck?" Travis pushed away from the table and getting to his feet. His booming voice punched through the silence and made Dave turn around.

"Travis, language," my mother admonished, turning her attention to Dave who stood in the doorway.

"I'm sorry, Mom, but seriously." He leveled his stare at Dave. "I know you aren't just dumping my sister's suitcase and then jumping on a plane and leaving her here."

Dave shrugged, his voice complete devoid of emotion. "She's

with family, where would you like me to leave her?"

"You *don't*, asshole," Travis spat back, moving toward the door.

I grabbed his arm, stopping him from getting closer. "Travis, don't."

"No, he needs to explain himself." Travis shook off my hands, facing Dave and folding his arms across his chest. "We're waiting."

Dave's eyes connected with mine but they were too difficult to read. The kindness I'd seen less than a day before was completely gone. "Look, I've got nothing personal against your sister, but this is a little more than what I signed up for. I've got a career to think about, I really don't have the energy for the . . ." He waved his hand. "Supportive boyfriend stuff."

"Are you kidding me? You can't waltz in here pretending to be part of this family and then waltz out. What kind of man are you? When your woman needs you, that's when you step up to the plate, not run and hide like a coward," Travis's voice exploded.

"Travis, please just let it go." I looked at Dave, the pain I was feeling so real even though I knew what he was saying wasn't. "I wish you the best of luck, Dave, thanks for everything."

I wanted it over, I wanted him to walk out of the door, because the longer he stood there, the harder it was for me to not to throw myself at him and tell him I'd made a mistake. But I had to remember *why*.

He wasn't mine to keep.

Dave just shrugged, looking at me one last time before he went to turn. "Yeah, okay."

"You've got some fucking nerve." Travis lunged at him, Dave ducking out of the way before the fist connected with his jaw.

"Travis," I screamed, jumping out of my chair and grabbing his arm. Amy latched on from the other side, neither of us doing a great job of trying to contain him.

His face was red, advancing toward Dave despite having a

woman hanging off each arm. "That shit might fly in Hollywood, but you're in Louisiana now. You just be grateful I left my gun in the car."

"Well lucky for me I don't live in this backward place and am going back to where that shit *will* fly. And no offense, Trav, but last time I checked you weren't the person I was dating. She's more than capable of speaking for herself, so maybe back off."

Travis lunged again, Dave managing to deflect. "You better get out of here, asshole."

He took one last look at me, shook his head and then walked out. I had no idea what was going through his mind or where he was going. The opportunity to ask slipped through my fingers as I heard the revving of the Mustang outside and the skidding of tires as he drove away.

I sunk back into my chair feeling relieved, but still shattered at the same time.

He'd not only managed to facilitate our breakup, but made *himself* the bad guy. Leaving me to be devastated in front of my family while he pretended to be the hurtful dick. It was definitely an award-winning performance. And as stupid as it sounded, it just made me love him all the more.

God, I hoped when it was all over, I'd still have him in my life. Even if I couldn't have him the way my heart wanted him, I couldn't bear the thought of losing him completely.

I looked down at breakfast, deciding I was no longer hungry. "I'm going to go get changed."

"Baby, I'm sorry." My mom stood, opening her arms for me. I sank into them, welcoming their comfort as I felt my eyes water.

As she rubbed my back, I choked out a sob. "Oh, Jessica. I promise it will be all right."

I couldn't help crying, but not for the reasons she probably assumed. It was because I was in love with a good man, and he'd deserved better. And I deserved better from myself.

Unable to deal with the concerned looks of my family any longer, I excused myself and went upstairs to my room. My suitcase was still by the front door but I grabbed an old bathrobe from my closet and took off my dress. It was when I tossed my clothes onto my bed that I saw there was an unread message sitting on my phone.

Hope they bought it. See you in L.A.—D

My heartbeat jumped as I messaged back.

Thank you x

My fingers hovered over the keys, wanting to write more but I didn't. There was no way I could begin to convey what was going on in my head and my heart with a text message, so I didn't bother to try. Instead I switched off my phone and hoped that its inactivity would minimize the temptation to call him.

I was already struggling and didn't expect it to get any easier.

Taking a deep breath, I walked out of my room, locked myself in the bathroom and stood under the shower until I felt like I was no longer going to cry.

Maybe someday, when all of the shit was behind us, we could start again.

And the next time around, it would be just for us.

No performance.

No money.

No lies.

Not right now, but eventually . . . at least that was what I hoped for.

Because the alternative—that it had all been for nothing—was unthinkable.

CHAPTER #20

DR. BARTLETT WAS concerned about Gran's low blood pressure but wouldn't know anything more until he ran additional tests. She was tired and wanted to go back to her home and he saw no reason to move her to a hospital.

She continued to be annoyed at the fuss we were making, perking up when I snuck into her room with some contraband wedding cake Mom had brought home.

"Aren't you flying back today?" Gran asked as I took a seat beside her bed. "And don't look at me like I'm about to keel over. I know I had a bit of a spell yesterday, but I'm not dead yet."

I smiled, shaking my head at her choice of words. "You didn't just have a spell, Gran. Dr. Bartlett needs to run more tests. And we're just worried about you because we love you."

She folded her arms across her chest looking inconvenienced. "You didn't answer my question. I thought you were leaving today?"

"Anyone would think you were trying to get rid of me," I laughed. "I decided to stay another day so I changed my flight until tomorrow." Or at least that was my plan; I still needed to clear it with Jeremy.

She tilted her head like she knew there was more to the story.

"Is Dave staying too, or did he have to get back for work?"

"Well, about that." I took a deep breath. "Things didn't work out the way we'd hoped and we decided to go our separate ways. I honestly think it's for the best though, and I'm sure there is someone else who is just right for me out there. You will just have to make sure you stick around so you get to meet him."

"You broke up?" Gran's eyebrow rose. "You want to tell me what happened?"

It would have been easy to throw Dave under the bus and say he was an asshole. Or take his lead, pretending he was too busy with his career to deal with me and our "relationship." He didn't want to be tied down . . . blah, blah, blah.

But I couldn't do it, the words so incredibly vile they gave me heartburn, the acid rising up my esophagus just at the thought.

"Nothing really happened, I guess we just wanted different things. Maybe it just wasn't the right time?"

Even if he wasn't around to hear it, I wouldn't vilify him for my benefit anymore.

He deserved better.

"Well, that's a shame," she said with a silent grin. "I guess things work out the way they're supposed to."

I narrowed my eyes wondering if the low blood pressure was making her act weird. "Yeah, I guess they do."

"As long as you're happy, sweetheart, I'll be happy." She pushed back the comforter, slowly swinging her legs around. "Now, help me up out of this bed, I want to get dressed before I go back home."

While I was glad Gran wasn't upset, she had taken my break up with Dave better than I'd expected. Perhaps she'd been given happy pills instead of a sedative, or it was one of those conversations she wouldn't remember later, but her lack of concern was surprising. I assumed she'd be a little bit more . . . *something*.

Pushing it out of my mind, I helped her get out of bed and into her clothes. Holding her arm, we managed to get her downstairs, my mother irate we hadn't called for help.

"LeeAnn, I've told you a million times you need to stop hovering. Jessica and I were more than capable of getting down those stairs." Gran waved off my mother. "Now be a dear and bring the car around."

Mom didn't argue, rolling her eyes at us both as my dad went and got the car. While we waited, Travis and Amy shared their good news with Gran, Amy showing off her shiny new ring. Gran Shelly beamed with pride, happy there was going to be another wedding soon.

It would be a cold day in Hell before anyone attended mine, ironic that for the first time ever there was actually someone I would consider marrying.

It wasn't until after Gran left with Mom and Dad that Travis dropped the smile with his annoyance from earlier resurfacing. "I've already told Dalton and he's tipped off his buddy who works with the TSA. He's going to hook us up and make sure fuckface gets pulled aside for a thorough search." He cracked his fingers as the devious grin spread across his lips.

"Travis, you can't use the TSA as your own personal revenge squad. Not only is it against the law but I don't need you fighting my battles for me." I yanked on his ear. "Now, call Dalton back and call it off. I don't want Dave messed with. And if anything happens to him that I can tie back to you, it won't be him you'll have to worry about."

He threw his hands in the air, blowing out a breath of frustration. "Jesus, Jess, you are no freaking fun. And just so you know, this has nothing to do with you not being able to fight your own battles. We're family and we stick together. If this was Dalton or Mel, I'd be just as mad."

I rubbed his arm, knowing his heart was in the right place.

"I know, and it's sweet that you want to protect me, but I think this is all for the best. It's not the right time in my life either. I'm so busy with work and we probably would have broken up later anyway," I tried to reason, hoping to convince myself as the words came out of my mouth.

Part of me had to wonder—in a different time, in a different place—if we could have made it work. Or maybe I was just delusional and had started to believe my own fucking bullshit PR.

"Plus, you don't want to date someone who the whole world has seen with their shirt off," Amy added, trying to be helpful. "Not that there is anything wrong with men showing their chests, and his was pretty darn nice."

We laughed. Her effort to convince me I was better off completely missed the mark, but I appreciated the sentiment. His chest *was* pretty damn nice and I didn't care who else had seen it, I just wanted it—like the rest of him—to be mine.

Assuring them both I was fine, I pushed them out the door to leave me alone in the house.

I couldn't take it any longer.

Taking the stairs two at a time, I raced to my bedroom and grabbed my cellphone. I powered it up as fast as I could, the moments ticking painfully slow until the screen lit up with the background picture. My fingers scrolled through my contacts, thanking the Lord his name was at the start of the alphabet as I paused and hit dial.

"Hey, it's me." My heart stopped the minute he picked up, hoping he was able to talk and not about to board a plane or worse, already in one.

"Hey." The one word not enough as I willed him to say more.

"It's the first opportunity I've had. Gran's gone back to my aunt's and everyone's left the house." I settled onto my bed, kicking off my shoes as I got comfortable.

Please talk to me, I begged. *Please, give me something—anything— just so I can keep you in my life. Even if it's just as a friend. Even if you don't love me the way I love you.*

"How is she?"

A long breath blew out from between my lips as my head rested against the pillow. "Hard to say, they're going to run tests and see if anything comes up. Of course she's acting like we're all fussing for nothing and almost didn't die a few months ago."

"Well, if she's angry that's probably a good sign."

"Yeah," I agreed, remembering her laying on the bed and her skin the color of ash. "I . . . I told her about us. About us breaking up."

"And how did she take it?"

I shook my head, still a little surprised by her reaction. "It was weird, she didn't seem to really care. Gave me some line about things working out for the best or some shit like that. I don't know, I thought she would have been more disappointed."

Lord knows I had been disappointed. And not that I'd wanted to upset her, but I assumed she'd give me more than advice I'd have easily found in a fortune cookie.

"That is strange. Anything more you need from me?"

Come back.

Let's start again, and this time it can be for real.

"No." I gripped the phone closer to my ear wishing we were still in the same room. "You were brilliant. Not that I ever doubted your ability, but everyone bought the whole thing. I couldn't have asked for a better costar."

"Well, I'm glad it worked out the way you wanted. Pity I won't get recognized by the Academy." He chuckled, the humor missing from his laugh.

"Yeah, sorry about that. Your next role will though. You start filming soon, right?"

I'd hoped the change in the conversation would help, moving us back into familiar territory. Work had been our common ground, and right now it was the only ground I was still sure we shared.

"Yes, soon."

He gave me nothing.

Keeping his answers short and concise with zero emotion. I had no idea what he was thinking, or whether he even wanted to talk at all. At this point, he no longer owed me anything, so he could have easily hung up.

"So . . . where are you?"

Like a pathetic loser, I tried again. With still no idea what I was hoping to achieve.

"Dallas. I jumped on the first flight out and am waiting for a connection to L.A. I didn't want to hang around Shreveport and risk blowing our cover. With us broken up, I had no reason to stick around."

He was right, of course. It wasn't like he could hide out in Shreveport until I was ready to leave. But the logic didn't matter, his departure stinging all the same.

"Dallas, huh? Going to pay that sex club a visit? You'll have to tell me if it's worth the trip." I shook my head, wondering what the hell I was saying.

"Yeah, I forgot about that. Thanks for the reminder," he chuckled. "Have you decided when you're flying home?"

It was an interesting choice of words, and not just because I'd been hoping we'd be taking the return trip together.

I'd always looked at Shreveport as home, and L.A. as just a place I lived. But the more I thought about it, the more it felt like the other way around.

"I'm catching a flight tomorrow morning. Jeremy is probably going to pitch a fit but he'll just have to deal. What time is your connection?"

"In another hour." The disappointment laced his words. "I have to meet the director in the morning."

"That's so great. This is a big opportunity, and you really are perfect for the part." I tried to hide my own disappointment, knowing I was running out of reasons to keep him talking. "Honestly, Dave. You're going to do so great."

There was a pause, neither of us saying anything as the silence stretched out uncomfortably between us.

"So, do you still want to go to Jimmy's exhibit?" He was the first one to speak. "The opening is Friday."

"Of course, I want to go. We had a deal, remember?"

The exhibition had been the furthest thing from my mind, but there wasn't anything that would stop me from keeping up my end of the commitment. It was the least I could do. Besides, as tragic as it sounded, I'd go to a thousand exhibits—a million—willingly, and use any excuse possible to see him.

He blew out a breath, sounding tired and maybe a little frustrated. "Yeah, we had a deal."

"Jessica?"

I heard my name being called from downstairs; my parents already back home.

"Shit, I need to go. Message me when you land in L.A." I stood up, knowing our time was coming to an end.

"Yeah, okay. Bye, Jess."

The call ended just as my mom opened the door, her eyes looking around the room like she expected someone else to be there.

"Hey, baby, what are you doing up in your room alone? I hope you weren't sitting here being sad?"

"No, Momma. I just needed to make some calls; I still haven't called my boss. I'll be down in a minute."

"You take whatever time you need." She straightened her string of pearls. "And don't let that heathen give you any lip. He's lucky to have you."

Yeah, well that wasn't true. I wasn't sure *anyone* was lucky to have me. But saying that out loud would get me a three-hour lecture from LeeAnn Dawson listing all my virtues, and I didn't have the energy. My mother didn't do wallowing and wouldn't accept anyone else to doing it either.

"Thanks, I'll be down soon." I held up my phone up and waited for her to leave.

Calling Jeremy to give him bad news was never a fun conversation, calling him on a Sunday when he and his wife were supposed to be having *couple time* was even worse.

"I swear to God, Jessica," he answered, barely taking a breath. "Unless you are calling me from a jail cell or the inside of some gator's stomach, you better be coming back tomorrow."

"I'm coming back tomorrow." I winced before adding, "Just a little later than expected. My flight leaves in the morning, so I'll get there sometime in the afternoon."

"Fuck," he shouted into the phone. "Two days with Katrina is giving me an ulcer. On Friday, she put Julian Schubert on hold. JULIAN SCHUBERT. I had to kiss his ass for twenty minutes and then promise him my first-born. And you know there is *no way* I'm ever having kids."

I cringed, hoping there was only so much damage she could do in the time before I got back. My work was the one part of my life where I had my shit together; I didn't need it going down the tubes because of carelessness and my own stupidity. "I'll call her and run through anything important. I have your schedule synced to my phone."

"Fine, do what you got to do." He hung up, not bothering with a goodbye.

I tentatively made my next call, praying Katrina could handle L.A. while I dealt with my own drama in Louisiana.

"Jess!" Katrina squealed into the phone. "Oh my god, I've missed you. You have to tell me everything? Did your family freak out when you arrived alone? They understood when you told them the truth, right? What am I saying? Of course they did, they're your family."

As far as Katrina and Liz were concerned, I went home alone. Once there, I would confess everything and beg for forgiveness. Which left them completely in the dark about my elaborate plan with Dave. It made sense to involve as few people as possible, minimizing the chance of something screwing up. Of course, them not knowing meant I also didn't have anyone I could confide in either, my misery remaining my own.

"I'd rather not talk about it." I coughed, not wanting to even think about it right then.

"It went that good, huh?" She laughed. "Okay, I'll let you off for now but tomorrow you're going to tell me everything."

I took a deep breath. "Well, that was part of the reason I was calling. I'm going to be late tomorrow, so I need you to cover for the morning. But Katrina, you can't screw up, Jeremy is already pissed about Friday."

"That wasn't my fault. The guy had an accent, and it was hard to understand him. I made one mistake and Jeremy flies off the handle. I swear you are a saint for putting up with him."

"Just get through tomorrow, I'll be back later in the afternoon," I begged.

She agreed, grumbling that she would be on her best behavior and see me tomorrow.

Well, at least the drama of work would keep my mind off Dave—and what would happen the next time I saw him—and my grandma whose health was still questionable.

After changing my flight with the airline, I trudged downstairs to where my mom and dad were sitting at the kitchen table. Deep lines of concern covered their faces, their masks of happiness returning the minute they'd noticed I was back.

"Jessica." My mom stood, the smile not hitting her eyes as she held out her arms for a hug. "You have everything organized with your boss?"

"Yes, everything is organized. I'll fly out tomorrow morning. Hopefully by then we will have some more answers on Gran." I wrapped my arms around her, sensing her tension.

"Good, I'm glad to have you home for an extra night. We can have a nice dinner at the house or we can go out, whatever you want." She played with my hair like she always did when she was nervous.

"Mom, she will be okay." I made assurances I had no right to make. "And we can do whatever you want to do."

She collected herself, pushing back the concern. "Well, what I want is a tall gin and tonic, and some of Gran Shelly's fudge. Maybe you can help me get together the ingredients and make sure your daddy doesn't eat the whole batch before it's cooled."

"I can't help it, LeeAnn." My dad laughed, giving my mom a kiss on the cheek. "That fudge is pretty hard to resist."

We set about making fudge and a bunch of other baked goods and waited to hear news on Gran. I was still unsure about leaving in the morning but staying indefinitely in Louisiana wasn't an option.

"You want to talk about it?" My mom wiped down the counter, putting the last of the dishes in the sink.

I'd been trying to push it from my mind, but the look on Dave's face when he left still gave me chills. "Not really, I'd rather not."

She nodded, her sympathetic eyes revealing she wanted to ask more but was giving me my space.

I'd have thought I'd have been relieved when it was over. Grateful that I no longer had to keep up the pretense of a fake relationship. But I didn't feel good at all. Instead I felt empty, like my emotions were adrift and grieving the loss of something that hadn't even been mine in the first place.

It was supposed to be easy. Our performance putting the lie to bed with our eventual break up. It would set me free, allowing me to save face in front of my family and not admit to what I had done.

But what I felt was far from free.

Instead, I felt like I had made the biggest mistake of my life and let go of the only man I really loved. And what was worse, I had no idea what he felt in return.

And now I might never know.

I wasn't sure what had been the bigger lie.

That I'd convinced myself we were pretending.

Or that I was capable of letting him go.

CHAPTER #21

ARRIVING BACK IN L.A. was both a blessing and a curse. The anxiety of my family hadn't left me even though I'd left the state—doctors still not sure on Gran's condition—and I was suddenly confronted with the problems I had set aside to deal with later.

Later was suddenly now.

I didn't bother going home to my apartment, instead going straight to the office. Jeremy dropped to his knees, welcoming me back in exaggerated gratitude. He "rewarded" my return with a to-do list as long as my arm as I sat at my desk. Apparently he hadn't trusted Katrina, so he saved it for me like a special gift.

Katrina was also relieved, deciding her previous ambitions of a promotion weren't really for her and she liked not having the extra responsibility.

Matt picking her up at her desk after work meant I'd been momentarily spared her inquisition. She was still demanding I tell her all about how understanding my family had been, but I didn't have it in me to lie. Liz sent me similar messages, but they were easier to avoid. I knew I would eventually have to tell them something, I just couldn't deal with it now.

Thankfully the day passed quickly, and other than a brief

message to Dave that I'd landed, I hadn't heard from him.

"Nick." I looked up to see Dave's younger brother standing in front of my desk. On instinct my head turned, discreetly trying to see if he was alone. "Hey, I don't have you down for a meeting, Did you and Jeremy have an appointment I didn't know about?"

"Yeah, five thirty. It's not like you to forget." He grinned, the famous Larsson smile making me want to throw up for the first time in history.

Ignoring his smile, I checked the schedule again, making sure Katrina hadn't screwed up and entered it in wrong. "Sorry, Nick, but I don't have you down for today."

"Are you sure? I've set up a reminder and everything." He pulled out his phone and scrolled across what I assumed was his calendar.

"Shit, my bad. It's for tomorrow. I could have sworn it was for today." He shook his head, seeming to be annoyed.

It was startling how much he looked like his older brother. Same brown eyes, same light brown hair and when they smiled, it was almost identical.

"I'm sorry, Nick, but Jeremy has already left for the day. He had a meeting with a studio head." I bit my lip, checking Jeremy's schedule to see if he was coming back.

Nope.

No such luck, he was heading straight to a dinner and wouldn't be in the office until tomorrow morning.

"No drama, it's my own stupid fault for not checking before coming down here." He ran his hand through his hair. "I guess I'll be seeing you tomorrow then." He gave me a wicked grin.

Between Dave and Nick, Nick was definitely the bigger flirt. And while both were equally charming—able to bring women to their knees with just a look—Dave had something extra that I just couldn't place.

Not that it mattered now.

"I know seeing me is the highlight of anyone's day. Try to contain your excitement." I tried not to sound too pathetic, faking a laugh as I shut down my computer and grabbed my things.

It wasn't a huge consolation, but at least I was done for the day. Leaving me free to go back to my apartment and wallow in peace.

"You're going home?" He looked at the purse slung over my shoulder as I stood from my desk and pushed in my chair.

I nodded, checking my phone one last time to see if there was a message from Dave.

There wasn't.

Not sure why I expected one.

"Yeah, I flew in this morning from out of state and I'm looking forward to getting back to my apartment. My plans for the evening include getting comfortable, eating something from a takeout container and doing as little as possible."

His eyes widened, clutching his chest in faux shock. "Wow, I don't think it's me who's in danger of too much excitement. Takeout, alone, in your apartment—here I was thinking that *my* plans for the night were a little out of control."

I grabbed my suitcase, wheeling it out from behind my desk. "Oh, har-har. And what are *your* plans for the evening? A hot date with a posse of beautiful women? Don't mock me."

I imagined that was what all the Larsson men did, because dating one woman would surely be a waste. I also didn't want to think about whether or not my description of his evening plans would also extend to his brother.

"That was yesterday. Tonight is just Dave and I drinking and eating pizza. He just got back from some bullshit shoot in Texas." He laughed, staring down at my suitcase. "You have a ride home? I have my car."

What I should have done was politely declined his offer of a ride, called a cab and gone home to my plans of eating dinner alone in my apartment. Then I could continue wrestling with my emotions a little while longer and obsess about how Dave was spending his night. But of course mention of his name made the offer too tempting to ignore, the opportunity presenting itself in what I could only assume was fate.

Nick's wrong appointment time, mentioning his brother, and offering me a ride home—surely it was too much of a coincidence to ignore.

"I would love a ride home, as long as you're sure it's not out of your way. I would hate to derail your fun night of pizza and gossip with your brother."

While I attempted to sound casual and uninterested in Dave and the mention of his "bullshit" shoot, internally I was screaming, wanting to know all the things. It was junior high all over again, hanging out with your crush's best friend and pumping them for information, hoping to find out if they'd *mentioned* you. In a perfect world, I wouldn't have cared, but I was struggling not knowing.

"Pfft, he's been in a bad mood since he got back anyway." He grabbed my suitcase and wheeled it into the hall. "Besides, he's probably not even home yet, I've got all kinds of time."

"Well, if you're sure. That would be great." I didn't argue, leading the way out the door.

"So, business or pleasure?" Nick looked down at my suitcase as we traveled in the elevator down to the lobby.

"Family, my cousin got married in Shreveport and I went back for the wedding," I answered, unable to make direct eye contact.

"Shreveport, isn't that only a few hours from Dallas?" He held the metal doors open as we stepped out of the elevator.

I coughed, the question catching me off guard. "It's about three hours. Not very far."

"Wow, you two should have caught up. Sounds like he could have used someone to keep him entertained. Apparently the director was a real asshole."

"Well, I was really busy with the wedding and all." *Do not panic, he has no idea you were together.* "Wait . . . he said the director was an asshole?" My head snapped around, Nick getting my full attention.

Did that mean he thought I was the asshole?

Considering I was the architect, there weren't a lot of other people it could mean.

"Yeah." He looked at me with hesitation like he wasn't sure if he should have mentioned it. "I assumed he would have called you guys."

My hand gripped tight around my handbag, trying to play it cool. "Maybe he called the office," I offered knowing full well that he didn't. "I was out of town so . . . what else did he have to say? I mean, it would be good to give Jeremy the feedback. This was for the *independent* project we sent him on, right?"

Not that there was a chance he was talking about some other project he'd been working on, but I'd hoped there might have been a miscommunication.

"Yeah, he was cagey about it, said he'd signed an NDA." He rolled his eyes; clearly not impressed he didn't know more. "Anyway," he continued, pointing out his silver Mercedes coupe. "From what I could gather it was a complete waste of his time. Lucky for him it was only four days. At least he's getting paid for it."

Ah. Shit.

I'd had every intention of paying him. We had an agreement, and it was only fair that he was compensated for his time. But him leaving so suddenly meant I hadn't had a chance, which also meant I still needed to do that.

Just thinking about it made my skin crawl, the reminder of the cash transaction made our time together seem tainted. It had been a job, it was only right he got paid. But Jesus, I hated the thought of him being a date for hire.

What would be worse? If I paid him, or I didn't?

A knot tightened in the pit of my stomach as Nick tossed my suitcase in the back and opened the car door.

I slipped inside, acting casual as he got behind the steering wheel and started the ignition. Torn between wanting to ask more questions and scared to hear the answers.

Nick turned his head and laughed. "You going to tell me where you live, or am I supposed to guess?"

"Shit, West Hollywood." I rattled off my address as I settled into the seat and stared out the windshield. "Thanks."

He nodded, pulling into traffic and heading toward my apartment.

We made small talk as he drove, me leading the conversation to safer waters and asking about him and his work. I nodded, hmming in the right places as I tried to sound interested, but I couldn't get my mind off Dave and what he'd said to his brother.

They were family; there was no reason for him to not tell him the truth.

The irony was killing me.

"Here you go." He stopped in front of my apartment building, getting out of the car to pull out my case. "Need a hand getting it up the stairs?"

I stepped onto the sidewalk, grabbed the handle of my suitcase and shook my head. "Nope, I've got it. Thanks." My eyes shifted to my apartment, a tight grin forming on my lips. "I better go get started on my *big* plans. I still haven't decided which takeout I'm going to order."

"You want to come to our place and hang out?" he asked with no hesitation.

I stopped, wondering if I'd actually heard him correctly "You want me to come hang out? With you and Dave?"

"Why not, it's not like we don't know each other and haven't

hung out before. Unless of course you're serious about wanting
to spend the night alone in your apartment. No judgment here if
you do." He held his hands up as he relaxed against his car.

Say no, damn it.

Tell him you want to soak in the tub with an overpriced bath
bomb until you turned pruney.

Or that your plans involved mindless television and junk food
without the audience.

Or even that you were so tired you were going to crash and
not up for any kind of human interaction.

Anything.

"I need to change," I heard myself say, my mind rearing back
in horror as my mouth continued unauthorized.

"I can wait, I'm in no hurry." He grabbed the suitcase back
out of my hands and carried it toward my gate. "You need a code
for this thing or key?" He tossed the words over his shoulder while
I stood on the sidewalk wondering what the hell I'd just agreed to.

By some miracle I was able to get my feet moving, entering
the code and opening the front gate. Nick waited, letting me take
the lead as I strode to my apartment on the first floor, my hands
barely able to get the keys in the door and open the goddamn lock.

"I'll just be a few minutes." I tossed my keys into the dish on
my sideboard, wondering what the hell I'd been thinking when
I agreed. "Make yourself at home, there's drinks in the fridge if
you're thirsty."

"Take your time, like I said, we're in no rush."

As he took a seat on my sofa and picked up a copy of *Vanity
Fair* I had laying on the coffee table, I thanked God I'd cleaned before leaving town. Not that my level of cleanliness mattered right
now, especially when throwing myself into the unknown was the
bigger problem.

Grabbing my suitcase and shutting myself in my room, I had

a whole new level of panic.

It would be the first time I'd seen him since the fake showdown at my parents' house. We'd had a brief conversation after and things had been icy since. So as vain as it sounded, I didn't want the first time he saw me post-breakup to be looking like shit. Which I knew was completely stupid and yet, didn't bother fighting it.

Taking Nick at his word of not being in a hurry, I threw myself into my shower, quickly reapplied my makeup and then sat in front of my closet mumbling obscenities under my breath. I had no idea what to wear, not wanting to come across as trying too hard and not wanting to look like I didn't give a shit. I finally settled on a white maxi dress and teamed it with a denim jacket, hoping it made me look cool and causal instead of the hot mess that I was.

Tossing on a pair of strappy sandals and taking one last look in the mirror, I quickly wrote out a check for five thousand dollars and stuffed it into the pocket of my jacket. I wasn't sure how I was going to broach the subject of payment, but I'd decided regardless of how awkward it felt to pay him, he'd earned the money fair and square.

"Wow." Nick smirked as I emerged from my room. "You really know how to make those few minutes count, don't you?"

"If working with Jeremy has taught me anything, it's how to get ready in a hurry." I walked over to the sideboard and grabbed my keys. "I'll follow you in my car so I can drive myself back."

He shrugged, lifting himself off the sofa as he followed me to the door. "If you're tired from your trip, one of us can drive you home. We don't live far."

As tempting as the offer was, I didn't want to be reliant on either of them to get home if shit became weird. Hell, my impromptu visit might only last an hour, my excuse of being tired already stowed away in case it was needed for an early getaway.

"Thanks, but it seems silly for you guys to drive me back. I'm good to go." I jangled my keys even though I was far from ready.

Nick followed me out, waiting for me to lock the door before we descended the stairs into my courtyard. While he went out the gate to where his Mercedes was parked, I got into my car and drove out of the apartment block, meeting up with him on the street.

He pulled out in front, taking the lead even though I already knew where he and his brother lived. Their duplex wasn't far, with both of us pulling up in front of it not long after.

Nerves plagued me as I followed him up the stairs to his front door, watching him push it open and stepping inside.

"Honey, I'm home," he called out, shooting me a grin. He closed the door behind us, tipping his chin to the living room.

"About fucking time." Dave's voice floated in from another room. "I was going to order without you, I'm freaking starving."

My eyes widened as he walked in, a towel around his waist while he casually dried his hair with another. His chest was still damp, a tiny rivulet of water traveling across his muscles I was dying to lick.

And having done it in the past and knowing what it felt like, just made it more difficult to resist.

Nick laughed, tipping his chin toward Dave. "Hey Bro, you might want to throw some clothes on. Jess doesn't want to see your junk."

The hell I didn't.

I waved lamely as I took a seat on the sofa.

"Jess, what a pleasant surprise." He folded his arms across his chest, making no moves to change his state of undress. "To what do we owe this pleasure?"

"Nick invited me," I blurted out, hoping he believed I hadn't engineered the whole thing. "I think he was jealous of my plans of takeout and television."

"Indeed, she just got back from Shreveport. Family wedding."

Nick grabbed his phone and started dialing. "What pizza am I getting?"

Dave tilted his head to the side, his acting talent getting a workout. "Huh, is that so? Welcome back. I'll go put some clothes on." He turned to his brother. "Get whatever."

He disappeared down the hall to where I assumed his bedroom was, shutting the door with a slam.

Nick rolled his eyes, offering an apologetic smile. "I told you he was moody, you good with sausage?"

"Yeah, whatever is fine."

If I were a normal person, I would have assumed from Dave's frosty reception that he wasn't pleased to see me. Of course, I wasn't a normal person so I wasn't about to take the hint. Instead I was intrigued, curious to see how the night panned out, like an experiment in torture or something.

Nick gave the phone his attention, ordering pizzas while directing me to go grab some drinks from the kitchen. Which I was more than happy to do considering it gave me the chance to explore Dave's habitat and generally be nosey. Not sure I was going to find any answers behind the condiments, but it beat sitting in the living room waiting to see if his mood had improved.

"Looking for something?"

My head snapped up when I heard the voice behind me. My interest in the fridge and trying to decipher which of the ten different varieties of beer would best suit pizza was no longer important.

Thankfully he was dressed, hiding that delicious body of his in a pair of jeans and a T-shirt, which would hopefully reduce the temptation. Not that I didn't know what was underneath, my brain being an asshole and filling in what we couldn't see.

My eyes shot over his shoulder, checking to see if we were alone. "If you want me to go, you should just ask me to go."

"Did I say I wanted you to go?" He bent down, reaching across and grabbing three beers, his body just barely touching mine.

"No, but I would hate for you to have to put up with an *asshole director* all night." I stood defiantly, the refrigerator door still open while I dared him to deny it.

He laughed unapologetically as he twisted the caps off the bottles and handed one to me. "Well that's just part of the job now, isn't it? Not complaining while I stand there, look pretty, say my lines and then leave."

"It wasn't like *that*," I hissed, trying to keep my voice low. "You knew there was a plan. We had to stick with it."

"Yeah, the plan. It was just a job, wasn't it? My mistake." He took a long pull from his beer, his Adam's apple bobbing as the liquid traveled down his throat. It was as if he was trying to be intentionally sexy, teasing me with what I no longer had a right to have.

"Actually, about that." I dug out the check I'd stuffed into the pocket of my denim jacket. "I didn't have a chance to give this to you before, but here." I held it out in my fingers.

His eyes dropped to the paper, reading what it was and then flashed back to me. "Are you fucking kidding?" If he'd been frosty before, he'd turned down right icy now, the bones in my body chilling from his glare alone.

"Look, I know it's not a lot and you deserve more. And I will reimburse you any other additional costs—"

"Keep the fucking money," he sneered, moving closer and lowering his head so his face was inches away.

All I had to do was reach up and I'd be able to kiss him but I didn't dare, too worried he wouldn't kiss me back. I may have made the biggest mistake in my life, but I still had my pride.

"Yo, what's taking so long on those drinks?" Nick called from the living room.

"Be there in a minute," I shouted back, quickly shutting the fridge door and grabbing another bottle from Dave.

I strode out to the living room, settling back on the sofa and handing Nick his beer. I didn't bother drinking mine, setting it down on the coffee table as I pretended to be interested in the conversation.

"So how's the break? I'd have thought you would have taken a vacation after wrapping for the season?"

Dave joined us, drinking his beer as he turned on the television.

Nick ignored Dave who was channel surfing, taking a sip from his bottle before answering. "Jeremy is trying to get me a part in this movie while we're on hiatus. I didn't want to take off until I knew if I had a chance."

"Hmm." I nodded, trying to concentrate on the words he was saying while pretending to ignore Dave. He could have literally told me he was giving up acting and joining a circus, and my response would have been the same.

He shrugged leaning back into the sofa. "Anyway, no point talking about it, it's either going to happen or it isn't."

"How very pragmatic, brother." Dave laughed.

I hadn't meant to turn my head, deciding the best course of action was to pretend he was invisible. But the minute I'd heard his voice, my head rotated all on its own, like a homing beacon had been activated.

"Well that's a good way to be," I offered. "I don't think half the directors in Hollywood know what they want anyway. Hopefully they'll see reason soon enough."

"Interesting concept." Dave stroked his chin, giving it some consideration. "Directors are generally self-centered pricks, so there isn't a lot of room for *reasoning*."

Ouch.

"Well, *some* directors have a really tough job," I spat back defensively. "It's not as easy as it looks. If it were, then everyone would be doing it."

Dave threw his head back, his body shaking as he laughed. "You're a riot, Jess. Seriously, no wonder Jeremy loves you. You can sprout bullshit and sound convincing doing it."

"Dude." Nick shot his brother a look of irritation. "I know that gig in Dallas was shit, but it's not Jess's fault."

Nick couldn't have known.

Known that it was *exactly* my fault and I was the reason his brother had such a terrible time in "Dallas." I was the *asshole* he was mad at.

"You're right. No one held a gun to my head, and I should have left." Dave's feet dropped to the floor and he stood up. "Let me know when the pizza gets here, I'm going to run lines in my room." He turned, taking his beer and strode down the hallway away from us.

Nick shook his head, rolling his eyes at his brother's behavior. "I always thought Roman was pricklier, but Dave is giving him a run for his money at the moment. Try not to take it personally, he probably just needs to get laid."

Great.

Because I didn't have enough anxiety, I needed to think about Dave having sex with someone else as well.

And as much as I wanted to go down that hall and ask him why he was so upset, I couldn't. Because I had no right to. We'd had a friendship and *I* had ruined it. Possibly even making him feel used when I'd hired him to be my boyfriend. What was worse was that I blurred the lines by sleeping with him and kissing him. And not because I didn't want to do those things—because I did—but I'd wanted him to know he'd been doing them with me. Not Jessica his *costar* or the idiot who'd hired him, but me, the person who had fallen so head over heels for him she was scared to even admit it to herself.

"So how is Roman doing?" The option to change the subject too tempting to resist.

Nick's face lit up, excited to talk about his older brother. "Can you believe he's getting married? At first I assumed there was something wrong with her because who in their right mind would marry Roman? But no, she's brilliant and beautiful and just unlucky enough to fall for my brother."

I sighed wistfully, the change in subject not going to plan. "You know, they say that you don't really choose who you fall in love with. Love chooses you."

"Pfft, sounds like a load of bullshit if you ask me. Meh, whatever, as long as everyone is happy, who gives a shit. I'm in no hurry." He took a sip from his beer and turned up the television, his smirk widening. "One of Eric's movies is on, we should watch and live tweet it. It drives him fucking insane."

I shook my head, turning to the screen as the opening credits rolled. "Tweeting is for suckers, let's Snap it instead."

"Fuck yeah." Nick clinked his bottle against mine and grabbed his phone.

It was a distraction, and one I was desperate for. Hoping the silliness would get my mind off love, my gran and all things Dave Larsson, I gave Nick my full attention. It was a good excuse to stay and I'd even managed a real smile or two.

Dave emerged when the pizza arrived, surprising us both by sticking around. While I assumed he would have snagged a couple of slices and disappear again, he didn't, watching me as I joked with Nick.

Eric sent us a bunch of eye roll and middle finger emojis, but overall was a great sport about our online shenanigans.

Dave wasn't so accommodating. He didn't speak, just watching us curiously while Nick remained oblivious to the heated glares Dave tossed my way.

And I had no idea what those heated stares meant, if it was anger or jealousy. Surely he didn't think I'd moved on to his brother.

Or was it lust that simmered beneath.

Because as pathetic as it sounded, I couldn't turn that part off.

Even though what had been between us was so much more than sex, when he looked at me the way he did, it had the power to undo me.

Even if he hated me, I *still* wanted him.

Clearly I was a glutton for punishment.

CHAPTER #22

THE WEEK HAD been a busy one. Not only had things been hectic at work, but I also made sure I called Gran every opportunity I got.

She was still with us, insisting there was nothing wrong despite a decline of her organ functions. It was only after a conversation with my mom that I got the truth, the doctor saying it was only a matter of time. Of course, Gran continued to believe she was fine. Even though her body was slowly giving out, her spirit was still fighting. She'd joked that as the only one of her grandkids still single, she was holding out for me to find my other half. And I'd have stayed single forever if it meant keeping her around.

But even burying myself in distractions couldn't make me forget about my date with Dave on Friday night.

I'd assumed our date for Jimmy Ferrara's opening was still on given he hadn't called to cancel. But then again, he hadn't called to confirm it either.

More to the point, he hadn't called for *any* reason.

Which was why on Friday evening, when I was sitting around my living room in a black cocktail dress and heels, I almost expected to be stood up. I wasn't even angry about it, knowing that I was probably the last person he wanted to see, even if our date was supposed to be professional.

We hadn't even discussed if we were meeting at my apartment or his, or at the gallery—the plan completely hinged on a commitment made over a month ago, and then casually mentioned last weekend. It was stupid to even expect he'd remember, let alone want me to still go.

Deciding to swallow my pride, I grabbed my clutch, locked my apartment and went down to the courtyard where my *Lyft* driver was waiting. I reasoned that I wasn't driving so I didn't have the hassle of trying to find a parking spot. Because hoping he might drive me home and giving me the opportunity to talk was even too tragic for me to think about.

The driver did his best to make small talk, probably assuming I was the rudest customer alive when I returned his efforts with one-word answers. My nerves were wound too tightly to talk; the mental energy required to maintain a conversation being used to calculate how long I should stand outside the gallery like a loser before I went home.

"Thank you." I opened the car door and stepped onto the sidewalk, my arrival in an ordinary car getting some serious side eye from the valet.

The beautiful people had already started to roll up, black shiny limos spewing out women in evening dresses and men in tuxedos.

"Do you have a ticket, ma'am?" A man—who was older than dirt—dressed in livery looked at me like he knew I didn't have one.

Pushing my shoulders back and refusing to be intimidated, I responded, "I'm waiting for a friend."

Done thumbing his nose at me, *Old Man River* gave his attention to other guests, making his face crack with smiles as he directed them inside.

"Something on fire?" A suited-up Jeremy looked at me with concern. His wife, Hilary—who was decked out in more Harry

Winston than a Fifth Avenue window—hooked her arm around his as she shook her head.

"Jeremy, you promised." The words barely audible from the caged teeth of her fixed smile. "At least *pretend* you're not working tonight."

She was a smart woman and knew the score with events like the one she was about to step into. They were more about networking than about any of the art on the wall.

"I'm here for pleasure," I lied, smiling like I wasn't skulking around the doorway like a thief.

"Good for you." Hilary gave me a reassuring rub on the arm. "If Jeremy had his way, I'm positive you'd be chained to your desk. And thank you for my anniversary present last month, you have excellent taste."

Jeremy laughed nervously, tapping his wife's hand. "What are you talking about, honey? I went to Tiffany's myself."

"It was *Cartier*." She rolled her eyes. "And I *know* it wasn't you."

While being pulled into a domestic dispute on the sidewalk sounded like a good way to pass the time, I resisted. Instead I gave some bogus explanation that she calmly accepted, smiling even though she knew it was horseshit. I should probably look into some kind of meetings for Dishonesty Anonymous; the lies I'd told recently far outweighing the truth.

Jeremy and Hilary disappeared—like all the other people of note—through the double glass doors under the guise of getting their culture on. While I stood outside looking a high-priced hooker, checking the time on my phone and counting down the hour I had mentally agreed to wait. I figured an hour would be reasonable, giving him the chance to show, without totally decimating my self-esteem.

The hour was almost up when I stepped away from the door. I was undecided if I was glad or sad that he hadn't showed, resigned that the outcome was one I had expected. My finger hovered over the app to book a ride when a sporty black BMW pulled up. Dave stepped out in a designer suit—no tie with the buttons popped on the shirt—and handed the valet the keys.

"I went to your apartment." He kept his eyes on me as he strolled over to where I was. "I wasn't sure if you were dodging me or had gone out."

He smelled good, the freshness of his cologne all-encompassing as he moved closer.

I tossed my phone in my bag, trying to act like I wasn't about to leave or doubt that he would show at all. "I assumed we were meeting here."

His hand went to my lower back, leading me back to the door. "Perhaps I should have clarified."

I didn't bother pointing out that *clarifying* would have meant talking to me, which he didn't seem too enthused to do. So instead I smiled smugly at the old dude at the door as Dave flashed our tickets.

My skin electrified as he pressed his palm to my back. Even through the fabric of my dress it tingled, my body seeming to forget that the casual touch was all we were going to get. But ignoring that logic, I—as discreetly as humanly possible—leaned back into his touch to allow maximum contact.

"Champagne?"

We were greeted by a waiter balancing a tray of tall crystal flutes. Thankfully he was about five decades younger than his buddy at the door and seemed to be in a better mood, managing a smile as he offered refreshments.

I was just about to reach for a drink and tell him not to go too far when Dave snagged two glasses, thanking him before passing one to me.

He lifted his glass in a wordless toast, bringing it to his lips as he swallowed.

I hated the uncomfortable silence.

Wishing he'd say something—*anything*—to me, but likewise worried anything *I* said was going to be embarrassingly emotional.

And it was only going to get worse unless I thought of something fast.

"Julian Schubert is by the large red canvas." My head tilted in the direction of the huge red painting as I took a sip. I'd hoped by slipping into professional mode I could avoid a mental breakdown in public and stop myself from asking him to love me.

Because *that* would make sense.

Dave turned casually, spotting the popular director by the large abstract. "He won't even consider me for work. He once called me a poor man's Eric Larsson," he said with a chuckle.

"He loves your brother." I tried not to laugh while secretly being elated he had said more than five words to me. "But he's big on first impressions. He once hired a guy who washed his car because he thought he had the right look for a movie. The man had zero acting experience, but Julian couldn't be swayed."

Dave's eyebrow rose, shifting his gaze back to me. "So what am I supposed to do? Go over there and ask to wash his car?"

"No." I shook my head, knowing it would be the only chance he'd probably get close to Julian in a social situation. "His wife died a month ago, but it's not public knowledge. He bought her a Collie last Christmas, Roger, who for all intents and purposes is their child. He's a sucker for pet talk and could literally spend hours telling you about the new jacket he bought for his dog. If I were you, I would casually mention how Jimmy Ferrara started off painting puppy portraits at Central Park. I bet that would not only get his attention, but engage him as well." I looked over at Julian who was ignoring almost everyone around him. "It's not like you have anything to lose."

His brow furrowed, narrowing his eyes. "How do you know all that?"

"I work for Jeremy, it's my job to know." I took a sip from my glass, hoping the champagne would make me less jumpy. "Go, that's why we're here, right?"

He shifted uncomfortably on his feet. "Yeah, that's why we're here."

"So go, I don't need to be entertained. I'm just going to wander, look at the art and ooh and ahh like I know what it all means." I waved my glass in the direction of the paintings.

He nodded but seemed to hesitate, not moving from where he was standing.

"It's okay, Dave, honest." I nudged him with my shoulder. "Go."

Figuring I'd make it easier for him, I turned and walked to the nearest painting. I didn't bother turning around to see if he was still standing there, doing my best to give him permission to ditch me. It was what we'd agreed to, and considering he hadn't taken a cent from me, it was the least I could do.

"It looks like someone shot a bunch of paintballs on a canvas." A voice came from behind me, forcing me to turn around.

The owner of the mystery voice was gorgeous. Shorter than Dave, but still taller than me, his sandy-colored hair longer at the front, flipped to the side to reveal his green eyes.

"I think it's interesting." I turned back around, examining the work that indeed looked like it had been shot with paint pellets.

He came to stand beside me, tilting his head to the side like he was studying it from a better angle. "Nope, it still looks like shit."

It was curious that whoever he was, he didn't seem worried someone might overhear him. He didn't look like an actor or model—even though he was handsome enough for it—and he seemed too young to be a director or producer. Maybe he was some famous musician?

"So, do you generally hate art, or just Jimmy's work?" I asked, hoping to find out more about him.

"Just Jimmy's." He smiled.

I was almost positive he was feeding me a line but I was intrigued nonetheless. "Well why are you here? On opening night? These tickets were almost impossible to get."

"And yet, here we both are." He laughed, grabbing a glass of champagne off a tray from a circling waiter. "If I had a choice, I'd be somewhere else, but as his brother, I'm expected to show up."

"Ooooooh?" My eyes flashed in surprise.

Jimmy Ferrara was a New York native with dark hair, dark eyes, and a stunning olive complexion. He was a world away from the light-haired, green-eyed, and pale-skinned man standing in front of me now.

He chuckled. "I never get tired of the reaction. I'm adopted. Lachlan." He held out his hand. "Lachlan Ferrara."

"Pleased to meet you." I returned his handshake. "Jessica Dawson."

"Well, Jessica." He held my hand even though we'd stopped shaking, his lips spreading into a grin. "I might not admire what is on the wall, but I am definitely a fan of what's in the room."

"Thank you." I politely extracted my hand. "But I'm here with a date."

While that wasn't technically true—and Lachlan was incredibly handsome—it just didn't feel right to allow him to flirt. And yes, I knew Dave could just as easily be making gaga eyes at someone else at the same exact moment, but I couldn't let that be the reason I pretended to be interested in Lachlan.

Because that's what it would have been.

Pretend.

"Your date is an idiot." He leaned in closer. "There's no way if I was here with you, I'd be anywhere but by your side."

"Maybe my date knows I'm not the kind of woman to be tempted by mysterious strangers," I countered, his compliment saying more about him than it did about me. "Do you travel from gallery to gallery picking up women on your brother's coattails? Or was it just this one?"

"Beautiful and smart, your date *is* a lucky man." He grinned. "But I have to do something to keep myself entertained."

I turned back to the painting, my eyes floating over the canvas as I finished what was left in my glass. I was positive my date didn't consider himself lucky. "Well hopefully you'll have more success with your next target."

My body froze as an arm wrapped around me, a hand gripping my hip.

"Hey, beautiful, what did I miss?" Dave sidled up, pulling me closer as I turned back around.

"I was just talking to the artist's brother, this is Lachlan Ferrara." I introduced the man who, despite my disinterest, hadn't left.

"Dave Larsson." He didn't bother extending his hand, leaving it possessively fixed around my waist. "Your brother is a talented man."

"As is yours." Lachlan raised his glass. "I was just passing the time with your beautiful date."

"*Girlfriend*," Dave corrected him as I tried not to look surprised.

"My apologies, *girlfriend*." Lachlan looked anything but apologetic as he turned to me. "Jessica, it was a pleasure meeting you. Maybe I'll see you in another gallery." He shot me a wink before taking his leave.

"Was he harassing you?" Dave asked coolly, tipping his head in the direction Lachlan had walked.

I shook my head, placing my empty glass on a nearby table. "I had it handled. He might have been flirting, but he was harmless.

At no time did I feel threatened."

"Does that happen a lot at these sort of things?"

He hadn't moved his hand, holding me tight even though Lachlan was no longer watching.

"What?" I lifted my chin, realizing how close we were. "Me feeling threatened?"

He blew out a breath, his gaze locking on mine. "No, men flirting with you."

Was he jealous? Curiosity spiked in me as I folded my arms and narrowed my eyes. "Why don't you tell me, Dave? Do you flirt with a lot of women when you're at these sorts of events?" I tilted my head, waiting for his response.

"I wasn't tonight."

"That wasn't the question."

He didn't need to confirm it; I'd seen him in action. Hell, he'd been on a date the night he'd met me in the coffee shop. So not sure why he had suddenly decided to play coy.

"So, how did your meeting go?" I decided to shake off feelings of him with other women and focus on what I was here to do—be his arm candy.

His gaze softened, a boyish grin spreading across his lips. "Your approach worked, it's the first time he's said more than two words to me."

I squeezed his arm, genuinely pleased. "Good, I'm glad." My eyes moved from his face to where his hands were still on me. "You can let go now, Lachlan left a while ago."

Dave seemed to hesitate but finally let go, sinking his hands into his pockets. "Sorry, old habit."

"Yeah, I guess so." His words feeling like an insult even though he'd probably not meant as one. "You don't have to worry about me, that's why I'm here instead of someone else."

There was no doubt he could have gotten another date, and

to be honest I was surprised he hadn't. But then he didn't want to seem rude, leaving her to wander while he networked. And with me he didn't have to worry.

About leaving me *or* being rude.

"Why don't you come with me?" he suggested, shifting awkwardly on his feet.

I looked around, confused. We were already in the gallery, where the hell did he want to go? "Go *where* with you?"

"To meet people, have conversations." He gestured to the crowd.

If he'd asked me the minute we'd walked in, I'd have probably been excited. Because I was lame and wanted him to want to spend time with me. But his suggestion had come after he'd seen me talking to someone else, which made me feel a little like he didn't want someone else playing with his toys. Not that I was his toy or anyone else's toy—damn it, it was a bad analogy.

"Don't worry, I'm not here to flirt or make you look bad, if that's what you're worried about," I assured him, trying to keep the hurt out of my voice.

His hand reached out, grabbing my arm. "That *wasn't* what I was worried about."

I glared at his hand prompting him to lift it, raising his palm in surrender. "Look, I'm sorry. I need you, okay. I need you to help me with all your insider information."

His honesty made my heart sink. He didn't want me to stand beside him while he chatted and laughed with important people, he wanted my brain. To use me for the information that I could provide him with, which was fair considering I'd used him too. But deep down, I wanted to be more than that.

"Sure, whatever you want. Lead the way." I plastered the smile on my face waiting for him to take the lead.

"Jess."

There was regret in his voice, but I didn't want to hear it. There was no point in him being sorry, he was just sticking to the plan. I was the one who should be sorry.

"It's fine, Dave. Let's go, I'll help you wow them." I slid my arm under his, pretending everything was fine. I'd been doing it a lot lately, so I should have been an expert by now.

His eyes dropped to my arm, standing up straighter. "Let's go."

As we wandered around the gallery it was like I was his chief of staff whispering into the ear of the president.

With his natural charm and my additional insider information, it was no wonder he had everyone eating out of the palm of his hand. And the stellar impression he was making was for more than just being Eric Larsson's brother. And while I was merely performing some duty, after a while it didn't seem so bad. I relaxed into the role, forgetting the obligation and enjoying the evening more than I thought I would.

"Is there a reason you're here with Dave Larsson?" Jeremy startled me, waiting until Dave had gone to the bathroom before sneaking up on me.

Hilary groaned, her hands anchored on her hips like she'd been trying to keep him away. "I told him to mind his own business."

"Thanks, Hilary."

It had been a challenge avoiding the conversation, and I was impressed I'd managed to make it this long. Our paths had crossed a few times over the course of the night, and I could see the vein bulging in Jeremy's forehead with his need to know.

"Dave and I are just friends. I'm helping him network."

For a refreshing change, it was the truth. Although the jury was still out on the *friend* part. But other than networking, there sure as hell wasn't any other reason why we would be together. Especially not now.

Jeremy laughed, the tension in his face fading as he gripped his chest. "Oh thank Christ. For a second I thought you were on a date and I almost had a stroke. But, you being with him is fucking brilliant, it will make sure he meets the right people and doesn't say something stupid. Only person better to hold his hand would be me, but we all know I don't have the patience for that shit."

"He doesn't need his hand held," I shot back defensively, not allowing my boss to take potshots at Dave when he wasn't there to defend himself. "I'm doing this as a friend, but he is more than capable of handling this on his own. You really underestimate him, you know that? "

Jeremy narrowed his eyes, waiting like he was expecting a punch line. When he didn't get one, he did what he always did and tried to smooth it over. "Of course, of course. I'm just saying I'm glad you're here. Makes me worry less."

Hilary sighed, shaking her head at her husband. "You're so giving, Jeremy. I don't know how you haven't been recognized for sainthood yet."

"Probably because I'm not a catholic." He shrugged, answering the question like she'd been seriously wondering why.

Dave returned from the bathroom, seeing Hilary and Jeremy but still put his arm around me. "Hilary, you're looking lovely tonight. You know you're too good for him, right?"

She threw her head back, giggling like a teenager as she slapped his arm playfully. "I'd divorce him, but I've already broken him in. I don't have the energy to start again."

Jeremy rolled his eyes, forcing the smile. "Yeah, yeah. Hilarious. Meanwhile the man is trying to steal my personal assistant *and* flirt with my wife."

"I wasn't flirting with your wife," Dave responded calmly. "The personal assistant part, well the night is still young." He turned to face me. "You ready to go?"

My chest hurt as I sucked in a huge gulp of air, holding it as

I let the words settle. He hadn't meant it—that part about trying to steal me. Instead he was probably just needling Jeremy because he thought it would be funny.

The crowd had already started to thin, with most people making plans to move to some after party I had no interest in attending. And Lachlan had managed to secure two new friends, giving me a wink as he waltzed out the door. "Sure, if you're done?"

"Jeremy, Hilary, we'll see you both later. Let's go." Dave brought me closer and led me to the door.

"You're going to give him a heart attack." I chuckled, glad things weren't as strained between us as when we walked in. "You know he's going to spend the next three hours obsessing whether or not you were serious about stealing me. I hope Hilary didn't have plans for them tonight."

"So let him obsess."

When we stepped outside, *Riff Raff*—the old doorman—had disappeared. The two younger guys who'd replaced him were pulling valet duty with startling efficiency. If only I could implement the same system to my life, maybe I wouldn't be in this mess. Although, to be fair, parking a Porsche three streets over and then bringing it back was a hell of a lot easier than unraveling my chaos.

Dave handed over his ticket, one of the guys disappearing to retrieve his car.

"I'll see you next time you're in the office." I gave him a quick hug, pulling away before I did something stupid like lay my head on his chest. I distracted myself further by fishing inside of my clutch for my phone.

My hug surprised him, his hands not having time to react as I pulled away, his eyes still wide as he watched me silently.

"Ma'am, you have a ticket?" one of the valets asked, wrongly assuming I was looking for my stub.

I pulled out my phone and waved it victoriously. "Ah, no.

Thanks. I'm just going to get a cab."

"You're not getting a cab, I can drive you home." Dave didn't so much as offer as declared, finding his voice as his black BMW pulled up to the curb.

The valet hopped out, standing at the driver's side while Dave held open the passenger's side door, ignoring everyone but me.

"Are you sure? I don't want you going out of your way." I hesitated.

I'd wanted nothing more than to be alone with him the whole night. And in my head, I had imagined the conversation, asking him if we could find our way back to friends. I knew things were irrevocably changed, and it wouldn't be the same as it had been before, but I hoped there'd be a chance to find something new. Through the evening I'd seen glimpses, small windows of hope that I held onto, praying it wouldn't slip through my fingers like sand.

His arm rested on the door waiting for me, his voice was so sincere. "It's not out of my way. It would be my pleasure."

"Okay," I agreed, hoping to God I wasn't pushing my luck too far for one night. After all, we had managed to get through most of the evening acting fairly cordial, I didn't want to ruin it at the end.

I slipped into the seat and he shut the door, walking around the driver's side and hopped in. The car pulled away from the gallery, the engine rumbling as we merged into traffic.

It was so familiar, the two of us being in a car together, going home after a night out. Even though we'd only shared it briefly in Shreveport, it was amazing how good it felt sitting beside him.

And then I remembered, we weren't going home together, and things weren't the same.

No, I wouldn't allow something like reality affect my mood, watching his hands locked around the steering wheel as I indulged my stupid fantasy.

"What are you thinking about?" Dave speared me with a look

before returning his eyes to the road.

My back relaxed against the seat, stretching out my arms in front of me. "Who says I'm thinking about anything?"

He laughed, pulling his lips into a smirk. "You have a *look*."

"Well you're wrong. I wasn't thinking about anything. My mind was totally blank." I did my best to neutralize my face, annoyed it had betrayed me in the first place.

His eyes cut back to the road and I could tell he didn't believe me, choosing to drop it as he continued to drive in silence.

And suddenly the situation had become very real.

With the date now completed, all our transactions were finished.

There was no reason to see him outside of work—no more obligations to fill—and that thought alone was enough to terrify me.

Our relationship—both real and fake—was well and truly over.

CHAPTER #23

THE ENERGY IN the car only intensified by the time we'd gotten to my apartment. Not entirely sure what an appropriate goodbye would be, but I reached across and gave him an awkward one-armed hug.

"Enjoy the rest of the weekend," I said, sounding like I had just bagged his groceries and was giving him the change.

His arms—both of them—wrapped around me and stopped me from leaving. "Don't," he whispered, bringing his face closer. "Don't pretend with me."

I should have mumbled something incoherent, said goodbye and got the hell out of Dodge while I still had possession of my faculties. That would have been the smart thing to do. Instead I lifted my eyes—bad move.

He was so close, every part of him overwhelming me in the tiny space of the car.

"Dave." I said his name because I wasn't capable of saying much else.

He brought his mouth closer, skirting the edges of my lips. He didn't kiss me though, just hovered, driving me crazy. "Invite me in."

It was a bad idea.

Terrible.

Completely the wrong thing to do.

"You want to come into my apartment?" I asked like a moron because stalling for two minutes while I got clarification would suddenly make it easier to resist him.

"Just to talk, I promise." His thumb caressed my cheek, not convincing me it was talking he had on his mind. "But either way, we need to be done with this bullshit between us."

On that, we could agree.

I wanted the chance to apologize and see if there was a way to set it right. I wasn't sure how I was going to do that, but I knew getting out of the car and leaving things as they were wasn't an option.

"Dave, come inside with me."

He slowly released me, taking away his beautiful lips as he undid his seatbelt. I quickly undid mine, exiting the car, hoping the night air might clear my head.

It didn't.

He was out of the car, stalking toward me when I turned and headed to the courtyard. I couldn't stop, scared that without the restraints the car had provided us, I wouldn't be able to resist touching him. So instead I quickly opened the gate, climbing the steps to my first floor apartment like the heavy footsteps behind me were that of an assailant I was trying to outrun.

My key slipped into the lock and I twisted the knob, saying a silent prayer before I opened the door.

Please Lord, whatever happens, don't make it any worse.

He was right behind me as I entered, shutting the door as I turned on the light.

Being in the dark wasn't smart. It would have made it too easy to forget we were there to have a conversation, and instead find my way back to his lips. Talking was so overrated anyway, and I missed kissing him so damn much.

"I'm sorry." It rushed out of my mouth before I had a chance to chicken out.

He took a step forward, closing the gap between us. "What are you sorry for exactly?"

"For everything. It was a stupid fucking idea."

I wanted to grab him, pull him close and forget the past week. For him to touch me like he did in that hotel room in Shreveport, to have permission to touch him back.

"No, Jessica. You need to be specific." His hands cradled my chin, lifting it so he could look in my eyes. "Are you sorry we had sex?"

"No." I answered without hesitation. "I could never regret that. And I'm not sorry for the time we spent together. But I am sorry I lied to my family, to you, and most of all to myself. It wasn't supposed to be like this, I never intended to feel this way."

His head dipped, his nose skating mine. I was positive he wasn't trying to seduce me but my hormones didn't much care for his intention. "I'm sorry too."

It was like a slap sobering me, my feet taking a step back as my eyes widened. "What are you sorry for?"

He dropped his hands from my chin and raked them through his hair. "Take your pick. For being a prick, for wanting to hurt you, but most of all for agreeing to walk away."

I wasn't sure what that all meant—especially the part about him agreeing to walk away—and I would get to all of that in a minute. But the *hurt* part stuck out the most.

"You wanted to hurt me?"

I knew he was angry, and I wouldn't have blamed him if he hated me, but I never thought he was capable of wanting to hurt me.

"Yes. I was so fucking mad." He shook his head, gritting out the words from his clenched jaw. "I couldn't believe that after everything, you would still go through with that bullshit. And I know you had your reasons, and to you they were valid, but none of it made sense."

"I know that, I was just—"

"Jessica, please let me finish." His finger rested on my lips. "Asking me to break up with you sucked. I hated it. I hated saying all those lies in front of your family and pretending I could leave you without giving a shit. But what killed me more was that you still thought of us as a transaction. Like nothing had changed. *Everything* had changed, Jess. It wasn't a job to me. *You* were not a fucking job. You shut me out, and you wouldn't even consider an alternative. In the end, I wasn't even sure if you gave a shit."

"I had to." My voice louder than I'd intended it to be. "Dave, she was going to die and if she believed—"

"If she believed what, Jessica? I know you've convinced yourself that if she believed you were miserable, she would stick around. But did you ever think maybe you were doing more harm? She's not an idiot, and she deserved the truth. We both did. Which was why I wanted to *hurt* you. I wanted you to feel how fucking horrible I felt."

"Don't think for a second it was easy for me." The tears welled in my eyes even though I promised myself I wouldn't cry. "I was desperate. I would have tried anything. And I wasn't sure what you felt."

His eyes widened, stepping back like I'd punched him in the face. "Jesus, Jess. I'm not that good an actor."

My mind swam, trying to sort out my feelings and thoughts while still trying to remain upright. He'd asked me not to go through with it—that we would find another way—but I hadn't wanted to hear. I couldn't. I'd just assumed that a relationship that had started out pretend would be destined to fail anyway, so why prolong the suffering.

"I was scared, okay?" I stalled out, not sure anything I was going to say was going to come out right. "We were pretending and then we weren't. And I wanted to believe you felt the same way but I wasn't sure, and I was too scared to ask. And maybe I was stupid, and using my grandma was an excuse, because admitting to you that I was falling in love with you was almost as terrifying as losing her. My heart wouldn't have been able to take it if you didn't feel the same way."

I hated my vulnerability, exposing myself so much that there was literally nothing more to hide. But it was too late, my mouth had opened and I wasn't able to make it stop.

My parents had raised me to be strong, resilient, and self-reliant. It was how I was able to leave the cocoon of my hometown and come to L.A. with a badass attitude and drive to succeed. I didn't think I *needed* anyone. But those days with Dave showed me how wrong I had been, and I needed and wanted him so goddamn much my heart hurt without him. It was easier to shatter it on my own terms than leave it in danger of being torn apart.

His lips came crushing down on mine before I had a chance to continue, pulling me against him as he hauled me off the ground. "Fuck, Jess. I think I started falling in love with you that night at the coffee shop."

I couldn't speak, losing myself in his kiss as my fingers clawed at him, needing to be closer than I felt I could get.

"I'm sorry, I'm so sorry." I mumbled it again and again against his lips, wishing I could go back and undo all the hurt.

He lowered me, brushing his fingers against my lips and silencing me. "No more apologies, we've wasted enough time, okay?"

I nodded, my arms still wrapped around him, scared to let go.

"No more wasted time."

His hand brushed against my hair, holding me close to his body as his lips brushed against my neck. "Does this mean we're making up?"

"No," I shook my head. "It means we're starting over. No more pretending, no more lies. I want you, and I want you to have me."

I felt his lips touch my skin so gently, and it wasn't enough. I was needy, wanting more of him on me as I grabbed his shirt in my hands and bunched it in my fists. "No more games, Dave. I want it to be for real this time."

"It was *real* the first time."

I didn't get a chance to respond. His lips claimed mine, kissing me like I'd always been his. My mouth opened, letting him in as his tongue stroked mine. I moaned, moving my hands up his chest and threading them through his hair as he gripped my ass.

There was more of the conversation that needed to happen, but I didn't care and just wanted him to kiss me.

"I need you," I moaned, unashamed of how much I wanted him at that moment. "I need you so goddamn much."

He didn't stop, his lips moving across my mouth to my neck as he kissed and licked my skin, neither of us able to get enough. "You have me. I'm right here."

"Are you still mad?" I asked, my fingers desperately sliding off his jacket.

He lowered me slowly, my feet touching the floor before he turned his attention to his shirt and yanked at it. Buttons went flying as he pulled the two halves apart, stripping it from his body and dumping it on the carpet. My fingers floated over his naked skin, touching the smooth firm muscles of his chest.

"It would be impossible to stay mad at you." He swept me off my feet, carrying me to the sofa.

My body bounced as he dropped me onto the cushions, toeing

off his shoes before covering me with his body. "Fuck, I've missed you," he groaned into the curve of my neck.

"I've missed you too." I kissed him, my fingers scrambling with the zipper at my side in an effort to get naked.

He took over, lowering it the rest of the way, bunching the fabric at the seam and lifting it over my head. He hovered above me, staring down at me as I lay in my underwear.

His eyes darkened as he dipped his head, lowering his mouth to the swell of my breasts and kissed each one. I writhed underneath him, feeling the familiar pull at the base of my gut as my body tingled. "Take it off." I moaned as he kneaded my breast through the lace, teasing me with his tongue and teeth.

Nodding, his hands disappeared, flicking free the clasp of my bra, the lace going slack against my skin. With his teeth he lifted it off, tossing it aside before returning his mouth to my nipples to worship them.

My hands fumbled with the front of his pants, wanting to get them off.

"Impatient." He laughed against my skin, lifting his body so I could unbutton them and lower the zipper.

I kicked off my heels while he lowered his pants, his hard cock straining against the front of his boxer briefs. My hand pressed against the bulge, rubbing up and down his length until he groaned in frustration.

"Impatient." I smirked back.

He stripped off in a rush and dumped his clothes on the floor before turning his attention to my panties.

His eyes feasted on my body as his fingers looped around the waistband and slid them down my legs. He leaned back on his heels, taking a moment to admire what was in front of him.

"Kiss me," I groaned, reaching across and pulling him toward me, his mouth landing on my thigh. My body wiggled, loving the feel of his lips on my skin as his fingers brushed against my pussy.

"So wet." He plunged a finger inside, making my back bow off the sofa. He took that as an invitation and added another, thumbing my clit as I rocked my hips.

"More, more," I panted, his hands not enough for me as I lifted into a sitting position and grabbed his cock. "I need more of you."

He continued to pump with his fingers while I stroked him, alternating between watching his hand and watching mine.

"Please tell me you have condoms in this place." He pulled out his fingers and brought them to his mouth. His eyelids dropped to half-mast as his lips curled around them, savoring what I'd given him as he pushed up to his feet and stood above me.

It was sexy and seductive and it was driving me crazy. "Give me a second." I leapt off the sofa, annoyed I hadn't stashed some protection in my purse, and ran to my bedroom. I carried the pack back to the living room like a conquering hero.

"Good, you brought the box." He grabbed it from my fingers, pulling one out and opening it with his teeth. I watched hungrily as he rolled it down his length and gave himself a stroke.

"Jessica." His hands lost interest in his erection, planting themselves on my hips as he guided me back to the sofa. He sat, pulling me down onto his lap and kissing me.

"What do you want?" he growled, the head of his cock rubbed against my opening, teasing me as I twisted against him. "Because I want you to ride me right now until you don't know your own name."

"Yes," I panted, reaching down between us and lining him up. With a single thrust, I pushed down hard, taking his entire length. I gasped, my body not fully ready and needing a moment to adjust.

"You okay, beautiful?" His lips pressed against my forehead, holding my hips still with his hands.

I nodded, slowly grinding against him as my body heated from the inside. With my fingers clamped on his shoulders, I rocked against him, slow and steady, watching his face as I rode him.

"That's it," he encouraged, pulling me down on him harder and deeper as I picked up speed.

Every part of me tingled as I lost myself in the rhythm, feeling myself climb higher as he filled me again and again. "Fuck me, Jess." His lips curled around my breast, sucking hard as I rocked. "Fuck. Me."

My orgasm tackled me from behind, racing up my spine and overwhelming me in a rush. I collapsed against him, breathing heavy against his neck as he continued to thrust. He was so hard, stretching me as he drove into me again and again.

"Fuck," he shouted, wrapping his arms around me and pulling me against his chest, his cock pulsing as he exploded in me.

I couldn't move, the waves of pleasure washing over me as I panted against him. His arms were like a cage, holding me prisoner as he kissed my neck.

"That was probably a little more than just talking, wasn't it?" He laughed against my skin. "I guess tonight I'm the liar."

I lifted my head, focusing on his beautiful eyes as I kissed him on the lips. "I don't think you got here on your own, buddy. And I wasn't interested in just talking."

"Ah, I see." He smirked, his hands moving up my back in a soft caress. "You were just using me for my body."

"No, I never used you for that." My hands locked around his face holding it still. "When it was just us, it was just us. It wasn't an act."

A smile edged across his lips. "I know." He dropped a quick peck on my lips. "Why don't we move this to the bedroom. I don't think either of us are done just yet."

My feet dropped to the floor as I lifted off him, his eyes followed the lines of my body as I stood.

"I will never get tired of that view, you're fucking stunning." He shook his head as he joined me on his feet. "And I'm the luckiest bastard alive right now."

I was just about to argue that I was the lucky one when my phone rang, the clutch I'd dropped on the coffee table when we'd walked in, vibrating across the surface.

"Why don't you get that and I'll get a shower started." He playfully swatted me on the ass. "And if it's Jeremy, tell him to fuck off, he can survive one night without you."

I smirked, watching him walk toward my bedroom as I picked up my clutch and dug out my cell. The caller ID made my heart stop, the bold capital letters on the screen spelling out MOM.

"Mom?" I answered, almost fumbling the phone and dropping it. I pressed it against my ear, and said her name again.

"Hey, baby."

She sound tired, completely wrung out, making my pulse spike.

"Is it Gran?"

Ice filled my veins as I dropped to my knees, hearing words I knew eventually would come, but I hadn't been ready to hear. She wasn't gone yet, but she didn't have much time left.

I tossed the phone aside, racing across to my desk, sinking into my chair and turned on my laptop. It was late but if I could get on a flight to anywhere, I was going to book it. I didn't care if I had to fly to Atlanta and drive from there, the alternative of not going was not negotiable.

"Book two tickets." A voice came from behind, Dave's hand gently brushing the hair off my shoulders. "I'm coming too."

"Dave, you don't have to. This is going to be intense and I haven't had time to explain to my family . . ." Visions of my brothers laying into him the minute he walked through the door made me want to puke. "It's probably better you don't."

He took my chin in his hands and kissed me deeply before pulling back. "Better for who? Certainly not for you. I don't give a shit what they think or what they're going to do, you are not doing this alone."

"Travis is probably going to want to take a piece out of you." I shook my head, terrified not only of losing my gran but the family drama that would erupt the minute we walked through the door. No man would put up with that kind of crazy, and it was too soon to worry about losing him. Not when I had just got him back.

Dave turned me toward him, shaking his head as his finger traced my jaw. "You think I haven't been in a fight before? You know I have *four* brothers, right? It was like a constant cage fight in our living room so I can handle anything your brother throws at me. What I can't handle is watching you get on a plane, knowing you're going to need me, and me not being there. Book the tickets, Jess, I'll go get dressed."

There was no more time to argue, precious moments ticking away as I tried to find a flight.

"Damn it." I stared at the screen, the time difference and the distance making it almost impossible to get home as quick as I needed.

"Try Houston." Dave was back, fully clothed minus the buttons on the front of his shirt. "It's not that much further."

I could get us on a United flight just after one in the morning. It would land in Houston shortly after six. Then driving the four hours to Shreveport. It wasn't ideal but we were running out of options.

"I'm going to go grab some clothes and pack a bag real quick." He watched as my fingers booked the flight. "I'll be back as soon as I can and we'll head to the airport."

I nodded, watching him dash out the door while I printed the ticket confirmation. The next step was to get dressed and pack, the latter consisting of grabbing random shit and tossing it into an overnight bag and hoping for the best. It would be potluck on what actually made it in, my concern getting out the door and not whether or not I had matching socks.

With my bag packed, I sat on my mussed up sheets and waited.

I didn't know what I needed but I needed to do something to keep my mind busy until I could get to her. So I started reciting my truth.

The one where I told her everything—the lie, finding Dave, and then letting him go. I didn't care anymore about saving face or if my actions made me look like the dumbest person alive.

I *was* the dumbest person alive.

Not only had I lied to someone I'd loved my entire life *and* to the new love I'd found, but also to myself.

I closed my eyes and for the first time in a long time I really prayed.

I prayed with all my heart that whatever happened, I got there in time.

Not only to say goodbye, but to finally tell her the truth.

CHAPTER #24

I ALMOST HAD no recollection of the flight or the road trip, muscle memory enabled me to walk, talk and breathe—going through the motions until we finally arrived at my Aunt JoAnn's house around ten thirty. My heart thumped in my chest as I stared at the front door, scrambling to get out of the car and terrified we had gotten there too late.

The driveway was filled with vehicles, and I knew just about everyone I ever loved was standing on the other side of the door. Thankfully there was also someone I loved standing beside me, Dave putting his hand around my waist as my trembling hand hit the buzzer.

It felt like my bones had disintegrated under my skin, my body sagging under its own weight as he held me tight and supported me.

The look on my aunt's face when she answered the door was enough to tear me apart.

"Jessica." Spoken with such anguish, I actually hated the sound of my own name.

"Is it too late? Did I miss—"

She pushed open the door, beckoning us inside as she shook her head. "She's holding on, but she's very weak."

Her glare fell on Dave but thankfully she didn't say anything. Stepping aside so we could both walk past and no doubt saving her choice words for another time.

"What the hell is he doing here?" Travis's voice boomed the minute we'd stepped into the living room. "Dalton, you want to help me take this shithead outside?"

"It will be a pleasure." My older brother stood, cracking his knuckles as he came toward us.

The room was packed with members of my family camped out in chairs, sofas and even on the floor. Every set of eyes turned toward us, their attention on Dave as they quieted down to a hush, probably expecting a showdown in my aunt's living room.

"You need to stop." I put my hand up, my eyes flicking between my two brothers. "I will explain everything, but not now."

"No need for you to do anything, little sis. We'll take Dave out for a little chat, and he can *explain* whatever needs to be explained." Dalton might have lowered his hands but his posture still meant business.

Travis laughed as he continued to advance. "Yeah, we just want to talk to him."

Dave stepped in front of me, his body separating me from my brothers when he was the only one in danger. "Go see your grandma, I'll handle your brothers."

"No, no one is handling anything." I grabbed his arm, knowing the only reason they wanted to tear him apart was because of me. It was my fault and even though I was positive he could hold his own, I didn't want any more people to get hurt.

"He didn't break up with me," I spat out, needing for everyone to know the truth. "I broke up with him, and then made him pretend like it was his fault. So shelve the macho bullshit, because if there is anyone who acted like an asshole, it was me."

"Jessica?" My mom wandered into the living room, her eyes

doing a quick survey of the room.

I turned, throwing my arms around her. "Hey, Mom. I got here as soon as I could."

Her hand patted my back while she kept her gaze fixed on Dave. "I know, baby. Why don't you go see Gran, and we'll talk later."

I nodded, grabbing Dave's hand to pull him into the hall, his body resisting against my tug. "You go, I want you to have time with her, and I'll be waiting for you right here."

I glanced at my brothers who hadn't returned to their seats, me taking responsibility for the breakup doing nothing to diffuse the tension.

"Go." Dave kissed me gently on the lips. "I've got this."

Instinct screamed at me to go to my gran but I hated leaving him in the lion's den. "If they do anything—" I said it loud enough for everyone to hear.

"They won't. Go, everything else can wait."

Shaking my head—and trusting my brothers not to behave like animals—I left them in the living room and walked down the hall to Gran's room.

My sister Melanie was sitting in my grandfather's rocking chair beside the bed, her hand on her swollen belly as she dabbed away tears. "Jessica, sweetie, you must have been traveling all night."

"It's okay, how is she?" I tipped my head to the bed, Gran's eyes remaining closed.

Melanie stood, walking over to me, rubbing my arm as she gave me the rundown. Gran had been sleeping a lot, waking occasionally, but became tired after the conversation. She gave my hand a quick squeeze before she left, giving me some time to be with Gran alone.

My head hung low on my neck, the weight of my thoughts crushing me as I stared at her frail wrinkled hands, unconsciously reaching for her as my eyes welled.

"Jessica." Her voice croaked like she'd swallowed a bag full of marbles, her fingers doing their best to close around mine.

"Hey, Gran." I forced myself not to cry. "I just wanted to sit and keep you company, if that's okay with you."

"Of course." Her lips did their best to spread into a smile, but she seemed exerted by the effort. "Talk to me a spell, I love hearing your stories."

It felt like there was a boot crushing my chest as I struggled to take a breath, the slow drag in and out making my lungs burn. But blinking away the tears, I opened my mouth and found it miraculously still knew what to do, words coming slowly at first until they found a sense of rhythm.

I told her everything, all about how I'd lied when I thought she would no longer be with us. How it led to my stupid intricate plan, and how I'd recruited Dave to play the part of my fake boyfriend. As the words spewed out, I felt liberated, stripping away all the layers I'd fabricated since that terrible initial lie.

I confessed how much I had fallen for Dave, how incredibly stupid I was for breaking up with him, and how glad I was we were getting another chance.

When I'd finally petered out—no words or confessions left to be said—I looked into her pale blues eyes and hoped I wouldn't see disappointment.

"Sweet child." Her soft gray lashes closed. "I love you so very much. But when you get to be my age, you get to know a thing or two." She tried to laugh, her breath wheezing like a car that wouldn't start.

"Gran?"

The air seeped slowly from her lips as her eyes flickered open. "One look at the both of you and I could see you were crazy in love with each other. It doesn't matter how it came to be, there wasn't a doubt in my mind that he was the one for you."

"But Gran, I *hired* him. And when it was time to break up, I let him believe that it had all been pretend." Just saying the word made me disgusted, I could only imagine what he must have felt.

"The night he left, he came to see me in my room. He knocked so quietly on the door I thought I had dreamt it at first." She patted my hand, working hard to get the words out. "He sat down beside me and thanked me. When I asked what for, he said that I had been the push you both needed to uncover what was already there. He also told me that no matter what happened between you, he'd never stop caring for you."

"What?" The air pushed out of me in a rush. "Why didn't you tell me?"

She turned her head, doing her best to focus. "Because love is one of the things a person has to come to on their own. I loved your granddaddy, and I've missed him every day since he's been gone. He was such a good man, Jessica, and I hope that you and Dave have the kind of love we had." She closed her eyes, her chest falling heavily after a breath. "Oh, I'm so tired. I think I just need a little more sleep."

As she settled back on her pillow, her breathing evened out and she fell asleep. There was more I wanted to ask her about the night Dave had left, but what little she was able to say had already wiped her out. I sat a little longer, taking comfort in the rise and fall of her chest.

I wasn't sure how long I'd been in the room, desperately committing every line of her face to memory. It was only after I felt a hand on my shoulder that I'd realized I'd fallen asleep.

"Hey." Dave thumbed my cheek. "You want some company?"

My eyes opened as I reached up to his face, twisting it both ways to carefully examine him for any obvious marks. "Are you okay?"

He chuckled, brushing his lips against mine as I held his face. "You know, not all men settle things with their fists. We just talked, Jessica. Everyone is fine."

"I'm so glad." I breathed a sigh of relief. "Help me up, I need to stand."

Dave held out his hand as I slowly rose from the chair. My body was stiff, my muscles protesting as I stretched, my eyes making sure Gran was still okay while I regained the circulation in my limbs.

"You want to stay or do you want to go out for a bit?" Dave's arms wrapped around me. "I think there are a few people who would like some time with her too."

I nodded, turning into his body as I reached up to kiss him. "I should let someone else sit with her."

Giving Gran one final look, we walked to the door. We hadn't gotten more than a foot outside when my one of my aunts slipped in past us, giving us a smile as she took my spot.

We were almost back in the living room when Dave stopped suddenly and turned. "I need you to know something, before we go back in."

My throat constricted, not sure what he was going to say. "What do you need me to know?"

"You're not in this alone. And I didn't come here because you asked me to pretend with you, or offered to pay me, or out of some stupid sense of obligation. Never, Jess. Not even the first time. I need you to know I'm here because I want to, and because there is nowhere else I'd rather be."

I gripped the front of his shirt, losing the battle with the tears I'd managed to keep at bay. "I don't know what I did to deserve you, but I promise, I will never take it for granted."

He lowered his lips to mine and kissed me, holding me against his chest while I tried to compose myself. My heart was simultaneously breaking for the loss I knew was inevitable, and rejoicing for the love I'd found.

Wiping away my tears, and after taking a deep breath, we walked back into the living room. Family were floating in and out, eating sandwiches on paper plates while talking in low voices. It was the quietest family get together I'd ever seen, and somehow, the lack of noise made it worse.

We all knew, bracing ourselves for the impact that was coming but trying to keep a brave face. And I couldn't stand it any longer.

"So, I lied." I stood in the middle of the living room, everyone's attention suddenly on me. Not that I'd given them much choice, short of getting a bullhorn and holding up a sign, my raised voice had easily carried over the muted chatter.

Dave's hand threaded through mine, squeezing tightly. "You don't have to do this."

"Yes, yes I do." I turned, finding a smile as I looked into his eyes. "I *need* to do this."

It was difficult to face my family, to admit to the charade, but more than that, admit that I had pretended to be something I wasn't. And it didn't matter what my intentions were. Because I'd hurt more people with the lie than I ever could if I'd just told the truth.

That wasn't who I was, at least, not who I wanted to be.

Pushing my emotions to the side, I did what I should have done the minute I'd received my cousin's wedding invitation. Every stupid decision I'd made, every little white lie, every deceit, was laid bare. I cut myself open and bled in front of them just as I'd done with Gran. And as my burden lifted, I felt myself get lighter, no longer worried about the silence.

I'd wear the consequences, I'd take their anger, their hurt, their distrust—I'd take it all and pay whatever penance they believed I'd deserve.

Because I couldn't let another second pass without owning my truth.

I waited.

And waited.

And waited some more.

But those words of condemnation, of hate, of anger just didn't come. I was hugged, and there were tears, and even poked fun at a little. But the concerns I'd had didn't eventuate, with my family loving me all the same.

And after all the hugging and crying was done, Dave and I snuck out to the porch and found a moment for ourselves.

"I am the biggest idiot alive." I buried my head in his chest, taking the first full breath since we'd left L.A. "You need to know that, because if we're going to date, I don't want you to be surprised if I make other questionable decisions."

"What do you mean *if* we're going to date? I didn't think it was a question." He dropped a kiss on the top of my head as his strong arms engulfed me.

Tentatively, I lifted my head trying not to cringe. "Well, I'm giving you the opportunity to change your mind. Just in case you've gotten your fill of crazy and want to go find a nice girl who isn't insane."

"And miss all of this. My first starring role as a lead?" He held out his hands, his face lit up with excitement.

I jabbed him in the ribs, not forgetting what he'd told his brother. "I thought you said the director was an asshole?"

"Maybe I like asshole directors?" He laughed. "They seem to get the best out of me."

"God." My head fell in my hands. "Do we really have to tell your family?"

Not to mention my boss.

And Katrina.

And Liz.

Ugh.

I groaned, "I am such an idiot."

"Think of how hilarious this is going to be when we're eighty and sitting on a porch just like this." He wrapped his arms around me. "And besides, what would be the alternative? We'd still be flirting with each other across a desk. You'd probably be dating some boring guy you couldn't stand, and I'd be wasting time playing dating roulette."

"My guy might not have been boring. Lachlan at the gallery seemed interesting enough." I tipped my chin in defiance.

I mean, he *was* right. In the last couple of years, I'd had more interesting nights with a glass of water and an Ambien than I'd had on most dates. But I wasn't about to admit that.

He brushed my hair back, kissing my neck before responding. "Lachlan at the gallery was a tool, and there is no universe where he'd ever be good enough for you. And yeah, I was jealous but that wasn't the reason I wanted you with me that night. I wanted you by my side because that's the way it's meant to be. It was always supposed to be us."

"Well then, someone is going to need to break it to all your *many* female friends. There will be a trail of broken hearts all the way down Hollywood Boulevard."

He'd made no secret of his casual love life prior to our fake / real relationship. And while I didn't doubt his fidelity, I was positive there was probably more than one woman who would mourn the loss. He wasn't an easy man to let go. Lord knows I hadn't been able to.

"And you honestly believe that I'd be interested in any of them now that I have you? But if it makes you feel better I will call every single one of them and let them know my current relationship status." His hand slipped from me and dove into his pocket, trying to fish out his phone.

"Please, I said I was an idiot but thankfully I'm not *that* needy."

I yanked his arm, stopping him from pulling out his cell.

He laughed, leaving his phone safely where it was and dropped a soft kiss on my lips. "No calls then, but you need to stop calling yourself an idiot. I won't have you talking about my girlfriend in that way."

"*Girlfriend*," I tried the word out, testing how it felt as I said it out loud. I liked the way it sounded, probably more so when he was the one saying it.

I followed his eyes as they returned to the screen door. It was only a couple of feet, and almost felt wrong that we were laughing and joking while on the other side of that door there was so much pain.

"I'm glad we had this." I was the first one to speak. "I know we don't have much time, and are going to have to be back in there soon, but I'm glad we were able to take the minute."

"Me too. We didn't do a lot of talking at your apartment."

"No, we didn't." I bit my lip, feeling guilty for thinking about our memorable reunion at a time like this. "But I don't regret it. That *or* this."

Brushing myself off, he helped me to my feet and we walked back inside.

I'd expected the same sober mood we'd left—and I wasn't sure if it was my confessional, the food, or something else—but thankfully it wasn't so quiet anymore. People were talking and there were even a few laughs—the noise and the bustle more what I'd expected from my family when they were all packed in together.

And while it gave us all a false sense of everything being okay, I knew no one was fooled. But it was what we needed, allowing us to find a way to honor a woman who thrived on a house filled with people. Which was exactly what we did. Until nine fifty that night, when Gran took her last breath.

Her memory though, would always be with me.

I was in the arms of the most honest man I'd ever met, and had promised to never let him go.

He'd whispered that he loved me possibly a million times that night, and I'd return his I-love-yous at least a million and two.

But I realized that night that my number one lie hadn't been my fake relationship, the whole stupid charade, or even our manufactured breakup.

It had been the day I looked into Dave's kind loving eyes all those years ago and ignored the whisper in my heart that told me he was my one.

Lucky for me, I was a terrible liar.

EPILOGUE

JEREMY HAD BEEN more understanding than I'd expected—proving he had a heart—organizing Katrina to cover for me and telling me to take as much time as I needed. He'd even shuffled things around for Dave so he didn't have to leave either. Of course that happened *after* the stream of swear words had come out of his mouth when I told him Dave and I were dating.

To say he wasn't pleased was an understatement, giving me a million reasons on why he thought it was a terrible idea and how bad it would be for business. Which was when I offered to resign, solving any issues of impropriety, leaving Dave and I to date with no restrictions.

He suddenly decided it wouldn't be that big a deal.

We stayed in Shreveport until the day after the funeral, kissing my family goodbye and promising to come back soon. It would be different from here on out and not because Gran was gone.

I was different, and I liked the change.

"So you hired Dave to be your boyfriend and then fell in love with him?" Liz looked at me with a mix of awe and surprise. "Girl, here I've been wasting my time picking up men at parties when really I should just be setting up auditions. I think I might have found my new approach."

My body shook as I laughed, glancing at my boyfriend who

was walking toward us with his brother Nick. "Yeah, maybe don't take dating advice from me. I think our story is more of an example of what *not* to do."

"Jessica." Nick smirked, throwing an arm around me because he knew it pissed off his brother. "I can't say I'm surprised you decided to settle down with a Larsson, pity you picked the wrong one."

I gave him a quick squeeze before moving toward Dave. "I think you'll find, I very much picked the *right* one."

"Funny how she had the same opportunity to date you and never bothered." Dave shrugged, not taking Nick's bait. "You might have also noticed that she picked me for the acting part *and* the relationship, pretty much proof of my superiority in all areas, little bro."

While parts of our history still made me cringe, we didn't try to hide it either. Why bother? The truth eventually always came out, and there was no way to keep track of which version everyone knew.

So there was only one version—the one we were both living.

"Maybe Liz and I should date?" Nick winked at my friend, blinding her with his famous flirty grin.

She rolled her eyes, shaking her head. "Nice try, Larsson. But I am sworn off actors, too much ego. I need to find me a regular guy, someone who isn't going to act like a diva because I'm more successful than him."

"Not all of us have egos," Dave added, wrapping his arms around me and giving me a kiss. "But we can't help it if we're amazing. I mean, I could have started my own cult down in Shreveport. Still not convinced it isn't a good idea."

Liz laughed. "And I rest my case."

"Nah, Liz is right," Nick agreed. "You can't have two famous people."

"You can't have two famous people for what?" Katrina joined

us, followed by Matt. Then again, there weren't many places he wouldn't follow her and it was adorable how smitten they were with each other.

Katrina no longer lusting after my boyfriend made the situation easier. It wasn't like I needed help making things awkward, so that was a positive.

"Liz and Nick need to find "regular" people to date because apparently two famous people doesn't work out. Egos," I explained, grinning at Dave.

He laughed, kissing me on the neck and not caring who saw. "Yeah, it was my big *ego* that you fell in love with."

Liz smirked, pointing at Dave. "See what I mean, he's just like the rest of us."

The plan had been to have dinner and drinks before heading to Eric's. Dave had already told his family, so at least it wasn't going to be a huge surprise, but I wasn't sure if they were all going to be as accepting as Nick.

Roman didn't seem to like anyone, so I wasn't expecting much from him. But Eric and I had always been amicable, so the last thing I wanted was for him to believe . . . I don't know, that I'd manipulated Dave?

"Your table is ready." The hostess smiled with a wave of a hand. "We have you set up in our private dining room, we wouldn't want you disturbed while you're enjoying dinner."

"Gotta love the perks." Nick grinned, following the hostess as we continued through the restaurant toward the back.

While I hadn't requested the private dining room, with three recognizable faces in our party, I guess it sort of made sense. Not that I was complaining, but in a city literally filled with celebrities, we'd managed to have dinner other times and never needed the extra precautions.

Maybe it *was* an ego thing?

Who knew.

Regardless, I was determined to enjoy a relaxing evening with friends before obsessing about the rest of Dave's family. As much as I would love to pretend I wasn't nervous, my new vow of honesty had meant I'd stopped lying to myself.

The hostess stood at the doorway and smiled. "Here you go."

If anyone else thought it was odd that she was directing us to a room and dumping us, they didn't show it. Each of them stepped inside ahead of us, like it was the most natural thing to do. And not that I'd expected someone to personally seat us or anything, but I'd assumed she would have at least walked us to our table and maybe taken a drink order.

"Could you have picked a place any more pretentious?"

My body froze at the sound of Roman's voice.

Dave didn't miss a beat, putting his arm around me as he guided me through the door. "Well, in order for us to invite you, we needed to find an establishment that allowed pets. No offense, Lauren."

"None, taken." The petite brunette standing next to Roman smiled.

Roman laughed, slapping his brother on the back. "Well, if anyone would know a place that served the finest canine cuisine, it would be you."

And if it had just been Roman and his girlfriend in the room, I might have been able to recover.

But, no.

No. Such. Luck.

"I have to say, I'm a little offended." Eric tipped his head to the two of us. His look turned serious as he leveled his stare at me. "I have an Academy award and you still casted *him* as your pretend boyfriend? It's because I'm blond, right?" His mouth edged into a grin.

"Jesus." I managed to squeak out, feeling the air return to my lungs. "I swear you guys are killing me."

Dave flipped his older brother off. "Big shot, you wouldn't have stood a chance. That role was mine, I owned it."

Tia, Eric's wife, slung her arm around her husband as her lips twitched into a grin. "It's totally because you're blond."

"I thought we weren't seeing you until later?" I anchored my hands on my hips, raising an eyebrow as I ignored Dave and addressed Eric. There were so many blinding Larsson smiles in the room at one time, I was positive the earth was going to tip off its axis.

"Your boyfriend was worried being at my place would be intimidating." Eric rolled his eyes. "It's sort of cute how protective he is." He reached across and tapped his brother on the shoulder.

"You did this for me?" I turned to face Dave, praying like hell I didn't cry. It was one thing to be emotional in private, but to ruin my makeup and get all blubbery in front of an audience wasn't cool.

He nodded, pulling me in for a kiss. "I told you, the two of us side by side, Jess. It's how it's meant to be. Friends, family—yours or mine. I love you."

The faint sound of collective awws in the background were drowned out by the beating of my heart.

"I love you, Dave Larsson. Kiss me."

"Always." He dropped his lips on mine, in front of everyone and gave me the best kiss of my life.

Not hard to do when he was the love of my life, and the Best. Kisser. Ever.

THE END

ACKNOWLEDGEMENTS

I HAVE SO many people to thank, the acknowledgements probably need their own book. This one was tough. It still is, and without you all, it wouldn't have been written. Thank you—those words seem so meager but alas, they're all I have. I adore and love you all without question or limit.

To my family, Gep, Jenna, Liam and Woodley—you are my superpowers, making me capable to do all that I do. I strive to be yours.

Thanks to the rest of my family, especially my mum who didn't laugh at me when I wanted to make pasta sauce live on Facebook. It has nothing to do with this book but is indicative of what she has to put up with having a daughter like me. Shenanigans are worth it in the end, thanks for your ongoing support.

Thank you, my support crew. Calling you just friends is an insult, you're family. Hugs!

My agent, Kimberly Brower from Brower Literary and Management—Thank you.

MK, you are a rock star. You can beta a book like no other. #Respect.

Hang Le—Ninja. Covers, teasers, badassary in general, you do it all with such talent and grace. A million thanks, and then a million more.

Thank you so very much to my editor, Nichole Strauss from Insight Editing. I didn't think we were going to get there with this one, but you manage to get the best out of me. I'm eternally grateful for your patience, understanding, and talent, but mostly for your kindness.

Christine Borgford—from Type A Formatting—you are a superstar. Love working with you. Thank you so much for your beautiful hand and making my words look pretty. I adore you.

Special thanks to my proofreaders MK, Danielle K, and Rosa. You find those pesky mistakes every time.

Thank you to all my author friends, you make "coming to work" so much fun. It's a solitary existence but knowing you are in my corner makes all the difference. We seriously need to see each other more, I miss you all so much.

Thank you a MILLION times to all the bloggers and reviewers! The love you give me and my books is priceless. Whether you're new to the T Gephart train or you've been with me from the start, I am grateful for the support.

To the T Gephart entourage, as always, many muches of thanks. I don't regret that it's not a street team, we have so much more fun discussing general silliness than just talking about my books.

And of course, my last and grandest thanks is always to YOU, the person reading this book. Thank you for supporting me, loving my words, characters and worlds, and allowing me to keep doing it book after book. Every time you buy, share, review, tell someone about it, or read my books—an angel gets its wings. Not *really*, but it gives me mine. Full disclosure, I'm not an angel.

ABOUT THE AUTHOR

T GEPHART IS a USA Today and International bestselling author from Melbourne, Australia.

 With an approach to life that is somewhat unconventional, she prefers to fly by the seat of her pants rather than adhere to some rigid roadmap. Her lack of "plan" has resulted in a rather interesting and eclectic resume, which reads more like the fiction she writes than an actual employment history. She'd tell you all about it, but the statute of limitations hasn't expired yet. But all those crazy twists and turns have led her to a career she loves—writing romantic comedy.

 When she isn't filling pages with sassy and sexy characters with attitude, she's living her own reality show in the 'burbs of Melbourne with her American husband, two teenage children, and her fur child—Woodley.

 She loves adventure, to laugh, travel, and strives to live her life to the fullest.

CONNECT WITH T

www.tgephart.com
Facebook
Goodreads
Twitter

BOOKS BY THIS AUTHOR

The Lexi Series

Lexi

A Twist of Fate

Twisted Views: Fate's Companion

A Leap of Faith

A Time for Hope

The Power Station Series

High Strung

Crash Ride

Back Stage

The Black Addiction Series

Slide

Sticks

Stand

#1 Series

#1 Crush

#1 Player

#1 Rival

#1 Lie

#1 Muse

#1 Love (coming 2019)

Collision Series

Train Wreck

Car Crash (coming soon)

Standalones

The Fall